0 Goalie Night

K.M. Gillis

This novel is entirely a work of fiction. The names, characters and incidents portrayed in it are the work of the author's imagination. Any resemblance to actual persons, living or dead, events or localities is entirely coincidental.

Cover Design: Fleurie Design

Editor: Carley Sugeng

Published by Literary Lupin Publishing Inc.

For everyone who's ever fallen for a fictional character.
Just because they weren't real doesn't mean your love for them wasn't.

AUTHOR'S NOTE

This book takes place in Canada and uses Canadian spelling. Some words may be spelled differently than what you're used to and the extra U's and double L's are intentional and not typos.

CHAPTER 1

FOSTER

"Do you know why you're my best friend, Fozzie?"

Here we go.

Anytime Ben Michaels starts a conversation with those words, I can be certain of two things:

1. He's about to compliment me until I'm uncomfortable.
2. He's going to ask me for a favour.

I sigh and continue stripping out of my goalie gear. It's just the two of us left in the locker room; the rest of our teammates are either still in the showers or gone for the day. "No, man. Why am I your best friend?"

He sits down on the bench next to me and I brace myself for the imminent praise.

"Because you're selfless. Even though you're one of the top goalies in the NHL, you always put your friends first. You look out for me off the ice like I look after you on the ice. I know that I can always count on you at any time of any day to drop what you're doing and help a brother out. I love you, man."

Christ. He's laying it on thick today.

I manoeuvre out of my shoulder pads and turn to face him, biting back a laugh at the expression of sheer earnestness on his face. He's looking at me like a kid begging for the puppy he knows his mom is allergic to.

"Why do I get the feeling that you're about to ask me for a kidney?"

His facade crumbles as his face splits into a grin, those famous dimples making an appearance. "I promise, you won't need general anaesthesia for what I need you to do."

"Spit it out, Michaels. I need to shower."

"You remember my sister, Beth?"

"I remember Beth," Austin Crawford pipes up as he struts in, fresh from the showers, a towel wrapped loosely around his waist. Stopping at his locker on the other end of the room, he removes the towel and runs it roughly through his wet hair. He pumps his eyebrows and grins at Ben who tosses a dirty towel at him as he tells him to fuck off.

I happen to know that Ben has three sisters. "Which one is Beth? The teacher, the one who married the clown, or the one that scares the shit out of you?"

He rolls his eyes. "Ally married a magician, though he is a total Bozo. And it's Tara that scares the shit out of me."

"Isn't she barely more than five feet tall?"

"Terror knows no size limitations, Fozz. Have you ever seen a tarantula? They're also a lot smaller than I am, and, like my sister, fucking terrifying. Now, back to Beth."

Right. Beth. My brain conjures up a memory of meeting his sisters after games. Beth was the taller one? The school teacher with big brown eyes? "I vaguely remember making awkward conversation with her once or twice."

"Most of your conversations are awkward, big guy," Ben drawls, causing Austin to snort with laughter as he pulls on a pair of jeans.

He's not wrong, but I glare at him anyway. I don't mind talking to people one-on-one, but I've never done well in crowds. There are too many distractions and I have a hard time focusing. I'm usually so worried that I'll say the wrong thing around people I don't know well that I opt to say nothing at all. "You know, I'm pretty sure I'm busy tonight, so–"

"No, no, no. I take it back," he begs. "You're a sparkling conversationalist. A real crowd pleaser. You talk so, soooo good."

"I'm going to shower." I stand and start tearing off my remaining sweat-soaked gear.

"Please man, I'm desperate. Beth got a job at an elementary school in Stittsville. She wasn't supposed to start until the new year, but the teacher whose maternity leave she's covering needed to go on bed rest, so they asked her to come early." He's talking very fast now, pleading his case before he loses me.

"Where exactly do I come in?"

"She was supposed to be arriving this afternoon, but her flight got changed and now she's due to arrive tonight at six. I've got plans to go to a restaurant opening with Valentina that I can't get out of."

I frown at him. “Can’t you pick Beth up and just show up to the restaurant a bit late?”

His shoulders slump as he mumbles, “Valentina said that wouldn’t be possible.”

“Hold on.” I run a hand through my hair that’s drenched in sweat from the two-hour practice that just ended. “You can’t pick up your little sister at the airport because you’re going to a party with the model you’re fucking?”

“Don’t minimise my relationship, man. What I have with Valentina is special. I think we’re soulmates.”

Valentina is a model Ben met three weeks ago at some fashion show in Toronto. Eighteen days ago, to be exact. How do I remember that? Because the idiot has done nothing but talk about how he’s sleeping with a supermodel for the past eighteen days.

To be honest, it’s out of character for him. The guy hasn’t had a girlfriend in the four years I’ve known him, preferring to keep things casual with one-time hookups. He meets Valentina and suddenly she’s the centre of his universe. If he hasn’t already gotten her name tattooed somewhere on his body, I’d bet my Olympic gold medal that he’s going to soon.

I resist the urge to tell him I’m pretty sure a soulmate would alter her evening plans to help one of his family members. It’s not like it would make any difference. Besides, I’ve been letting him talk me into things I don’t want to do for the last four years. Why stop now?

“So, you want me to pick her up at the airport?”

He nods enthusiastically. “And drop her off at her new apartment.”

“I’m available,” Austin offers, now fully clothed and

sporting a shit-eating grin. The team's hotshot rookie never passes up on an opportunity to stir the pot. He's not a bad kid, but he's got more charisma than common sense and a smile that will either land him on the cover of a magazine or in prison. "I'd *love* to pick your sister up."

Ben lunges for him, but I step between them, blocking his assault. Austin blows him a kiss before striding out of the locker room, laughing his ass off.

I exhale defeatedly and start for the showers. "Fine. I'll do it."

Before I can get past him, Ben throws his arms around me and lifts me off the ground. As a 6'2" man that weighs 210 pounds, I'm not used to being picked up and I don't like it. Especially when I'm naked.

"Put me down, Jackass." I growl, shoving him away from me. "Text me her flight info and the apartment address."

"I will. Thank you, Fozz. You're the best friend I've ever had." He continues to shout as I walk away. "You're a god. A king amongst mortal men. I don't know what I'd do without you. You're the greatest thing that's ever happened to me, after Valentina."

I don't know if he's finished praising me or if I'm just out of earshot, but I welcome the silence. I stride into the shower room and am greeted by wet floors and lingering steam. Most of my teammates book it to the locker room as soon as practice is over, but not me. I'm always the last player on the ice and that's how I like it. Not only does it give me extra time to work on strategy with the coach, but the locker room is usually cleared out by the time I get there.

Unless an annoying friend is waiting to ask me for a favour, like today.

Don't get me wrong; I like my teammates. For the most part, I've gotten along with the guys that have come and gone on the team. I even consider a couple of them to be close friends, especially Ben and another defenseman, Will.

But I've always felt the need to keep a bit of distance between me and everyone else. I need a certain amount of solitude to be at my best both on and off the ice. When you play at this level, you're often surrounded.

I replay the butterfly drills my goalie coach just put me through in my mind as I shower. I've become a lot better at staying tight to the posts, but there's always room for improvement.

Once I'm clean, I head back to the now empty locker room where I dry off and dress quickly, eager to get home and grab something to eat.

"Excuse me, Mr. Foster?"

Tony, one of the arena's security guards, waves at me as I'm on my way to the parking complex. I smile at him as I approach.

"Just Foster is fine, Tony."

The guy is a few years older than me, but insisted on calling me "Mr. James" when he started. I told him to call me by my first name and since then it's been "Mr. Foster."

"My nephew, Hunter, is turning ten this weekend. He's a huge fan of yours. I was hoping you'd sign his jersey for him?"

"Of course," I answer without hesitation, taking the marker and pint-sized jersey from him. This isn't the first time I've signed merch for him or even the tenth, but he's a good guy and a loyal fan so I'm more than happy to oblige. I scrawl my illegible signature to the top left shoulder.

"Still the best-selling jersey on the team," Tony reminds me.

For five years straight.

I've been incredibly fortunate to play for this team. I was drafted by the Ottawa Otters at age eighteen late in the first round. I spent the next twenty months finishing up my junior career before moving on to Ottawa's AHL farm team, the Belleville Badgers. I got called up to the Otters five years ago and have been their starting goalie ever since.

Growing up in Renfrew, Ontario, the fans immediately embraced me as a hometown boy, making me a fan favourite from the very start.

I hand the jersey back to him and pat him on the arm. "Wish Hunter a happy birthday for me."

"Thanks, Mr. Foster. I will. And good luck in Florida this weekend!"

"Thanks, Tony. I'll need it."

We've lost the last two times we've played the Panthers on their home ice and I plan to end that streak on Saturday.

A text comes in from Ben with his sister's flight information and address as I'm climbing into my Lexus LX.

As much as I don't want to spend my evening making forced conversation with someone I barely know, it's not like I have anything else going on. I'll pick her up, drop her off, and still be home in time to stretch and be in bed early. We leave for a full week of away games tomorrow and I want to be rested.

When I pull out of the parking garage I'm momentarily blinded by the midday sun. It may look beautiful, but the temperature has been dropping steadily over the last few weeks. We haven't had any snow yet, but it can't be long now.

I turn on the radio hoping to hear the weather forecast, but instead the radio announcer gives me unwelcome news.

"It's November first and you know what that means! You better watch out and you better not pout! Only fifty-five days until Christmas, folks!"

As if on cue, snowflakes start floating through the mostly clear sky, melting the moment they land on my windshield.

Humbug.

CHAPTER 2

BETH

"Excuse me…I'm so sorry, could I just get by you… thank you…oh I'm terribly sorry…I just need to grab my bag."

I manage to make my way to the baggage carousel without stepping on anyone, but just barely. The flight in from Charlottetown was full, and apparently every single passenger checked a bag. I spot my luggage coming around the bend of the conveyor belt, easily identifiable by the shockingly pink scarf my mother insisted on tying around the handle before I left.

I don't even like pink.

My hand grabs the brightly adorned handle and I haul the overstuffed suitcase off the conveyor belt before it goes around for another trip, nearly pulling a muscle in the process.

Man, that's heavy. What on Earth did I put in this thing?

Oh, yeah. *Everything*.

I had a plan. I was going to spend the first three weeks of December prepping for my move to Ottawa. Then, the day after Boxing Day, I'd make the fourteen-hour drive with my sister, Ally, and her husband, Mitchell, in my dad's minivan. They'd help me move in, we'd do some touristy things, and then they'd drive home after New Year's.

It was a great plan and I was genuinely looking forward to having an adventure and getting to spend time with my sister and her new husband.

But plans change. One minute I was making road trip playlists on my phone of the bangers that got me through junior high school; the next, I was booking a one-way flight and attempting to pack my life into one regulation-size suitcase.

After reading a self-help book titled *The Answer Is Always Yes*, I've been trying to step out of my comfort zone. I've been getting steady work as a substitute in Prince Edward Island's Public School Board, but decided to look at job postings in other provinces.

Ottawa has always been one of my favourite cities and I cried when I received the offer to cover a maternity leave at Stittsville Elementary. My mom also cried, but those were tears of sadness about her baby moving thirteen hundred kilometres away.

"I just don't like the idea of you all alone in a big city," she'd said when I announced the move to my family over Sunday dinner.

"Ottawa is one of the safest cities in Canada, Mom," I insisted.

"But they have bears!" In my mother's defence, she has lived her entire life in a province where the largest wild animal is a coyote.

"Lots of places have bears, dear," my father told her gently as he passed me the mashed potatoes.

"Prince Edward Island is the only province that doesn't have bears," Ally confirmed, matter-of-factly.

"Don't waste your time worrying about bears, Mom. She's way more likely to get attacked by a human," my older sister, Tara, chimed in, unhelpfully.

After a lot of hand-wringing and reassurance from my brother that he'd look after me, my mother begrudgingly gave me her blessing. She also gave me bear spray which I "forgot" to pack.

Even though it didn't happen the way I planned, I couldn't be happier about the move. I can't wait to explore all the historic sites, museums, and restaurants that the city has to offer.

In addition to being excited about moving, this will also be the first time Ben and I have lived in the same city since I was twelve and I'm really looking forward to spending more time with him.

With my suitcase dragging behind me, its wheels straining under the weight, I scan the vast arrival bay for my brother. As I'm searching the area, my eyes snag on a wall of a man standing alone off to the side. He looks like he's trying to blend into the pillar he's leaning against, and failing miserably. When he turns his head I see his face in full profile and my stomach does a somersault.

That's Foster James.

What are the odds that the Otters' starting goalie is also picking someone up from the airport? I wonder if Ben knows he's here. Gripping my ridiculous pink handle, I debate whether or not to say "hi" to him. We've met twice before, although I doubt he'd remember me.

I don't have the same problem. The man is entirely unforgettable. He's tall and broad like every other hockey player I've met, but his face is one-of-a-kind. A chiselled jaw that looks like it never learned how to relax. Piercing green eyes a person could get lost in, and a mouth that looks inviting even when it's frowning. He's the definition of "broodingly handsome" and "I can change him" in one. Plus he seems to have all his original teeth, by some miracle.

I recently succumbed to clickbait ranking the hottest players in the NHL and was shocked to see him at number twelve. I'd have ranked him much higher.

Someone wheels a suitcase over my foot and I yelp in pain. The man throws an apology over his shoulder as he hurries away. When I look back up, Foster's steel eyes are narrowed in my direction.

He can't actually remember me, right? We talked so briefly each time we met. Actually, come to think of it, I don't think he spoke at all. It was just me babbling at him while he nodded politely and looked like he wanted to be anywhere else.

But what if he does recognize me and I ignore him? That would be rude and I wouldn't want to insult my brother's friend. Should I approach him?

The answer is always yes, Beth.

I square my shoulders and quickly close the twenty feet between us, dragging my comically large suitcase behind me.

"Hi, Foster." Why is my voice so high? Does it always sound that way? I swallow and try again. "I don't know if you remember me, but I'm Ben Michael's sister."

"Of course I remember you. How are you, Beth?" His

voice, both deep and powerful, elevates my blood pressure. Strands of light brown hair peek out from beneath his Blue Jays hat, somehow making his green eyes stand out even more.

"I'm good! Just arrived, obviously." I laugh to mask how nervous I am. Foster freaking James is just as impressive in real life as he is in the net. And he remembered me. "And yourself?"

"Also good," he nods.

"Good." I nod back. Conversation comes to a standstill as we continue nodding at one another like a couple of human bobbleheads.

Finally, he clears his throat. "So, are you good?"

Bless his heart, the man is gorgeous but he's even more awkward than I remember. "Yeah. I'm good." There's a stretch of silence that borders on uncomfortable.

"Great. Can I take your bag for you?"

"Take my bag where?"

Another awkward pause. "To my car."

My confusion must be written all over my face, because his expression clears and he shakes his head before continuing. "Your brother didn't tell you that he asked me to pick you up, did he?"

At first, I think I must have misheard him. I mean, there is no way that my brother would have sent Olympic gold medalist Foster James to fetch me like a chew toy, right? But then I pause long enough to think about some of the stunts Ben's pulled over the years. Like the time he made his buddy attend our cousin's wedding because he was too hungover to go. This is one hundred percent on brand for him.

Goddammit, Ben.

Embarrassment makes my face heat. I start to panic and when I panic, I ramble at warp speed.

"I'm so sorry that he imposed upon you like this. I'm sure you have much better things to do than chauffeur me around Ottawa. I mean, I get that he's busy, but he could have just told me he couldn't make it. I would have figured something out. I'd have gotten an Uber. I mean, I've never ordered one because we don't have them on the Island, but I'm not a complete moron. I'm sure I could have figured it out. I will figure it out right now. Is there a website or a phone number I can call?"

Please don't cry, I silently beg myself. Not yet, at least. *Once you make it to the new place, you can shut the door, curl into a ball, and cry as much as you like. Remember your mantras.*

I am self-sufficient.

My past does not define me.

Obstacles help me grow.

I risk a glance up at Foster whose narrowed eyes regard me with concern.

"Ben wanted to be here, but he had plans he couldn't get out of. He really wanted to make sure you made it to your new place safely." He's being so nice and it just makes me want to cry more.

"I understand, but did he have to send *you*?"

His eyebrows lift and I realise how rude that came out.

"I just mean, because you're you. You're Foster James. You're a Vezina trophy finalist with a ten-million-dollar a year contract. He could have asked someone else, like an equipment manager or the guy that wears the mascot suit."

Amusement flickers in his eyes and his mouth twitches. "It's actually a twelve-million-dollar a year contract. And our equipment manager has had it out for Ben since he pranked him last year. I won't go into the gory details, but it involved several gallons of maple syrup and an upsetting amount of human hair."

"I don't know whether to laugh or gag."

"Both are completely suitable reactions. As for Otto The Otter, he's almost impossible to book. We're lucky he still shows up to the games, he's that popular. Also, he's a shit driver. When he drives the zamboni at games, he's all over the place. He'd probably do better if he took off the mascot head."

This time, I do laugh and he quietly joins in. This is a side of Foster James I've never seen in person or on television. He's more relaxed and almost playful. I wonder briefly how many people get to see him like this.

"Let's try this again," he says, a gentle smile playing on his lips. "Can I take your bag?"

I sigh and pass my suitcase to him, not missing how he picks it up with ease. I'm still pissed at my brother, but I suppose there are worse things than spending my evening with Foster James.

CHAPTER 3

FOSTER

"According to the email their teacher sent me, they're just starting their World War I unit. It makes sense seeing as Remembrance Day is coming up in a couple of weeks. I've got this really great presentation on Vimy Ridge that I'm going to show the kids. It was developed for older children, but with a bit of tweaking I can make it suitable for fourth graders. After that, we start learning about hibernation. Which is an interesting subject too, to be sure, but I don't have any materials prepared to teach it."

Beth has been talking non-stop since we got in the car, but I don't mind. She talks with her hands like she's in front of a classroom or conducting an invisible symphony. So far I've heard about her flight, her plan to search for a used car right away, and her excitement for her new job.

Best of all, we're not talking about me. One of the reasons I don't usually like meeting new people is that I somehow always end up the focus of the conversation. And while I'm sure some people enjoy that kind of attention, I can assure you I'm not one of them. I end up feeling like I'm being interrogated.

But Beth just talks. It's almost like I'm privy to an inner monologue that she can't keep caged up. She's got the nervous energy of someone being strapped into their first roller coaster; terrified, but oddly happy about it. There's a wholesomeness about her that I don't see often and I understand why Ben wanted someone to look out for her.

I'm glad he asked me to pick her up and not someone else. If he'd sent Austin, he'd probably have convinced her to take a private tour of the city that ended at his condo.

None of us on the team are saints; I've had more than my fair share of hookups in random cities with random women. But Austin Crawford's exploits bring new meaning to the term "player."

The thought of him taking advantage of Beth when she's just arrived sets my teeth on edge. I'm so put off by the idea that I miss that she's trying to get my attention.

"I'm sorry, what was that?"

She lets out a nervous laugh and looks down at her hands. "No, I'm sorry. Am I talking too much?"

"Not at all. I just got distracted looking for the right exit to take. What were you asking?"

"I was just curious if you knew of any animals that hibernate. I haven't had much time to look into it yet and all I have so far are bears and bats."

I blow out a breath and shake my head. "I'm not sure. Do otters hibernate?"

"No, but they are fascinating. Did you know river otters can dive to a depth of sixty feet?"

I did not know that.

"Seriously?"

"Yes!" She pushes her dark hair behind her ears and twists in her seat so she's facing me. "They can hold their breaths for eight minutes under water. They're extremely intelligent and adaptable, and they mate for life."

I sneak a glance at her after that comment and have to bite back a laugh when I find that her cheeks have gone pink.

"Definitely talking too much," she mutters under her breath. Before I can argue that's not the case, she sits up in her seat and points to a house. "I think this is it."

I pull up in front of the two-storey house with white siding and park the car. It seems like a nice neighbourhood and the properties all appear to be well-maintained. I make a mental note to tell Ben as much as I'm sure he'll want to know.

I insist on taking her bag in for her. The thing is more beaten up than a retired boxer and must weigh at least eighty pounds. I have no idea how she managed to get it this far.

I'm almost sad it didn't take us longer to get here. I enjoyed talking to her. Or I suppose listening to her would be more accurate. She's funny and smart. Hopefully I'll get to see her again sometime now that she'll be living here.

As a friend, of course. Don't get me wrong—she's cute as hell, in that wide-eyed, girl-next-door way—but she's Ben's sister, and I would prefer my balls remain attached to my body.

"So you're renting a room, not the entire house?" I ask, eyeing the two Toyota Corollas parked in the driveway.

"Yes," she answers as she skips up the walk way. "I'm renting from a retired couple. They have an ensuite apartment, so I have my own kitchen and bathroom. They've been wonderful to deal with, especially considering I needed to move in on such short notice."

I set the suitcase down as she knocks on the door. She bounces on the balls of her feet as she waits, practically radiating excitement. After a few moments a teenage girl wearing headphones and a bored expression opens the door.

"Oh," Beth stutters, taking a step back to make sure she's at the right house. "Are Colleen and Brian here?"

The girl takes one look at the suitcase and rolls her eyes.

"Moooooom! We've got another one." The sour teen turns and walks away without another word leaving us standing in the open doorway.

I've got a very bad feeling about this.

A middle-aged woman appears, drying her hands on a dish towel. Her face falls when she sees us and she gives us a look of pure pity. I know before she opens her mouth what she's about to say.

"I'm guessing you're here about an apartment of some sort?"

Fuck.

"Yes," Beth says, giving her an anxious smile. "I got an email from Colleen yesterday confirming it would be ready..." she trails off.

It's clear that Beth knows something is very wrong, but she hasn't quite figured out what. Every cell in my body is urging me to throw myself in front of her to shield her from the disappointment that's coming.

"There is no Colleen," the woman says sadly. "And no apartment either. I'm so sorry, dear. You're the eighth person this month. I'm guessing you already paid a deposit?"

Beth gives a minuscule nod and whispers, "And the first month's rent."

Rental scams. Con artists using the housing shortage to prey on people. I've seen reports of it happening all over the country.

I'm so angry right now. Not only at the criminals who took advantage of her, but at Ben for not helping her find a safe place to stay.

"Do you need a drink of water, dear?" The sudden concern in the woman's voice brings my attention back to Beth who's gone paler than snow and looks unsteady on her feet.

Afraid she might pass out I put my arm around her waist for support and she sinks against my side. I thank the woman for her time and apologise for disturbing her.

"I wish there was something we could do. We keep reporting the ads to the police, but as soon as they come down, new ones pop up."

I thank her again and without removing my arm from Beth, pick up her suitcase in my free hand and guide her back to the car.

She says nothing as I help her into the passenger side, just continues to stare ahead like a lost soul. After I throw the suitcase in the back, I take my phone from my pocket and call Ben. I wait outside while it rings, cursing when it goes to voicemail.

"Ben, I need you to call me," I bite out. Then, realising

that might freak him out, I add, "Beth is fine, but I need you to call me right away."

I climb into the driver's seat and find that Beth is in the exact same pose I left her in; hands in lap, back straight, eyes staring blankly ahead. I slowly reach over and rest my hand on hers. They're freezing. I start the car, turning up the heater as well as the heated seat for good measure.

Seeing her so upset has me feeling helpless. Powerless.

What am I going to do with her? She's alone in a new city and I can't track down Ben.

"Are you okay?" I ask, knowing she's not. Given the circumstances, how could she be? She's so quiet. Too quiet. In the short time I've known her, I've gotten used to her incessant talking. I want nothing more than to go back to when she was excitedly spouting fun facts about water mammals.

She blinks in surprise, almost like she'd forgotten I was there. "I...yes. It's just...It was the school that sent me the ad, along with some others. I thought..."

"Hey." I lean forward until she meets my eye. "None of this is your fault. These assholes are very good at looking legit."

She closes her eyes. "I feel like such an–"

"Do not finish that sentence, Beth. Do you hear me? You didn't deserve this." No one does of course, but especially not her.

She opens her eyes and gives me a watery smile before nodding. "Okay," she sniffs. "I should call my brother."

"I just tried him. He's not answering his phone."

"Oh...alright." She swallows. That look of panic flashes in her amber eyes again and I can practically hear the wheels turning in her head. “You’ve already done so much for me, Foster, but do you think you could drop me off at a hotel?”

“No.” I answer, firmly. Her shoulders sink and I rush to explain. “Because you’re staying with me tonight.”

I didn’t realise I was going to say it until the words came out of my mouth, but it’s the only thing I can think of that makes any kind of sense. She can crash in one of my guest rooms for the night and figure out what comes next tomorrow. I’m sure Ben will want her to stay with him until they can find her another apartment. Preferably one that actually exists.

She shakes her head vehemently. “I’ve already inconvenienced you enough. I can’t ask you to put me up.”

“You’re not an inconvenience at all,” I insist. “And you’re not asking, I am. Beth, please do me a solid and stay at my place tonight so your brother doesn’t murder me for leaving you at a seedy hotel.”

A ghost of a smile touches her full lips. “I didn’t ask you to take me to a seedy one.”

I shrug. “Those are the only ones I know.”

Her giggle warms the interior of the car far better than the heater ever could. I release the breath I’m holding, relieved that she doesn’t look so devastated anymore. My heart couldn’t take another second of this girl looking so sad.

“In that case, I’d be very grateful to spend the night at your house.” She pauses. “Provided it’s not seedy.”

“Well,” I grin as I put the car in reverse. “Not *as* seedy, anyway.”

CHAPTER 4

BETH

I want to hibernate. Burrow into a hole in the ground far from the outside world and avoid the consequences of my actions.

No. This is not my fault, I remind myself. I am the victim.

Finding a place to live had been overwhelming to say the least. Every place I looked at required a first month's rent and a damage deposit up front. Early in my search, I'd reached out to several places only to be told that the apartment had already been rented.

And then I found what seemed like the perfect rental. Close to the school and in a nice neighbourhood. The rent was expensive but not unreasonable. After inquiring about it, I received a response from Colleen, or whatever her real name is, asking for a phone interview. She peppered me with questions about my lifestyle. Did I smoke? How loud do I listen to my music? Do I have any pets? We talked for more than twenty minutes and at the end she told me the room was mine.

I feel physically ill. She played me like a fiddle and I had no idea it was happening.

When we arrive at Foster's house, which for the record is beautiful and not even remotely seedy, all I want to do was go to bed and pretend the day had never happened.

Foster sets my suitcase down in the guest room he's just led me to. It's bigger than my room back home. The walls are painted a soft blue, enhancing the airy feel of the space. The only furniture is a queen-size bed and a simple white dresser.

"Are you hungry?" He asks, green eyes scanning me with concern.

I don't want to be but I am. My appetite disappeared with my three-thousand-dollar deposit, but my stomach doesn't know that. All it knows is that I haven't fed it since lunch.

"Not really," I lie. "I think I'll just go to bed."

"Here's the thing." He points at the bed. "The sheets should be washed. No one has ever stayed here and I certainly wasn't expecting anyone. But the sheets have been on the bed for years. Why don't you take a shower while I throw them in the laundry and make us something to eat?"

I bite my lip. A shower does sound amazing. I know I won't be able to scrub away what's happened and wash my disappointment down the drain, but I can try.

"That sounds great," I admit gratefully.

As I help him strip the sheets from the queen-size bed I'm struck by the intimacy of it all. On any other day, being alone in a room with Foster James would probably have sent my imagination into overdrive. But here we are, leaning over a bed and I feel nothing but my own sense of self-pity.

I'm broken.

The shower is incredible. I've never felt water pressure this powerful; it's practically massaging the balls of tension in my shoulders and neck. There is nothing on any of the shelves; not a bar or soap or a bottle of shampoo to be found. I have my own toiletries, so I don't mind at all, but I find myself wondering if it's ever been used. The tile is gleaming and I'm sure Foster has a cleaner come regularly to keep it that way.

I'm not sure how long I stand there, basking in the hot water, but eventually my growling stomach becomes more insistent and I get out. Once I'm dried and dressed in my oversized University of Prince Edward Island t-shirt and a pair of leggings, I make my way to the kitchen Foster pointed out on the initial tour of the house on the way to my room.

My host is standing at the stove with his back to me, his sculpted muscles visible through his thin t-shirt as he works. He must hear me approach because he glances back over his shoulder and gives me a smile that makes the lower half of my body tingle.

Maybe I'm not so broken after all.

"How was your shower?" His entire body stiffens and he immediately starts to shake his head. "Nope. Let's try that again. How are you now?"

A burst of giggles escapes me as a blush stains his cheeks. It's not like I thought he was asking for a detailed report, but his reaction is priceless.

"Better, thank you." I watch him plate our supper

before joining me at the island. He sets down identical plates of chicken, rice, and broccoli in front of us.

"It's not the most exciting meal," he says with an apologetic shrug as he grabs forks and knives from a nearby drawer. "The team dietician gives us plans and I try to follow mine pretty closely. Would you like a glass of wi–"

"Yes, please."

He chuckles as he moves to the cupboard and removes a bottle of red wine and a stemless glass. "Yes, Ma'am."

I watch him search through three kitchen drawers before he retrieves a bottle opener. He removes the cork swiftly, his impressive bicep flexing as he pulls it from the bottle's neck.

Accepting the glass gratefully, I raise it to my mouth and take a large mouthful of the maroon liquid. My eyes close as the full-bodied wine hits my taste buds and I swallow, sighing contentedly.

When I open my eyes, Foster is looking at me expectantly.

"Is it okay?"

"It's wonderful. You're not having a glass?"

He relaxes, shaking his head. "Nah, I don't drink much. I'll have a beer with the guys when we're playing poker sometimes, but that's it."

I press my lips together, fighting a smile. "So you just keep a bottle of wine stocked for when you rescue your friends' sisters from sleeping on a park bench?"

"I guess so. For the record, I would have left you at a seedy motel before I let you sleep outdoors." The man has perfected deadpan and I laugh as I pick up my fork.

We eat in comfortable silence. The meal is simple, but

simple suits my anxiety-riddled stomach just fine. Though there is no way I can possibly eat all of it. Two chicken breasts, at least two cups of brown rice, and a mountain of broccoli. He probably doubled what he would normally make for himself.

As I sip my wine, I make a mental list of everything I need to do.

I'm going to need to call my parents. They will probably already be wondering why I haven't called them yet, but I'm dreading my mother's reaction when she hears about the apartment. Even though I wasn't in any actual danger, she'll act like I was robbed at gunpoint.

Then there's the matter of finding a new place to live. Even if I manage to find a suitable rental on short notice, I don't have enough in my meagre savings to afford another first month's rent, damage deposit, AND I still need a car.

UGH.

I feel Foster's gaze on me and worry that I just made that noise out loud. He's looking at me like he's afraid I'm about to erupt or crumble or both and I decide to deflect.

"Your house is lovely," I tell him as I look around and admire the custom-built cabinets and quartz countertop. It's minimalistic and it suits him. "How long have you lived here?"

"Almost three years. I lived in a condo downtown for a little while when I started with the team, but I tired of city life pretty quickly. I prefer the quiet." He glances at the phone screen next to him and frowns.

Suddenly I wonder if I'm intruding on his solitude. "You don't need to entertain me, you know. I'll just head back to the guest room and you can pretend I'm not here."

"No, please stay. I didn't mean it like that. I'm happy

you're here, really. You're the first real houseguest I've ever had."

I suspected as much, but hearing him confirm it surprises me all the same. "Really? My sisters and parents impose on Ben at least once a year. Has your family never stayed here? Oh, but I forgot you're from here, right? Do they live in the area?"

Foster doesn't look at me as he continues to chew the food in his mouth. When he finally swallows he takes a drink from his water glass before clearing his throat. "No."

I wait for him to continue, but he doesn't. "No, they don't live nearby or no, they've never stayed here?"

"Both." Pushing back from the table, he grabs his empty plate and walks to the sink without another word.

Way to go, Beth. Find that sore spot on the poor man and then poke it.

I open my mouth to apologise, but stop myself. Clearly, I've made him uncomfortable, but I feel like an apology would only bring more attention to what appears to be a sensitive subject. If Foster doesn't want to talk about his family, I will happily change the subject.

I step down from the stool and bring my plate to the sink. There is a lot of food still left on it, but I made a decent dent in it. Foster's broad back is to me as he washes the dishes. I note that there is a state-of-the-art dishwasher not two feet away from him, but don't mention it.

"No word from Ben yet?" I set my plate down next to him and grab the dish towel that's resting on the counter so I can dry.

"No," he sighs. "It's not unusual, though," he adds hastily, probably so I don't worry.

"Oh, I know," I laugh as I run the towel over the plate in my hands. "He probably forgot to charge his phone."

"Or forgot it at home altogether," he agrees, smirking. He probably knows my brother better than I do.

"Classic Ben." I'm reaching for a glass to dry as Foster adds another plate to the drying rack and our arms brush against one another. The contact startles me, but thankfully I manage not to drop the glass I'm holding. Our gazes meet, and, for a moment, it's like I can't look away.

Just then a buzzer sounds from somewhere in the house.

"That's the dryer," Foster explains, shaking the soapy water from his hands. "Your bedsheets are ready. I'll help you make the bed."

While it's kind of him to offer, I already feel like a child who's been coddled all evening. I draw the line at having this man make my bed and tuck me in.

"No, I've got it," I insist. "I'll make the bed and then call my parents. Just point me in the direction of the laundry room."

"Last door on the left."

"Perfect." I set down the dish towel and face him. "Thank you so much for everything, Foster. You really saved me tonight."

He rubs the back of his neck looking downright bashful. "Well, I'm a goalie. Saving is what I do."

I can't help but wince. "That was really bad."

"I regretted it the moment I said it. I'm so sorry." We both laugh at his failed joke and I start to leave, grabbing my phone from the island.

"Could I use your wifi? I hate that I have to ask, but my phone plan is awful and I can't use up all my data this early in the month." It's embarrassing to even ask.

"Of course. Password is Patrickroy33. All one word."

Grinning, I enter it into my phone and take it off airplane mode. As soon as it connects, my phone starts to ping with voicemail and text alerts from my parents and sisters.

Alright. Let's get this over with.

I take a final glance at Foster. He's watching me from the counter as he's drying off his hands, a serious look on his face.

"Goodnight, Foster."

"Goodnight, Beth."

CHAPTER 5

BETH

I never want to leave this bed.

Up until now, I've always thought my bed back home was comfortable, but after sleeping in Foster James' guest room, I may as well have been sleeping on an inflatable raft filled with dead leaves and branches.

As I stretch my arms above my head, I feel like every part of my body is being supported, cradled even. This bed is my holy grail. I want to live here. I want to make and raise a family here and, eventually, die here. And not just because I don't want to face the fact that I got swindled out of three thousand dollars I really couldn't afford to lose.

If I stay in this bed, I'll never have to.

Last night feels more like a fever dream than a memory. After taking my time making the bed with military precision, I texted my mom and sisters identical messages.

Beth: Hi! Arrived safely and all settled in. Sorry it took me so long to message– I just got the wifi password! Exhausted and turning in for the night. Love you! xoxoxoxoxoxooxoxo

Where's the lie?

I realise I'm going to have to tell them the entire story, and soon, but I just couldn't make myself rehash it all again. I would have cried and that would have upset everyone.

Instead, I turned my phone to silent and fell into a sound and dreamless sleep. It was bliss. I think I need to seriously consider never leaving this bed.

"Where the fuck is she?"

Perhaps not.

I throw the 500 thread count sheets off and hop down from the bed, missing them both immediately. After rummaging in my suitcase for my bathrobe, I throw it over the t-shirt I'm wearing and march down the hallway towards the smell of cooking bacon and the sound of my brother's hissy fit.

"You weren't supposed to take her home," he accuses as I round the corner to where he and Foster are standing squared off against one another.

"No, *he* wasn't," I say so loudly that both men jump and turn towards me. "*You* were." I may have been mildly irritated at Ben before, but hearing him chastise his friend who has done nothing but look out for me makes me positively livid. "You were supposed to pick me up at the airport and make sure I got to the apartment safely."

Ben takes a step in my direction, towering over me like he always has. His hair, the same shade of muddy brown as mine, is shorter than it was when I saw him in August. He crosses his arms across his barrel chest, clearly not ready to be held accountable for his actions or lack thereof. "What apartment would that be, Beth? Fozzie says it doesn't even exist."

Oh, you have got to be kidding me.

Foster gives him a hard glare. "This is your warning to tread carefully," he utters quietly.

"What apartment, Ben?" My voice is practically vibrating with anger. "You mean the apartment listing I sent you weeks ago, asking you to check out for me? The one you responded with a thumbs up emoji to?"

My brother's face goes slack and I think Foster's eyes might roll so far that they'll never come back.

"Seriously, man?" Shaking his head, Foster steps around my brother and hands me a green ceramic mug filled with coffee. "There's cream and sugar, if you want it. Or if you'd prefer, you could throw it at him. It might even give him second degree burns, if we're lucky."

"Thank you and noted," I say as we exchange conspiratorial smiles. I'm not used to having someone side with me, especially against my brother, and it's a refreshing change.

"What?" Ben uncrosses his arms and rests his hands on his hips. He's looking much less sure of himself now that the tables have turned. "The place looked fine."

"Exactly," I fume. "It did look fine. I don't need you making me feel like an idiot, Ben. I'm doing a pretty great job of that all on my own. How about we call Mom and Dad? Maybe put them on speaker and we can update them on the last twenty-four hours together?"

"Come on, Bug." He only uses that nickname when

he's desperate and given that he promised our parents he'd look out for me, he knows they'll be disappointed to find he didn't. "You know that will only upset them."

"You're right. They'd be very upset to hear that someone took advantage of me and you weren't there."

At that, his nostrils flare and he spins around to where Foster is leaning against the counter holding a spatula, observing our sibling squabble.

"What the fuck, man?" Ben demands.

I'm confused at first, not understanding his reaction, until Foster gives an exasperated sigh.

"She's clearly talking about the people who scammed her, you moron."

Ben visibly relaxes. "Right, I knew that."

Realisation dawns and my jaw drops so fast I'm shocked it doesn't dislocate. How could he have thought that Foster would make a move on me when I was in such a vulnerable state? Even if I wasn't, the very idea is laughable. He's Foster James. I have enough self-awareness to understand that there are leagues and he is far out of mine.

Ben's focus is back on me. "Look. I'm sorry that I wasn't there for you, Bug. Really I am. Are you okay?" He looks genuinely apologetic as he opens his arms to me.

I know I shouldn't let him off the hook this easily. I should stay mad at him in the hopes that he might actually learn something. But I'm so sad and overwhelmed, and right now I could really use a hug from my big brother.

The moment his arms are around me, I burst into tears. It's the first time I've cried since all of this happened and while I'm a bit embarrassed to be falling apart in front of Foster, I'm also surprised I managed to hold out this long.

"Awww, don't cry, Bug. It's going to be okay." He ruffles the hair on top of my head.

"How?" I pull away, wiping at my tear-stained face. "I start my new job on Monday and I don't have a place to live."

Ben places a hand on his hip and runs the other over his face as he blows out a breath. "I'll put you up in a hotel until we figure something out."

A hotel?

Foster doesn't seem to like his suggestion either. When I look over I see his shoulders stiffen as he continues flipping bacon. "Why can't she stay with you?"

I'm so grateful he said it and not me. My entire family stayed with Ben the last time we were here. His condo is huge with three bedrooms and three bathrooms.

Ben suddenly looks very uncomfortable. "I would invite you to stay with me, Bug, I'd love to have you. But Valentina is there already."

"Who?" I have no idea who he's talking about.

"Your future sister-in-law," Ben states without a trace of sarcasm. "You're going to love her, I promise."

I try to hide my surprise at this revelation. Ben's only serious relationship ended close to a decade ago. He'd started dating Madelyn when they were sixteen, but they broke up when he was drafted after juniors and he's never so much as mentioned her or any other girl since.

Not that I'm one to talk. I've only dated a handful of guys and none of the relationships ever reached the meet-the-parent stage.

Foster shifts against the counter. "Don't you have several bedrooms?"

"Yes, but she's very private. I can't just tell her my little sister's going to be moving in."

"Why the fuck not?" Foster asks tersely. "It's not like you're asking her to babysit."

This is a new level of humiliation for me. Foster doesn't realise it, but he's pressing on an open wound. Everyone in my family already treats me like I need adult supervision. It's part of the reason I've been trying so hard to become more independent.

"It would be weird, okay? The relationship is too new. Besides," he glares at his friend before continuing, "I don't think you're one to give out family advice, okay?"

I watch Foster's jaw go rigid and his eyes harden before he looks at the floor. After his reaction to me asking about his family yesterday, I suspect there's more to that story than he'd like to admit.

"I'll find you a hotel," Ben repeats, bringing my focus back on him.

My shoulders sag. It sounds completely ungrateful, even to me, but I don't want to stay in a hotel. They're fine for short trips but not for extended periods. I want to have access to a kitchen, be able to do laundry, and not have to hear people moving around at all hours of the day and night.

Not to mention, hotels are very expensive. I certainly can't afford to stay in one for an extended amount of time. I know Ben will offer to foot the bill, but I hate the idea of taking a handout from my successful brother.

But beggars can't be choosers and I can't think of another solution.

"Okay," I manage to force a small smile. "Thanks, Ben."

"You can stay here."

At that, the two youngest Michaels children both turn to Foster and in perfect unison say, "What?"

He hesitates, as if unsure of himself. Leaning his weight back against the countertop like he's on unsteady ground, he seems almost uncomfortable as the sudden centre of attention.

"For the week, at least." He looks at me and then to Ben. "We leave tonight for eight days of away games. Her stuff is already here." He meets my eye for a brief moment before looking away and shrugging. "You're welcome to stay, if you want."

"Yeah?" Ben asks him before turning back to me. "What do you think?"

I hesitate. This move was about me becoming more independent and after being here less than twenty-four hours, I feel like more of a burden than ever. "I think it's too much to ask."

"You didn't ask, I offered," Foster insists, giving me a faint smile. "You'll have the place to yourself. You can even use one of my cars to get around, if you'd like."

My brother gawks at him. "But you never let me drive your rides."

"She knows the wifi password, too."

Ben gasps. "You told her your wifi password?"

"I did."

"I've been asking you for it for years."

"I'm aware." Foster deadpans before throwing me a wink and turning back to the bacon on the stove.

Ben scowls and I try not to laugh. I feel torn about

Foster's offer. I already feel like such a nuisance, but to stay here for a week? That's a very big imposition.

On the other hand, it's close to my new job and I'd be much more comfortable here than at a hotel. And being able to use his car would be so helpful.

"Well?" Ben asks, waiting for my answer.

Having an extra week to find a place would make my life so much easier. Besides, I wouldn't want to offend my host by turning down such a generous offer.

Foster remains facing the frying pan, but his head tilts to the side like he's listening to hear what I'll decide.

"I'd like to stay here." I can't be certain, but I could swear Foster's face breaks into a grin before turning away again.

"That settles it, then." Ben claps his hands together. "Fozzie and I will go on the road, you'll stay here, and no one will tell Mom and Dad what I did or didn't do."

Leave it to Ben to frame the situation around him. Heaven forbid his golden boy image be tarnished in the eyes of our parents. I've always found it impossible to stay mad at my brother and it's just as annoying now as it was when we were younger.

"I really am glad you're here, Bug."

"Thanks, Ben. Me too."

"And I'm sorry. Maybe I was being a bit of an asshole."

"You definitely were," Foster says without looking over as he grabs plates from a cupboard.

Ben glances over his shoulder at his friend before he whispers to me, "I need you to tell me what the wifi password is."

I tilt my head and with a placating tone usually reserved for the children I teach tell him, "Aww. Never."

CHAPTER 6

FOSTER

"Look at her cheeks!"

I do as I'm told and look at the picture on Will's phone of his newborn niece, focusing on the infant's cheeks. They're chubby like she's storing nuts for the winter. Her eyes are closed and her hairless head seems to be a bit misshaped. Is that normal? I don't know shit about babies.

"She's beautiful, man," I tell him because I know it's what he wants to hear. We're in our seats, awaiting take off, on our way to Tampa.

"Isn't she? I wasn't planning on going home until Christmas, but I might try to sneak in a quick trip." Will's from a huge African Nova Scotian family. When I say huge, I just don't mean in numbers. He's got five siblings, all over six feet tall—even his sisters—and at six-foot-five, he's the biggest guy on our team. When they come up for games, all proudly wearing their Oliver jerseys, they completely take over the friends and family box.

I wonder what that's like; playing knowing that you've got loved ones in the stands, cheering you on.

"The offer still stands, by the way," he adds, still staring at his phone. "You're welcome to spend Christmas with my family this year."

A nod is my only reply. He's made this offer several times and I've never taken him up on it. It's not that I don't appreciate it. Will Oliver is the undisputed gentle giant of the team. He loves to take care of us and I understand that he hates knowing I spend every holiday alone. But I'd much prefer to be on my own than spend Christmas being reminded of what I don't have.

"I hear you got yourself a new roommate, Fozzie Bear." Austin grins at me from the row ahead, kneeling on his seat to face us. His blond hair, long on top and buzzed on the sides, brushes against the cabin's ceiling as he leans in, as he awaits my response.

This gets Will's attention. He looks up from the pictures of his niece and stares at me. "You have a what?"

"As of yesterday, he's shacking up with Ben's sister."

I glare at him. "We are not *shacking up*. Beth's housing fell through and she's staying with me until she finds a new place."

Will brightens next to me. "Beth's here? I like that girl. She's such a sweetheart."

"You like everyone," I say dryly. Will's people skills far exceed my own. Where I get awkward around people I don't know, he becomes fast friends with everyone he meets. But I like Beth, too. She's easy to talk to and even easier to be around.

Not hard to look at either, but that's completely beside the point.

"Well, I still think I should have gotten her at the airport," Austin says as he stretches his back against the ceiling of the plane. "Teachers are so hot, with their hair pulled back in those tight buns and their glasses."

"She doesn't even wear glasses." My tone is clipped. He's annoying me even more than usual lately, which is saying something.

"I bet she would for me, if I asked nicely." He winks at me before sitting down, leaving me scowling at the back of his seat.

"That's really great of you to let her stay," Will says sincerely.

"It's not a big deal."

It's really not. Beth needs a place to stay and I've got lots of room. Ben and Will are the closest thing I have to family. I'd have done the same for any of their siblings.

I know that being alone for the first time in a new city is hard and she has already had a rough start. If I can do anything to make things easier for her, I will.

Since we don't seem to be taking off anytime soon, I decide to message Beth just to check in. We exchanged phone numbers in case she needs to get ahold of me, but I want to make sure she's got everything she needs.

Foster: Settling in okay?

The three dots appear almost immediately.

Beth: Yes

Huh. Her short response doesn't convince me.

Foster: You sure?

There's a longer pause and I wonder if maybe she's in the middle of something and I'm interrupting.

Beth: I can't turn on your tv

I laugh out loud, causing Will to look over at me.

Beth: You have too many remotes

Foster: I have exactly the right number of remotes

Realising I should have given her a tutorial before I left, I type out what each is used for.

Foster: Short black one = tv

Foster: Long black one = stereo

Foster: Blue one = fireplace

I stare at my phone, eagerly awaiting her response.

Beth: What's the chrome one do?

Foster: Nothing.

Beth: ??

Foster: It was for my old stereo system. When I upgraded I kept it

Beth: Why?

Foster: Because it's shiny and looks cool.

Beth: Wow.

The flight attendants have started their safety spiel and I tuck my phone away with a smile on my face.

❄

I'M on my way back to my hotel room the next day when I hear from Beth again. We had a team skate this morning after which I met with my coaches to talk strategy. I've just finished lunch and am going to have a nap before we head to the arena.

Beth: Hi! Sorry to bother you but do you have an iron?

I tuck my water bottle under my arm as I type my response.

Foster: Yeah. Closet at the end of the hall on the left

Beth: Thank you!

I've just closed the door to my suite when my phone lights up again.

Beth: Why do you have so many bottles of pineapple coconut foaming hand soap?

Foster: Because it's the best scent.

Beth: lol

I picture her standing in my hallway laughing at my soap supply.

Beth: You have thirty-two bottles of it!

Laying down on top of the covers, I decide to lean into it.

Foster: Only thirty-two? I need to restock.

Beth: You're weird

Foster: Thanks

I close my eyes and start the pregame breathing exercises I do before every game.

The phone buzzes again, but I don't check it immediately. When the second text comes in, I give in and reach for it.

Beth: omg I just used it and it's amazing

Beth: It's like washing your hands in a pina colada!

Foster: Told you so

I set the phone aside again, grinning. Having a roommate isn't half-bad.

❄

My ears are still ringing from the sound of outraged Panthers fans on my ride to the airport late that night. We stomped the home team three to nil, ending the losing streak in the most satisfying way.

I close my eyes, wanting nothing more than quiet as I decompress from the game, but I'm far from alone on a bus full of guys, unfortunately.

"Dude," Ben says from his seat beside me.

"What?" My eyelids remain closed.

"Did you see Valentina's Instagram?"

I'm not on Instagram or any other social media platform for that matter. He knows this.

When I don't reply, he nudges me and I begrudgingly turn my head and look at him. On his phone is a post of who I have to assume is his girlfriend. Only her eyes and the top of her head are visible, the rest of her is obscured by a massive bouquet of red roses.

"She used the hashtags 'best boyfriend ever,' 'keeper,' and 'couple goals.' Am I nailing this relationship or what?"

"That's great," I say without feeling and Ben's eyes flash to mine.

"What?"

"Nothing, man. Don't get me wrong, I'm happy if you're happy. I just have never seen you with the same girl twice. Seems kind of sudden is all."

A muscle in his jaw ticks before his lopsided grin returns. "I'm just ready to settle down, is all, and when you know, you know."

"That's great," I say again, with more conviction this time. "Tell me about her."

His brow furrows. "What do you mean?"

I thought the question was self-explanatory, but I elaborate further. "I mean, what's she like? Funny? Smart? Sweet?" Why am I spoon-feeding him personality characteristics?

"Ohh. I gotcha. She's smart, I guess. Really cultured and career focused. And, like, so hot, obviously." He doesn't continue.

Right.

"Cool," is all I can think to say, but it seems to work because he happily goes back to his phone.

It's not like I was expecting him to come up with a sonnet on why she's the one, but I was expecting more of an endorsement for the woman he's claimed he'll marry.

As someone who's spent most of their life solely focused on hockey, marriage is something I've never given much thought to. I'm not opposed to having a family, I just have a hard time imagining myself with one. Most of the women I've met since signing with the Otters seem more interested in my bank account than in actually getting to know me.

I check my own phone and see I have a new text from Beth.

Beth: Nice game! You didn't let any pucks in! Good job!

Man, she is such a teacher. I type a quick response.

Foster: Thanks. It's called a shutout

Her response comes in moments later.

Beth: It's got a special name? That's so neat!

I frown at the phone, surprised that she doesn't know basic terminology with a brother who plays professionally.

Beth: I'm screwing with you, btw. I know what a shutout is.

I snort with laughter before responding.

Foster: Oh, thank god.

"Who are you texting?" Ben asks, craning his neck to get a glimpse of my screen.

"My trainer," I lie, quickly putting my phone in my pocket.

I'm not sure why I lied. Okay, that's another lie. A lie on top of a lie.

I figured if I told Ben I was talking to his sister, he'd act like himself and overreact. We're just texting. She's staying at my house and we're keeping in touch. That's all that's happening and all that's going to be happening.

But even as I tell myself that, I can't deny that when I used the terms "funny, smart, and sweet" earlier, Beth's face was the one that came to mind.

CHAPTER 7

BETH

"Vimy Ridge was a big hill in France that was very important during the First World War. Many other countries tried to capture it, but no one could—until the Canadians came along. Our soldiers worked together, planned carefully, and on April 9th, 1917, they attacked. They fought bravely for days, and even though it was tough and scary, they didn't give up. In the end, they captured the hill."

I stare into twenty-four mesmerised faces as they look from me to the black and white pictures I've put on the smart board at the front of the classroom. The soldiers in the grainy photographs look so young that some of the children in the room could have older siblings the same age.

"This battle helped shape Canada into the country we know today. It was the first time all four Canadian divisions fought together, and it made people realise that Canada was a strong, independent nation."

A hand in the second row shoots up and I smile at the young girl it belongs to. "Yes, Amelia?"

"Were they really happy that they won?" Her pink scrunchie sits on top of her head like a crown.

I pause before answering. War is a hard subject for adults to truly comprehend, so it's very difficult for children to grasp the enormity of it.

"It was a very important win for the Allies, so I'm sure they were happy, in some sense. But you have to remember that they were also very sad. More than three thousand Canadian soldiers alone died fighting in the battle."

A bell chimes and the kids immediately start to put their school supplies away and prepare to go home. I look at my watch in complete disbelief. My first day absolutely flew by!

I know from my notes that once my students change into their outdoor shoes I'm to accompany them to the buses. The kids getting drives will meet their parents in the designated pick-up areas.

A flurry of new faces hustle by waving goodbye to me as they go.

"See you tomorrow, Miss Michaels!" Amelia calls as she's zipping up her puffy pink coat.

"Have a good evening," I reply as I head to the exit.

There is a chill in the air that nips at my nose and ears and I make a mental note to bring a toque tomorrow.

"How was day one? Are you thriving or surviving?" Tamara, another fourth grade teacher whose classroom is across the hall from me, asks as she joins me on the sidewalk. She's older than me, in her mid-thirties and was kind enough to check in on me a couple of times today.

"Definitely thriving," I laugh, unable to wipe the smile off my face.

Just like my brother knew he always wanted to play hockey, I knew at a very young age I wanted to be a teacher.

It's a challenging, ever-changing profession that demands a lot from you, but honestly, I've never been able to picture myself doing anything else.

It was only my first day and already I felt a real connection to several of my students. There's such a genuine curiosity at this age and I love being a part of their learning journey. Seeing their eyes light up when they grasp a new concept or reading to them and watching them get lost in the story is just so rewarding.

"You've got a good group of kids." She pulls her belted peacoat tighter around her and places her hands in her pockets. "But buckle up; as soon as the snow starts to accumulate, they'll go from angels to demons in the blink of an eye."

"Who's a demon?" The teacher from the classroom next to Tamara asks as he joins us. "Hey, Beth."

"Hi, Jacob." I'm pleased that I remembered his name. I've been introduced to so many people today and I just know I'm going to forget someone.

"The children are demons, in general," Tamara answers. "At least they will be when there's snow to pelt at one another."

Jacob nods, his blond hair peeking out under his knit toque. "Don't forget Skate Day."

"How could I?" She actually shudders.

When neither of them elaborates, I hesitantly ask, "What's Skate Day?"

"Every grade gets their own field trip before Christmas

break," he explains. "For grade four, that's a morning skate at an indoor rink."

"Oh?" My voice comes out higher than usual and I force myself to remain calm. "That's a big undertaking."

"Yup. Annually scheduled chaos," Tamara adds darkly.

My heart rate increases and I start to sweat despite the cold. "So...do just the kids skate, or...?"

Jacob shakes his head. "Kids, teachers, and some parent volunteers, too."

Dammit.

"And when does this field trip take place?"

Tamara answers. "It's always the last Friday before Christmas vacation, so this year that's the twenty-first of December."

After some quick mental math, I determine that means it's forty-seven days from now.

I have forty-seven days to either come up with a reasonable excuse for why I can't go, or teach myself how to ice skate.

CHAPTER 8

FOSTER

"Are you in or out? Where's your head at, Fozz?"

Wondering why your sister hasn't texted me back.

"Sorry," I say as I throw my pair of kings down. "I fold."

A chorus of "boos" rise from the small coffee table that four large men are crowded around.

I slide my phone out of my pocket and check my messages for the twentieth time today. There are no new messages from Beth since our brief exchange this morning where I wished her good luck on her first day and she sent me a gif of a very nervous looking kitten.

I'm not sure why I care so much, only that I do.

I can't remember the last time I felt this anxious about something that wasn't hockey-related, but Beth's had such a rough week; I want her to have a win. She deserves a big one.

"This is not your day, Fozzie Bear," Austin says as he slaps me on the back with his hand. I swat it away like you would any pest. "If poker is too challenging, we could play something more your speed. Go Fish, perhaps?"

"The authorities will have to *go fish* your body out of the canal after I drown you in it." This earns me a round of laughter from my teammates seated around the table.

Will makes a disgusted face and shudders. "Imagine the diseases you'd catch in that filthy excuse for a body of water."

"Crawford's probably already got every STI known to man," Ben snickers. "What's a few more?"

"Hey!" Austin protests. "I"ll have you know I have aced every blood test I've ever taken, thank you very much. I always wrap the Prince before any action."

We stare at him, horrified.

"Austin," Will says patiently. "Please tell me you did not just refer to your dick as 'the Prince.'"

He shrugs. "That's his name."

"I know I'm going to regret asking this, but why?" Will asks.

Austin forms twin pistols with his hands and points to his own chest. "Because his daddy's the King!"

Everyone collectively throws their cards at a very pleased-looking Austin, groaning.

"I swear, I get stupider the more time I spend with you." Ben gives him a look of pure disdain.

There's a surprising amount of downtime for professional hockey players. Yes, there's plenty of travel, games, and practices, but in between that there's a lot of hours to kill. In the evenings, a lot of the single guys go out looking for hookups, but during the day we tend to go through cycles of how we keep ourselves busy. Depending on where we're playing, we might go golfing or sometimes there's gaming in someone's hotel room. Lately, we've been passing the time with poker.

Why this poker game always seems to happen in my hotel room, I don't know. Maybe it's the price I pay for not being a slob like everyone else.

I need to leave soon for warm ups and I'd have a much easier time getting my head in the game if I know Beth got along okay at school.

Fuck it.

I leave my friends at the makeshift poker table and make my way to the in-suite kitchenette typing out a quick text.

Foster: How did it go?

The reply bubbles appear and then disappear.

"We're starting the next hand," Ben calls to me from the table.

"Play without me."

"We can't play with three guys, man."

"Then don't play."

"Fozz, come on. Please?"

Normally, I would, but, to be honest, I'm annoyed with him. He hasn't mentioned Beth once since we left on Friday. On top of that, I haven't forgotten the dig he took at my own family situation.

I don't think you're one to give out family advice.

He's not wrong, but I didn't appreciate the reminder.

I think about my brother Cody a lot, but especially this time of year. With less than two years between us, we were inseparable when we were younger. He's going to be thirty-one next month. The last time I saw him on his birthday, he was turning twenty-one. He'd gotten so drunk, I needed two other guys to help me get him home.

The urge to reach out and see how he's doing always gets stronger around Christmas, but I never do. Almost ten years ago he told me to lose his number and I haven't spoken to him since.

My phone starts to vibrate with an incoming call from Beth and I start for the door. Regardless of what she's calling about, I know I don't want to have this conversation in front of her brother, let alone the others.

"Where are you going?" Ben demands.

"Gotta take this," I say, slipping out of the room. I accept the call as I'm walking down the hallway. "Hello?"

"Hey," she answers and from that single syllable, I can tell she's smiling and I relax. "I just got home. Is it ok that I'm calling? My parents and sisters are still at work, and I haven't heard from Ben since you guys left on Friday. I understand if you're busy."

It doesn't escape me that not only did she call me and not her brother, but she just called my place "home." I'm surprised by how much I like it.

"How was your first day?"

"It was so great," she gushes. "The kids were wonderful. A couple of them are going to be a handful, but I know I can handle it. The school is beautiful!"

I picture her sitting on my couch, talking with her hands, her long brown hair falling over one shoulder.

"And the staff are all so nice," she continues. "Oh! I think I've found a place to stay."

A weight similar to disappointment settles in my stomach. I mean, of course she was going to find a place to stay, I just didn't think it would be so soon. "Yeah?"

"One of the VPs talked to me on my way out. He has a sister who was renting a room to a graduate student, but they'll be moving out at the end of next month. I won't be able to move in until January, but at least it's something. I was thinking that since I'll be going back to the Island for Christmas, I really only need something for six weeks, so I'm going to try to find an Airbnb in the area. Maybe I can find something that isn't too expensive since it's the off-season? What do you think?"

I lean back and let my head rest against the cool wall in the hotel hallway. It's not a bad plan. I'm sure she could find a decent place to rent for a short period of time. I should tell her that and offer to help her in any way she needs.

But even in the off season, those rentals are expensive and she still hasn't found a used car.

What if she finds a place and hates it once she moves in? If Ben and I are travelling with the team, she won't have anyone around to help her.

The solution is simple. I've got the extra room and spare vehicle and I'll be gone half of the time. Logically, she should stay where she is.

"Foster?" Beth's voice interrupts my thoughts. I should probably say something before she thinks the call was dropped.

"Why not just stay where you are until your new place is ready? It's only going to be a few weeks, right? I'm going to be gone half the time with games."

There's silence on the line and I worry that I've overstepped. We don't know each other well and I shouldn't have assumed that she'd want to stay at my place when I'm actually there. I'm about to tell her as much when I hear her sigh.

"Oh, Foster, I couldn't possibly ask that of you. I've already been such an in–"

"Beth Michaels, I swear if you refer to yourself as an inconvenience one more time, I will rescind my offer to introduce you to Otto."

Her laughter does something to my chest. It feels warm and tight all at the same time.

"I really do want to meet that otter." I can practically hear her chewing her lip as she decides what to do.

"So you'll stay?"

Why am I so nervous about her answer? Am I holding my breath? I really need to get my head on straight before we play tonight.

"If you're really sure that you don't mind."

"I'm sure." Surprisingly sure.

"Okay. I'll stay. Thank you so much Foster. I promise, I'll be the perfect roommate. You won't even know I'm here."

Somehow, I doubt that very much.

CHAPTER 9

BETH

"You look thin, Dear. Doesn't she look thin, Dale?"

I force a grin at my mother's concerned face looking at me from my laptop. I've been putting off this call all week, but it's Friday night, and I've run out of excuses.

"And tired. Are you tired? Dale, look how tired she looks."

My Dad isn't even on screen and I have no idea why she keeps asking for his input.

"I don't know what to tell you, Mom. I'm eating regularly and sleeping well." I'm the best sleeper in my family. As a baby, I'd sleep for twelve hours straight from the time I was six weeks old. Mom took me to our family doctor because she was worried there was something wrong with me.

Although, apparently, as a kid I would occasionally sleepwalk, if that's what you call it. I'd get up in the middle of night, walk around, and even have conversations with my family. In the morning, I'd have no recollection of even being out of bed. Even now, I set three alarms to wake me up every morning.

My mother sniffs like I've offended her. "Well, you look like a sleepy skeleton, that's all."

Patsy Michaels has been this way for as long as I can remember. Mom firmly believes that no one can take care of her children as well as she can, not even ourselves. When we'd spend a weekend with our grandparents, she'd pack days' worth of food, like she thought they couldn't feed us properly.

I steer the conversation away from my weight, which I'm pretty sure has not changed in the eight days I've been here, and fill them in on my new job. I tell them about the students, the staff, and the building itself, knowing my mom loves nothing more than getting as many details as possible.

"And what about your apartment? Can you give us a little tour? I want to see the space."

Okay, Beth. Just like you rehearsed.

"So there was a bit of a mixup with the place I was supposed to rent." My mouth has gone very dry, but I force myself to keep going, making sure my smile never fades. "Long story short, it didn't work out and I'm staying with a friend of Ben's, for the time being."

Were it not for her rapid blinks I would think the screen had frozen.

"Did you say Ben's friend?" My dad's head pops into view. His ears always perk up whenever his only son's name comes up. His grey hair is slightly matted to his head like he's had a hat on for hours and he's wearing one of the two dozen Otters t-shirts he's collected over the years.

"Yes, you've both met him. It's Foster."

"Foster? Foster James?" He barks.

Of course, Foster James, I think as I resist rolling my eyes. Do we know any other Fosters?

"The team's goalie?" Mom has regained her ability to speak.

"The very same." I'm smiling so hard that my face hurts. I know that I need to sell them on this so I play the ace up my sleeve. "Ben thought it was for the best."

The fastest way to guarantee my parents get on board with something is to tell them that Ben's all for it.

My parents exchange a long look and I wait for the barrage of questions I'm about to be hit with.

"Well, as long as Ben thinks it's a good plan," Dad says with a shrug.

My mother chirps her approval next. "Yes, Sweetie. Be sure to be a good house guest, though. Make your bed every morning and pick up after yourself."

Unbelievable.

Yes, I wanted my parents to be okay with my living situation, but I expected a bit more concern. I mean, come on! Their youngest child, who's never lived with a man that wasn't an immediate family member, is playing house with a single, professional athlete and they don't even bat an eye? As always, my brother's stamp of approval proves it is worth its weight in gold.

Mom starts to tell me about an upcoming craft fair at a nearby high school, and I follow along, agreeing with her at the appropriate times.

"Yeah, Mom, that's pretty expensive for a pair of mittens." I stifle a yawn. "I think I'd better get to bed. So I can look more rested the next time we chat."

We say our goodbyes and I log off, shoving my laptop to the edge of my bed. Even though I'm miffed at their lack of response, I feel lighter than I have all day having finally talked to my parents. Ben and I both agreed that there was no need to tell them everything.

I'm actually surprised that Ben didn't object when Foster told him I was planning to extend my stay, but he probably figured that if I'm safe and settled here, why go to the trouble of helping me find something else.

I pull out my phone and send him a quick text just letting him know that everything went swimmingly with Mom and Dad before heading to the kitchen in search of a snack.

There were several bare shelves in Foster's pantry when I got here and I took the liberty of filling them with my own groceries. I grab a bag of potato chips and make my way to the living room prepared to spend the next two hours scrolling hundreds of channels only to end up not watching anything.

I check my phone and see that Ben has responded to my message with his signature thumbs up emoji. Rolling my eyes, I'm about to set the phone down when it vibrates in my hands.

Foster: Sup?

If you had told me last week that my most active text chain would be with Foster James, I would never have believed you. But here we are.

Beth: Looking for something to watch on tv. You?

Foster: Beating your brother senseless at cards

I grin at the phone, shaking my head. Ben never had much of a poker face. Not that he's ever needed one, seeing as people tend to give him whatever he wants.

I start scrolling through the channel menu one section at a time. There really is nothing on and I wonder if Foster has any streaming services. I'm just about to give up when I notice I'm now in adult programming. I start reading the titles squealing with all the maturity of an adolescent boy when I find the holiday-themed ones.

Guy Hard

Hard for the Holidays

The Boner Express

I'm still laughing when another message comes in.

Foster: Find anything?

Beth: You have an insane amount of channels

Foster: And I only watch two of them

Beth: Are they porn channels? Because whoa that's a lot of porn channels

Maybe I shouldn't have sent that. I feel like Foster and I are becoming friends, but it's a new friendship for sure.

Foster: No. Weather and SportsNet

Foster: I only watch the porn channels for the articles

Beth: ☠️☠️☠️

The man is too many things. No one should be allowed to be that handsome, thoughtful, and funny. It's simply not fair. It's a threat to the delicate balance of our society.

Foster: Guys are threatening to take my phone. Have a good night.

Beth: You too.

I set down my phone and flop onto my back on the couch. My cheeks are warm to the touch and I'm a bit breathless from laughing. I feel a bit giddy over Foster texting me just to see how my night is going.

Don't read into it, I tell myself. He was probably just checking in to make sure I haven't burned down his house.

Desperate for a distraction, I grab the remote again and start flipping until I find myself on a local channel showing sports highlights. And who do they feature on his way to the locker room before last night's game?

My roommate.

Foster's expression is serious as he walks in looking gorgeous in his black suit. His teammate, Will Oliver says something to him before starting to laugh, but Foster doesn't join in, just offers a small smile while avoiding looking at the cameras surrounding him.

The sportscaster starts talking about his stats, but I'm

too busy thinking about the man behind the gear to pay any attention.

Annoyingly, I'm still thinking about him as I wash my face and brush my teeth. Even as I climb into my comfy bed I can't stop picturing his rare, unguarded smiles or the way his voice sounds when it says my name.

CHAPTER 10

FOSTER

It's after two in the morning on Sunday when I silently enter my house. It's always good to be home after a string of away games and I'm particularly eager to get back tonight.

I tell myself that it's because I'm looking forward to relaxing and getting back to my routine, but the real reason I'm so happy to come home is my new roommate.

I've never had a house guest. Sure, a few times Ben and Will came over and crashed after one too many beers, but this is different.

Beth has told me that she's fine and has everything she needs, but I'll feel better seeing her and knowing that she's settled.

Her brother made such a fuss about me letting her stay until the holidays. Forget just being his best friend, this one gesture made me the greatest man that ever walked the Earth. He all but promised to name the first child Valentina bears him after me.

I'm not sure what the big deal is. It's not like having her here inconveniences me in any way. Besides, I didn't do it for him; I did it for Beth. Her texts have been the highlight of my week, including my shutout in Florida.

Setting my suitcase down in the foyer, I slip out of my shoes before treading into the living room. I survey the dark space. It looks exactly the same as it did when I left a week ago, but it feels different.

I stifle a yawn. The post-game adrenaline has worn off and I am ready to get reacquainted with my bed. Making as little noise as possible, I walk down the hallway past Beth's room. Just as I reach my bedroom, the door to hers opens.

Jesus.

All the air leaves my body as my eyes greedily take her in. She's wearing a t-shirt that falls at her mid-thigh showing off long, toned legs. Two pert and perky nipples are visible through the thin cotton. Her long hair is mussed, making me wish more than anything I'd been responsible for that.

"Hi. You're back," she says in a hushed voice. A deep pillow creese is visible on her cheek as she gives me a sleepy smile and makes my heart thud.

I don't move. I don't even blink because that would mean losing sight of her and that is out of the question.

Devastating. The woman is absolutely devastating.

And Ben's sister. In other words, completely off limits.

"Hey." My voice cracks as I answer. Probably because my mouth has gone bone dry at the sight of her. "It's late. You should get back to bed."

She brings a hand up to cover her yawning mouth and her t-shirt raises another inch higher on her pale thighs. "Okay. I'm glad you're back." She gives me a little wave, her eyes barely open, before retreating back into her room and closing a door.

I lie in bed for a long time making a mental list of all the reasons I can't and won't act on this attraction. Eventually, I drift off thinking about messy hair and whiskey eyes.

❄

Morning comes, like it always does and I'm shocked when I look at my phone and see it's after ten. Sure, I was up later than usual convincing myself that sleeping with my best friend's sister is a terrible idea, but still. My internal clock rarely lets me sleep past eight regardless of what time I go to bed. At least it's Sunday and I've got nowhere to be.

After throwing some clothes on, I make my way to my kitchen to brew coffee, giving myself a pep talk along the way.

My reaction to Beth appearing like a vision last night was due to a combination of exhaustion and not getting laid in months. My body would have reacted the same way to any attractive woman standing half-naked in my dimly lit hallway.

Maybe it's time I take Austin up on his frequent offers to be my wingman the next time we're on the road for a long stretch. A one-night stand really doesn't appeal to me like it used to, but it might be the reset I need.

As I walk downstairs, I hear music coming from below and I frown as I recognize the familiar melody.

When I come around the corner, I freeze mid-step at the sight of Beth dancing in my kitchen. At least, that's what I think she's doing. Her limbs flail wildly, completely out of sync with the rhythm of the song as she quietly sings along.

She doesn't notice my presence. At least, I can't imagine she does the way she's moving. She's stringing together so many combinations of different moves it's almost as though she's having some sort of a fit.

I mean, wow. She is a terrible dancer.

I have to bite down hard on the inside of my cheek to stop myself from laughing. Because not only is she dancing like no one's watching in her oversized sweatshirt, tights, and ridiculous slipper socks, she's doing it to the worst Christmas song of all time.

When she starts to strum an imaginary guitar, my resolve breaks and I laugh.

At the sound, Beth spins around to face me, hitting her elbow hard on the refrigerator door. Her face distorts with pain as she winces and grabs her arm. My laughter forgotten, I rush to her side, reaching forward, but stopping before I touch her.

"Shit, I'm so sorry."

"For my arm? Or for laughing at my sweet dance moves?" she jokes, but I can tell she's hurting.

"Both. May I?"

She offers me her injured arm and I gently slide up the sleeve of her sweater, feeling around her elbow joint to assess if anything is broken. I try not to notice how soft her skin is or that she smells faintly like cinnamon. When I'm certain she's not seriously hurt, I release her, saying, "Your elbow is likely just bruised and should be fine in a day or two. As for your dance moves, I'm not sure anything can be done. And your taste in music is atrocious."

She gives me a gentle shove, using her good arm, eyes widening as she gapes at me in mock horror. "I beg your pardon? Taking Care Of Christmas is a Canadian classic."

"No. Taking Care of Business is a Canadian classic. Taking Care Of Christmas is an embarrassment to our nation."

"That's unpatriotic, Foster. Randy Bachman is rolling over in his grave."

"I don't think he's died yet."

"Well, he will someday and when he does, he'll be rolling."

I laugh again at the sheer ridiculousness of this conversation and she joins in, but grimaces when she straightens her arm.

"Do you need ice?" I ask when I see that it's already starting to develop a dark purple bruise. The sudden urge to lean forward and press my lips to it has me taking a huge step back.

Pull yourself together, man.

"No, I'm fine," she answers, tugging the sleeve back in place and giving her arm a little shake. "Though if you're going to maim me again, at least make a useful injury like a sprained ankle or a few broken toes. Coffee?"

Confused by her statement, I answer, "Okay."

"Okay, you'll aim for my feet next time? Or okay, you'd like some coffee?" She squints up at me, coffee pot in hand and I notice that her left eye gets the tiniest bit smaller than the other when she smiles.

It's fucking adorable.

"Yes to coffee. No to injuring you again."

"Pity," is her only response as she fills the mug almost to the top and passes it to me.

"Great game last night!" She walks back to the counter and starts to add pre-measured ingredients into a large mixing bowl. "The commentators were practically drooling over how well you were tracking the puck."

I don't want to talk about hockey right now. "Can we go back to the part about you wanting to be on the injured list?"

She's still smiling, but her shoulders sag a bit. "You don't want to hear about it. It's silly."

I join her at the counter and give her my most serious face before answering, "I'm very silly."

Her laugh might be the most joyful one I've ever heard in my life. It brightens the already bright room and floods it with warmth.

"It's not a big deal, really. There's a skating field trip for my class on the last day of school."

"And?"

"And I never learned how to skate."

I'm not sure what I was expecting her to say, but it wasn't that. Most of the kids I grew up with learned to skate before they learned how to tie their shoes.

"Oh." It's literally all I can think of to say.

"I actually have a big favour to ask of you." She's abandoned her mixing and has turned to face me.

"Yeah?" I already know whatever it is, I'm going to say yes.

"I had planned on inviting Ben over to my apartment for a late birthday dinner since we didn't get to celebrate with him this year. I've got all the ingredients to make my mom's lasagna – it's his favourite. Would it be OK if I invited him here tonight?"

"Of course."

"Really?" She gives me a smile that could bring a grown man to his knees.

This grown man, anyway.

"Thank you so much! You're going to love your first Michaels family birthday dinner. Mom's lasagna has four different kinds of cheese and three different kinds of meat. It will take years off your life, but it's totally worth it."

"It's cheat day anyway." As glad as I am to have made her so happy by granting such a simple request, I can't deny it's bittersweet. It's been a long time since I've had a family dinner and I can't help thinking about Cody and wondering if he's okay.

"I'm going to text Ben." As she skips out of the kitchen, the pompoms on her slipper socks bounce around her ankles. "Another fun fact about our family birthdays? We wear party hats."

I frown at her retreating form. "I'm not really a party hat person."

"Don't worry—you will be!"

CHAPTER 11

BETH

"Aww, fuck off," Ben says when he sees what I'm holding. "You added too many candles on purpose. There's no way I'm that old."

My brother looks like an overgrown toddler who didn't get his nap as he pouts at the five-layer chocolate cake I place in front of him. His cardboard party hat is slightly askew completing the look perfectly.

"Hate to break it to you, Benny-boy, but you are that old." I pull out my phone and start taking rapid fire pictures. "Oh! You look really miserable in this one. That's going on this year's Christmas card."

Foster laughs from the end of the table and I pivot to take a picture of him, too. I'm not surprised it turns out beautiful because, well, Foster is beautiful. Especially on the rare occasions when he laughs.

He scowls at me when he realises I took his picture, but I can tell his heart's not in it. There's such softness in his eyes sometimes.

Turning back to my brother, I say, "If you take a nice one for Mom, I promise not to sing to you."

His sour expression immediately transforms into a boyish grin and I take a few more pictures.

"Wow," Will says, still snacking on leftover garlic bread, as he observes my brother's rapid change from asshole to angel as he poses for me. "You really don't want to hear her sing."

"You don't either," he laughs.

"Hey, I'm not that bad."

"Beth," Ben says in a patronising tone before turning back to Will. "When she joined her elementary school choir, her music teacher told her just to mouth the words while the other kids sang."

My cheeks heat even as I try to laugh along with him and Will, but the truth is that Mrs. Doiron really hurt my feelings when she'd said that to me. I was only nine and I just wanted to sing with my friends.

Foster is the only one at the table not laughing. "Blow out your damn candles before you burn my fucking house down, Old Man."

"You're older than I am," Ben retorts.

"Smarter and better-looking too," Foster adds.

"He's got you there," Will agrees.

No arguments here, I think to myself.

I'm so glad that my brother has friends like these two. Real ones that will have his back, but also put him in his place if his head gets too big for his shoulders.

Ben blows out all twenty-nine candles with one breath and we all applaud.

"All that conditioning really paid off." He smirks as he starts to cut the cake into enormous portions and putting them on the plates I've given him.

Will eyes the dessert as it's passed to him. "Well, there goes my girlish figure."

I can't help but snort as I hand him a fork. He is the largest man I've ever met in real life, yet somehow the least intimidating. He's always got a smile and a kind word.

Right now, I watch him take a large bite of cake and chew it slowly. When he finally swallows, he looks me straight in the eye. "Beth, I'm going to ask you something, and I need you to really think about it before answering, okay?"

"Okay," I answer, hesitantly, bracing myself to hear that something is wrong with the cake.

"Will you marry me?"

Ben and I laugh and Will joins in, looking like he'd rather marry the cake he's devouring than me.

Foster chokes on the water he's drinking and I catch him glaring at an earnest-looking Will.

He can't actually think that Will is making a pass at me and even if he did, why would it bother him?

Not even Ben seems upset. If he thought Will was actually propositioning me, I'm sure he would challenge him to pistols at dawn, but he can obviously tell his friend is just being playful.

I wonder why that's lost on Foster.

I come to the conclusion that he must be concerned that Will is making me uncomfortable, though he needn't worry; I know the big lug thinks with his stomach.

Turning back to a seemingly oblivious Will, I smile. "I'm glad you like it."

"It's the best thing I've ever tasted," he replies. "And my dad's a pastry chef."

"For real though, Bug. This is incredible. Better than Mom's." Ben shovels another forkful into his mouth and I beam with pride.

"You're not having any?" Foster still hasn't touched his dessert, like he was waiting for all of us to be served.

That's sweet.

"Beth doesn't like chocolate," Ben answers with his mouth full of food. "Which is crazy."

Foster says nothing as he picks up his fork and starts eating.

After inhaling their desserts, Ben drags Will to the living room to play some sort of online video game and I get to work on the dishes. I expect Foster will join the guys when he finishes, but instead he gathers up everyone's plates and meets me at the sink.

"I can take care of these." I've been cleaning up after myself as I go all day, so there's only plates and utensils to wash now.

He shakes his head as he grabs a dishtowel. "That was the best meal I've had in years. The least I can do is help with cleaning up."

I look away, hoping I'm not blushing as hard as I think I am. I've never been very confident in my culinary skills, but after Will's proposal and Ben and Fosters' praise, I might be more talented than I thought.

Plunging my hands in the warm water, I grab a plate and start scrubbing, trying not to notice how close Foster is standing to me and how good he smells. I know he's done advertisements for athletic clothing and sports drinks, but someone should design a cologne line for him, because the man smells amazing. Like clean, mountain air at sunrise; rugged and fresh.

"So what do you like?"

Foster's deep voice startles me from my thoughts about how great he smells.

"Wh-what?" The oven has been off for hours, but suddenly it's stifling in this kitchen.

"If you don't like chocolate, what do you like?"

Calm down, Beth. The man is just making conversation.

"It's not that I don't like chocolate; I just don't like chocolate as a base." Vanilla ice cream with chocolate swirl? Great. A chocolate chip cookie? Wonderful. Chocolate cake with chocolate icing? No thank you.

He nods as he carefully dries the plate and I can't help but stare at his large hands and thick forearms.

"If you were to pick any dessert, what wou–"

"Lemon meringue pie." I answer without pause. "It's been my favourite since I was little. My mom makes it from scratch every year on my birthday." I may have mastered her chocolate cake recipe according to Ben, but I'm nowhere near close to replicating her pie crust. "I've always preferred tart desserts. Lemon meringue, strawberry-rhubarb, apple."

He nods thoughtfully. "Good to know."

"What about you?"

He rolls his lips together and I'm mesmerised by the movement. "That was the first dessert I've eaten in six years."

My jaw drops. "That's a tragedy. I would die."

His lips twitch as he scans my face. "Now *that* would be a tragedy."

"Come on. There has to be something you crave."

"Like I said: I follow the team dietician's recommendations pretty closely, with the exception of bacon. My mom used to make sticky date pudding a lot, though. It was one of my favourites."

"Oh, my grandmother makes that every Christmas. It's amazing." Just thinking about it is making my mouth water. I look forward to it every year. "Speaking of Christmas, when do you usually decorate?"

"I don't."

The slippery plate I'm holding almost drops from my hands, but I manage to hold on to it. "I beg your pardon?"

He looks almost sheepish, which, considering he's a rather large man wearing a cardboard party hat, is saying something.

"I don't really celebrate Christmas. I enjoy the days off we get, but that's it."

He goes back to his chore, clearly done with the conversation. I keep my eyes on him as I slip my hands back into the soapy water wondering what it would take to get him to open up to me more. I'm clearly not paying attention to what I'm doing because my finger scrapes against something sharp and I jump.

"Ouch!" I pull my hands out of the water, my finger stinging. Before I'm able to inspect the damage, Foster is by my side taking my hands in his.

"Where does it hurt?" His hoarse voice combined with the nearness of him makes me forget all about my hand.

He's close enough that his warm breath caresses my skin causing a shiver to run through me.

When his green eyes search mine I realise I never answered his question.

"I'm fine," I croak. "My finger must have grazed the knife I cut the cake with."

"Are you sure?" He's still holding my soapy hands in his.

"Positive. It's not even bleeding. It just surprised me."

Foster nods but doesn't move away. He looks positively stricken at the thought of me being hurt. Our faces are mere inches apart. All I'd have to do to close the distance is—

"Fozzie! We need you!"

We both react to Ben's voice like a jump scare. Stepping back from each other like we were caught doing something wrong.

"Go ahead," I tell him. "I'm almost done.

He dries his hands off on the dish towel and starts to leave.

"Beth?"

"Yes?"

He hovers in the entrance to the kitchen, watching me.

"Thank you for tonight. It's been a while since I've had a family dinner."

There are too many things I want to say back. I want to ask him what happened with his family. I want to thank him for everything he's done for me over the last couple of weeks. Most of all, I want to get inside his beautiful head and find out what he's thinking when he looks at me so intensely like he is right now.

"You're welcome."

His only response is a faint nod before he disappears around the corner, leaving me with sudsy hands and a smitten heart.

CHAPTER 12

FOSTER

"What do you think I'd look like with a moustache?"

Austin is gazing at himself in the reflective walls of the hotel elevator. He rubs his hand over his bare upper lip like he's trying to manifest one onto his face.

"A sexual predator," I answer.

"A nineteen-seventies pornstar," Ben quips, not looking up from his phone. He's been on it all day, texting all through the lunch we just had at a nearby sushi place.

"A young Tom Selleck," Will says and when he notices Ben and I looking at him sceptically he adds, "What? All white guys with moustaches look like Tom Selleck to me."

"Forget I asked," Austin huffs. "Speaking of forgetting to ask, I'm still pissed you didn't invite me to your birthday party."

Not this shit again.

"It's been four days, man." Ben sighs deeply. "You need to move on." Austin has brought the supposed slight up every day since then and we're all tired of it.

"Move on from what? From you guys throwing a party and not inviting me. You know how much I love parties."

"Like we told you the first half dozen times," Will sighs. "It wasn't a party. Beth made Ben a late birthday dinner and I happened to be there when she invited him. You weren't excluded on purpose."

"I'm just saying, she could have invited me, too."

"She barely knows you," Ben says, still frowning at his phone.

Austin licks his lips and grins. "Well, maybe I should get better acquainted with her."

I wait for Ben to threaten him, but he's too busy tapping away at his phone.

It is going to be a long week. Still, I've looked forward to this stretch of away games more than most. I need some distance from my new roommate. Beth Michaels has been consuming my waking thoughts and, as of last night, my dreams.

I close my eyes and once again attempt to block the image of her kneeling in the middle of my bed wearing nothing but my jersey, but it doesn't work. Nothing does.

I can't hold back a frustrated groan. Thankfully, my friends assume it's because I'm frustrated with Austin.

"Anyone want to hang out before the game? I've got the new season of Project Gingerbread House downloaded on my laptop." Will's favourite show follows a dozen bakers as they compete against one another in Christmas-themed baking challenges.

"I'm going to pretend you didn't just ask me that," Austin says disgustedly as the doors to our floor open.

"I'm going to take a nap," I tell him. Even if I wasn't, I wouldn't watch holiday reality tv with him on purpose.

"I've got to call Valentina," Ben grunts as he stalks down the hall, away from us.

Will and I exchange concerned looks. Ben's been in foul humour all week which is unlike him.

"Trouble in Paradise?" Will asks after Ben has rounded the corner. "Has he said anything to you?"

I shake my head. "Not a word."

"Maybe Valentina's pissed she didn't get an invite to the party."

"For the last fucking time, Austin," Will moans. "It wasn't a party. Besides, Ben said she was back in Toronto for work last weekend."

I'm not sure what's got my friend surlier than usual, but I wish he'd talk to me about it.

Like you're talking to him about your problems? I think darkly.

Obviously, his relationship problems and my feelings for his sister are not remotely the same.

So I've got a little crush on her. Who wouldn't? Beth's beautiful, but it's more than that. She has this sweet, genuine way about her that I can't help but be drawn to. And she's always making me laugh even when I don't want to.

A week away will give me some much-needed space to get these frequent thoughts and inconvenient desires under control once and for all.

As I enter my hotel room and close the door, the quiet wraps around me like a hug. The noise of my teammates fades away, leaving just the soft hum of the heater and the faint rustle of the curtains as they sway gently against the window. I sink onto the bed, letting the stillness seep into my bones.

A few hours of alone time where nothing is expected of me is exactly what I need before we play Pittsburgh.

I'm about to close my eyes and start my breathing exercises when I get an alert on my phone.

Pulling it up, I see it's a snowfall warning being issued for Ottawa. Fifteen to twenty centimetres overnight.

Fuck.

That system was supposed to miss the city entirely, but it must have changed course. Now they're about to get a storm and not only am I away, I haven't gotten the winter tires put on Beth's car yet.

I pull up my messages, trying not to read into the fact that I just thought of my Lexus as Beth's car and type out a message to her.

Foster: They're calling for a lot of snow tonight.

Beth: I know! 10-15 cm! I'm so excited!

Of course she is.

Foster: 15 to 20 now. The roads will probably be bad

Beth: I'll drive slowly

Beth: Or I can get an Uber if you're worried about the car

Of course that's what she'd think.

Foster: I'm not worried about the car, Beth

I'm sitting up in bed, pulling up a contact I haven't used in almost a year, my nap long forgotten.

Even in another country, this girl is driving me to distraction.

CHAPTER 13

BETH

Well. This is not what I expected to see as I'm leaving the house this morning.

The snow, sure. It's everywhere and it is glorious. There's nothing like the first heavy snowfall of the year. It covers everything like a blanket of white making everything sparkle in the sun. Apparently, we got almost twenty centimetres overnight, which is a lot for mid-November.

What I wasn't expecting was four men and some sort of oversized truck to be in Foster's driveway.

"Good morning, Ms. Michaels," one of the toque-clad men greets me while the others smile and wave. His grey beard is likely keeping his face warm on this chilly day.

I wave back, wondering what the hell is going on. "Good morning..."

"I'm Tucker. You're all set," the man says as he gives Foster's black Lexus an almost reverent pat with his gloved hand. "We've changed the tires and topped up your windshield wiper fluid. The roads aren't bad, actually. The snowplows have been out all night. But if you'd rather not drive, I'd be more than happy to take you to work and pick you up at the end of the day."

I'm so distracted by the strangers in the driveway that I don't notice the car which has been cleaned off and appears to be sporting four, shiny new tires.

Foster.

I'm not worried about the car, Beth.

My heartbeat quickens at the thought of him being so concerned for my personal safety that he sent a crew of men in the early morning to winterise his car. But that's just Foster, right? The man is a natural born protector who's done nothing but look out for me since I arrived. I'd like to spend more time unpacking this, but I have a job to get to.

I thank the men and assure them I'll be fine to get to work on my own. Once I'm in the car, I send Foster a message.

Beth: Thank you. You really didn't need to do that.

His reply comes so quickly that, if I didn't know better, I'd think he was waiting on my text.

Foster: Yes I did. Drive safely. Text when you get to work.

Foster: Please.

Grinning, I put my phone in my bag and start the car. The windshield is so clean it's as if it wasn't buried in snow an hour before.

Tucker was right; the roads have been cleaned up

nicely, especially considering how much snow came down. Still, I take my time, wary of any black ice that might be hiding.

The commute seems so different this morning, like the snow has softened the edges of everything. I catch glimpses of people shovelling their driveways, bundled up in puffy coats and bright scarves, their breath visible in the cold air. I sing along to the radio all the way to work.

I really love how close Foster's place is to the school. The place I'll be renting in the new year is twice as far. But at least it exists, unlike the last place I rented.

Once I've parked in the staff parking lot, I retrieve my phone from my purse and text Foster again.

Beth: Beth Michaels has been marked SAFE at Stittsville Elementary.

Foster: Thanks 🩷

If they weren't attached to my face, I'm certain my eyebrows would have hit the ceiling of the luxury SUV.

Foster: Shit. My finger slipped.

I break into hysterics thinking of the horror on Foster's face at sending me that little pink heart and decide to screw with him.

Beth: Of course it did 💋

Not expecting a reply, I grab my bag, but just as I'm about to climb out, the phone buzzes again.

Foster: Thanks for understanding 💪

I squeal and do a little dance in my seat. He's not flirting with me; not really. But it's likely the closest I'll ever get, so I plan to enjoy it while I can.

Beth: Anytime 🍑

❄

The kids are bouncing off the walls with excitement today. I'm not sure if it's because it's Friday, there is a coating of fresh snow to play in or the fact that every day that passes brings us one step closer to Christmas vacation, but they are like ticking bombs ready to go off at any minute.

I land in the staff room with my lunch bag feeling like I've crawled off a battlefield. The children, so sweet and attentive when I started last week, have gotten wilder and more unhinged as the days go by. And there are still five weeks of school before the break!

"Hey there," Jacob says, his face lighting up when he spots me. "You look like you could use this." He hands me a cup of coffee which I accept gratefully.

"Is it that obvious?" I croak, bringing the cup to my lips and making a mental note to check my appearance in the bathroom before the afternoon.

"Only a little." Jacob has been one of the most supportive new colleagues I've met since I started. He's always popping his head into my classroom to check on me and ask if I need anything. "I'll bring you something stronger at the staff party next week."

The Christmas staff party is being held at one of the vice principals' homes next Friday night and I'm looking forward to getting to know more of my new coworkers better.

"So what type of party is it?" So far I've only been given a time and place so I want to make sure I'm prepared and dressed appropriately. "Casual drinks and food? Or more formal? Will there be games? Don't get me wrong, I'm fine with that but if I'm going to be forced to play charades, I need a bit of warning."

"The first kind, thank God," Tamara answers as she joins us. "It's very low key. If we play any games, they're drinking games."

"Perfect," I sigh with relief unwrapping my sandwich and starting to eat my lunch. I used a fancy balsamic and black pepper mustard that I found in Foster's fridge on my Montreal smoked meat on rye sandwich and it is just delightful.

"I hope there isn't a hockey game on," she groans, stabbing her salad with a fork. "Last year, all the men were in the living room watching tv and the women were all in the kitchen getting drunk." She pauses, contemplatively. "Come to think of it, it was lovely. Go sports team."

"The Otters don't play next Friday. They're in Boston next Saturday," Jacob pipes up as he returns to the table with his own cup of coffee.

I shake my head, swallowing the food in my mouth. "No, they're in Boston next Thursday and next Saturday is a home game."

Is it weird that I've memorised the team's schedule for the next couple of weeks? Given that I'm living with one of the players, it seems perfectly logical to me.

Tamara quirks an eyebrow at me while Jacob pulls out his phone looking confused.

"Huh. You're right. I could have sworn they were in Boston next Saturday," he says looking at me with renewed interest. "You follow hockey?"

Here's the thing. Most people back home know who I am. People have been watching my brother with interest since he was six years old and I can't remember a time when I've been anything other than Ben Michael's sister to the general population. And while I don't plan to deny the fact that my brother is an NHL defenseman, I also wasn't going to volunteer the information. Not yet, at least.

I take another bite of my sandwich, chewing thoroughly and swallowing before replying, "I do."

"That's awesome," Jacob appears legitimately excited to learn this. "We should go to a game sometime. I can get us good seats." He adds with fake modesty, "I know a guy."

I hide a smile. *Me too.*

"Sure," I say with a shrug. I wonder how he would react if he knew who my brother is.

Or who my roommate is. I feel the colour rise in my cheeks again at the thought of Foster's texts. While he's been travelling for most of the two weeks I've been staying with him, I have really enjoyed getting to know him better. I think we're becoming good friends.

Which means I really need to bury this juvenile crush I have on him.

"Aren't you supposed to be on second duty, Jacob?" Tamara gives him a pointed look.

"Oh shit." Jacob stands and starts to leave before stopping and backtracking. "Let me know if you need a drive to the party next week, Beth?"

"I'm already taking her," Tamara says in a singsong voice.

"Right." He's clearly disappointed as he's pulling on his coat. "I'll see you ladies later."

The moment he's gone and we're alone, she turns to me. "He wants to woo you." There's no teasing in her tone; she says it like she's stating a fact.

"No he doesn't." Wait. Does he?

"Oh yes he fucking does. He's already started wooing."

"I'm not being wooed. I would know if wooing was taking place."

"Beth, that boy was pitching woo all over you. The entire room is covered in it. It absolutely reeks of woo in here."

"I don't think that's how wooing works."

"Maybe not. No one has wooed me in quite some time. But I recognize the act when I see it. The question is, do you want to be wooed?"

I give myself a moment to consider her question. Jacob seems like a really nice guy. He's nice-looking and employed and heaven knows I could do worse. But I don't get that flutter of excitement when I'm around him. When he smiles at me, I think "that's a nice smile" and that's as far as it goes.

When Foster smiles at me, I feel like my vital organs are all about to simultaneously malfunction, but, like, in a positive way.

"No," I answer, firmly. "I'm not looking to be wooed." At least not by Jacob. Part of me wishes I felt that way for him. It would certainly be easier than having an unrequited crush on my brother's best friend.

"I figured as much," Tamara nods solemnly. "You'll have to make that clear to him. He's a good guy, but he's the type who'll follow you around like a lost puppy unless you tell him to go home."

"I won't lead him on."

"Good," she stands and stretches, like she's limbering up for a fight. "Alright, Ms. Michaels. There are two hours left in the school day. If we stick together, we just might make it out of here alive."

Chuckling, I pack up my lunch bag, ready to return to class. "So the kids aren't just acting like this because I'm new?"

"Nope. The first snowfall makes them feral. Every damn year." I follow her into the bustling hallway, almost getting run over by a mob of children. "No running, Jeremiah!" Tamara says with a shake of her head. "By the time Skate Day arrives, they're more beast than children."

My stomach sinks as I part ways with her and enter my very active, noisy classroom. Skate Day is one problem I don't have a solution for yet.

CHAPTER 14

FOSTER

My alarm goes off at seven-forty-five. I roll out of bed and throw on a worn t-shirt and a pair of sweatpants. I don't normally set alarms this early, but I have a lot to get done today.

Alright, I don't. But I really want to see Beth before she leaves for work.

It's been nine long days since I've laid eyes on her. Yes. I've been counting.

I was sure that some time and distance were what I needed to find perspective and come to terms that regardless of my feelings, nothing was going to happen between the two of us.

I can't deny it anymore—I like Beth more than just a friend. It's ridiculous, really. I'm twenty-nine years old; I shouldn't get crushes like some awkward middle schooler. I've tried to remind myself of all the reasons I can't pursue this, mainly that she's Ben's little sister and my temporary roommate. But my brain won't listen to reason and I feel like a damn fool. My pulse picks up when I think about her. I can't stop checking my phone to see if she texted me. And when she does message me, it's like everything she says is the most interesting thing I've ever heard. Thinking about her has become a habit I can't shake and it's starting to mess with my head. A few days ago, I called her to ask if any packages had arrived. I wasn't even expecting a delivery, I just wanted to hear her voice.

There's no way I'm going to cross any lines. As much as I like her, she's the definition of off-limits. No matter how strong this feeling is, I owe it to Ben—and to Beth—to keep things as they are.

But that doesn't mean I'm going to avoid her. Regardless of my infatuation with her, Beth has become one of my few friends. She's easy to talk to and even easier to be around. Just because something can't happen romantically between us doesn't mean I don't want her in my life.

Also, our friendly, bordering-on-flirty banter is the most fun I've had in years and I'm not about to give it up.

I find Beth in the foyer slipping out of those ridiculous pompom slipper socks she wears whenever she's home.

She looks lovely. I mean, she always does, but today even more so. The dark green sweater dress she's wearing is simple, but it hugs her body, tracing the lines of her figure in a way that makes it hard not to notice. Her dark hair is pulled back in a low messy bun, with a few tendrils loosely framing her face.

She straightens when she notices me. "Hey you. Long time no see."

Too fucking long, I think.

"You look nice," I tell her, honestly. Her cheeks flush and she smiles shyly.

"Thank you. I have my staff Christmas party after

school today. I'll be going there straight from work, so I won't be in your hair."

I frown. I was kind of looking forward to having her in my hair.

"Where is the party?" I'm trying to sound casual and have no idea if I'm succeeding.

"One of the vice principals' houses. Don't worry, I'm going to get an Uber to work and then grab a ride with a coworker so I don't have to leave your car at the school. I have the app downloaded and ready to go." She waves her phone, excitedly.

Dammit. Why does she have to be so adorable?

"I can drive you," I say, already reaching for my coat.

She looks mildly panicked at the suggestion, though I have no idea why. "Oh, you don't have to do that."

"I know, but I don't mind. You can fill me in about your week on the way. Tell me what I've missed." *Aside from you.*

"But…it's just…you know." She's practically squirming with unease.

Has something changed while I was gone? We've spent the past week trading texts, each exchange of our banter easily becoming the best part of my day. Why does it suddenly seem like she can't get away from me fast enough?

"Okay," I laugh to mask my disappointment. "I can take a hint. Have a good time at your party." I shoot her what I hope is a convincing smile before I start to walk away.

"No one at school knows I'm Ben's sister."

I turn back around, not knowing what this has to do with me driving her to school. "Okay."

"And they definitely don't know I'm staying with you."

Ah.

"Beth," I hedge, playfully. "Are you embarrassed to be seen with me?"

She covers her face with her hands. "No! Of course not. But if they see you dropping me off, they're going to have questions. What if someone recognizes you?"

"I won't wear my goalie mask."

"Foster, please." Her hands find her hips and my eyes linger there for a moment too long. "People Magazine put you in their Fifty Most Beautiful Athletes edition last year."

I grin. "Did you purchase that magazine?"

"No." Her denial comes too quickly and she won't meet my eye.

"Oh wow, you did. Do you have it here? Do you want me to sign it?" I shouldn't be enjoying this so much, but she's so fucking cute when she's embarrassed. I hated every goddamn second of that photoshoot, but her reaction right now makes every awkward pose worth it.

This is the best day of my life.

"I hate you," she says pushing past me.

"Wait," I rush ahead of her, putting myself between her and the door. "I'll wear a hat and sunglasses. No one is going to recognize me."

"But they still might ask who you are."

I shrug. "Tell them I'm your boyfriend."

Am I a masochist? Maybe.

She looks shocked by the suggestion. I'd be offended if she wasn't blushing so hard. "No one is going to believe that, Foster," she takes her coat from the closet and throws it on.

"Why not?"

"Well, for one, this." She waves her hand dramatically like she's drawing an imaginary circle around me. "And then there's this." She repeats the motion only on herself this time.

"I'm not following."

At this she laughs, rolling her eyes. "Of course you're not. You know what, it's fine. Let's go, fake boyfriend."

We catch up on the drive to school. She talks about her students and what they've been working on in class. I update her on one of the team's forwards, Fischers, who got injured in the last game we played against Colorado. He's fine, but he'll be sidelined for at least the next three games.

When she informs me that she's found a yoga studio nearby and has attended a few classes I do my best to not picture her clad in lycra as she bends herself into various positions.

It's very difficult.

As I pull into the elementary school parking lot, the morning hustle is in full swing. Minivans and SUVs are lined up as kids with backpacks almost as big as they are jump out and wave goodbye to their parents.

There are a couple of teachers standing at the top of the steps in front of the main entryway. One is a guy around my age who definitely takes notice of our arrival. I track his movements as he steps forward smiling. He halts in his tracks when he notices there are two people in the car.

"Thank you for driving me on your day off."

"Hey, what are fake boyfriends for?"

"Like I said, no one would ever buy that," she laughs, unbuckling her seat belt and getting ready to leave.

"If you want to be really convincing, you could kiss me goodbye," I smirk at her from behind my sunglasses. Yup. Definitely a masochist.

Her mouth forms a perfect "o" shape as her eyes fall to my mouth. "That seems like overkill. I, um…I'll probably be home late tonight."

"Let me know if you need me to pick you up."

"That won't be necessary, but thank you. Don't wait up." Giving me a departing grin, Beth hops out and shuts the door. She quickly scurries across the pathway and up the stone steps.

The fuck I won't.

CHAPTER 15

BETH

Here's the thing: when people start drinking at four o'clock, they're usually trashed by seven. And tonight is no exception.

I've made a conscious effort to pace myself, slowly sipping my wine over the evening. The last thing I want is to wind up sloppy drunk and dancing on a table.

When school teachers let their hair down, they let it all the way down.

The VP's home is a lovely two-story, modern but very tastefully decorated. When I arrived, the first thing I saw was a towering Christmas tree adorned in shimmering silver and navy ornaments, twinkling lights, and delicate snowflake garland. After handing my coat to my gracious host, I was directed to the sleek kitchen where the scent of freshly baked gingerbread cookies immediately brought me back to my annual cookie baking days with my mom and grandmother.

Now, sitting in the spacious living room with a crackling fireplace that casts a warm glow over the room, I'm drunk on nostalgia rather than rum and eggnog and very homesick for my family.

But I have gotten to know some of the staff better and made some new connections. I met a Kindergarten teacher originally from Nova Scotia who invited me to join her book club and I made plans with a sixth grade teacher to go to a Christmas craft fair next weekend.

As the night goes on, however, the room keeps getting louder as my colleagues get rowdier. I narrowly avoid getting dragged into a conga line and am hiding near the fireplace when Jacob finds me.

"Hey," he opens with as he sidles up to me. He's dressed casually in jeans and a plaid shirt. There's a necklace of flashing Christmas lights around his neck.

"Hey. You look festive."

Jacob laughs, lifting the blinking lights from his chest before dropping them again. "When Principal LeBlanc gives you lights, you wear them."

"Well, you're pulling them off."

"Thank you. Are you having fun?" He moves a bit closer and suddenly our arms are touching as we stand leaning against the wall.

"Definitely, but," I have to pause to yawn, "it's getting a bit late." It's only nine o'clock, but the party seems to be trending from festive to feral and I think it would be in my best interest to leave sooner rather than later.

"Yeah," Jacob agrees as he straightens and looks at his watch. "I could drive you home if you're ready to leave."

"Tamara is driving me home, remember?"

He looks around doubtfully. "Are you sure about that?"

Before I can answer, Tamara appears. She's looking

very...merry. She staggers towards me throwing her arms around me and spilling her drink on my dress.

"Sorry!" she slurs before looking into her now empty red plastic cup. "How did that happen?"

"That's okay. I, uh, thought you were going to give me a drive home?" I'm not sure why I even say it. Right now she's not fit to operate a mechanical pencil, let alone heavy machinery.

"Ohhh, no love. I drive here, I don't drive home." She cradles my cheek in her hand. "Your skin is soft, like my cat. Have you tried the punch?" She raises her cup to take a drink and seems legitimately confused to find it's empty. "I'm going to go get some more. Looooove you!"

Now what?

I suppose when Tamara offered to drive me, I should have confirmed that meant both ways.

As I watch her disappear into the kitchen I evaluate my options. The simplest thing to do would be to order an Uber. I haven't done it yet, but it can't be that complicated.

Let me know if you need me to pick you up.

Despite the kind offer, I am not calling Foster. The man is not my personal chauffeur and I refuse to take advantage of his generosity more than I already have.

Pulling out my phone, I open the Uber app and enter my location and destination. A driver accepts my ride, but they're coming from Centrepoint and are more than 20 minutes away. I waver on what to do, not sure I want to be here for that much longer.

"So, how about that drive?" Jacob asks. "I'm heading out now anyway, if you're ready to go."

While I want to go back to Foster's sooner rather than

later, I definitely don't want to give Jacob the wrong idea by letting him drive me home.

Just then the sound of breaking glass followed by raucous laughter comes from the kitchen and I make up my mind.

Wincing up at Jacob, I say, "I'm definitely ready."

❄

"TAMARA WILL GET HOME SAFELY, I promise," Jacob assures me, patting me on the knee. His hand lingers a moment too long and I stiffen. We've been sitting in awkward silence since we got in the car.

"Hmm? Oh, of course. I know that." I tried to convince Tamara to come with us, but she was enjoying herself too much. While I felt confident that she wouldn't attempt to drive in her condition, selfishly I would have loved to have her as a buffer for this car ride.

It's becoming clear to me that her assessment of Jacob was correct. He seems to be interested in me. I've noticed the way his entire face lights up when he sees me and when he insisted on helping me put on my coat as we were leaving, I could have sworn he smelled my hair.

Even though my feelings are not reciprocated, I'm hopeful we can still be friends. After all, he's a really nice guy and we seem to have a lot in common.

I mean, we're both teachers, approximately the same age, and Otters fans.

But if we have any hope of being friends, I need to shut down any idea on his part that we will become anything more.

"Did you watch the hockey game last night?" he asks, breaking the silence.

"Yes! Great game. Heron's goal late in the third was beautiful. I thought for sure we were going into overtime."

"Same," he nods as he pulls onto Foster's street. "James should have stopped that goal in the second. He's really been off his game lately."

I scrunch up my face but say nothing. What games has Jacob been watching? Foster's been on fire this season and anyone who says otherwise doesn't know their ass from their elbow.

"It doesn't help that their defence has been a joke so far this season."

Deep breaths, Beth.

Look. I realise that it's common practice to talk shit about athletes. They make millions of dollars a year and because of that, fans feel like they're owed perfect performances. But the fact is, professional athletes are still human. They're out there working their asses off under unbelievable pressure and constant scrutiny. So when people who've never played the game anywhere near that level offer up their couch commentary, I get a little defensive.

Furthermore, Jacob is wrong. Foster's advanced stats have been excellent and Ben and the rest of the defence have been solid. Yes, they've lost a few games they probably shouldn't have, but that's hockey.

Foster's property comes into view and I point to his driveway. "This is me here. You can just pull over."

He doesn't listen and pulls into the entrance. "Wow," he says as he drives up the long driveway. Wow is right.

Foster's place is impressive. "Who did you say you're staying with?"

"A friend," is all I offer him. He puts the car in park and I say, "Thanks again for the ride."

"My pleasure."

I climb out of the car, intending to tell him that I'll see him at work, but to my absolute horror he gets out of the car and starts to walk towards the house. I'm frozen in place next to the car.

He smiles and motions me towards the house. "This is a door-to-door car service," he jokes.

"That's really not necessary," I insist, keeping at least five feet between us as I make my way up the steps. There doesn't appear to be any lights on in the house and I wonder if Foster has turned in for the night.

He could be out with friends. Or on a date.

I punch the security code into the keypad as I attempt to say goodnight once more to Jacob. "I really appreciate the drive home."

"Like I said, it was my pleasure." He stands in front of me, his hands in the pockets of his coat. "We should hang out sometime."

I open my mouth to respond, but can't decide on the right thing to say. Jacob takes the opportunity to focus his gaze on my parted lips.

Oh God, he wants to kiss me.

Is this what I look like when my eyes wander to Foster's mouth?

Jacob leans forward ever so slightly and I'm about to gently break it to him that I'm not interested in him that way when the front door opens. We both turn to gawk at the man who takes up the entire doorway.

"Hey," Foster says, his eyes sweeping over me as though he wants to make sure I'm in one piece. His gaze softens when it settles on my face and he leans a shoulder on the door frame. "How was the party?"

I stare into his eyes, unable to look away. "Good." Illuminated by the light of the moon, his skin almost glows. "Are you good?"

There's a glint in his eyes as he smirks at me. "Yeah. I'm good."

"Good."

"Good." He tears his gaze away from me and looks at my companion who I momentarily had forgotten was there.

"This is my coworker, Jacob," I offer, lamely. "He gave me a ride."

Foster nods. "Thanks for getting her home safely."

Jacob's eyes bounce between the two of us. It's obvious that he recognizes him, because of course he does. "Uh…yeah. No…no problem. Um…I'll see you Monday, Beth." He looks starstruck as he nods at Foster and then heads down the steps. When he reaches his car, he looks back up at us.

Foster waves at him and Jacob awkwardly waves back before climbing in and driving away.

I watch him go, certain that the anonymity I've enjoyed at Stittsville Elementary is leaving with him.

"He seems nice," Foster says as he moves out of the doorway so I can step in.

I roll my eyes as I push past him, pausing just long enough to slip out of my snow-covered boots on my way to my room.

"What?" He trails behind me down the hall. "Did I say

something to upset you?"

I turn on my heel and walk back toward him, crowding him in the dim confined space. I'm so frustrated with him that I don't even allow myself to enjoy his fresh, manly scent. Much.

"Do you remember me saying I didn't want everyone I work with knowing my brother plays for the Otters?"

"Yes, but—"

"Well, I don't particularly want them thinking I'm sleeping with their goalie either."

His mouth forms that sexy straight line that's not quite a frown and his jaw flexes.

"Why did you come to the door, Foster?"

He rests his hands on his hips and takes a deep breath. Then another one. He looks up at the ceiling, avoiding my gaze before finally answering. "Because it looked like he was about to kiss you. And, unless I was reading the situation wrong, I didn't think you wanted him to."

I cross my arms over my chest, unimpressed. "Why were you reading the situation to begin with? Were you lurking by the door?"

"I wasn't lurking. I heard the car and I happened to look out the window."

"And instead of letting me handle it, you decided to jump in and do it for me?"

"I didn't think–"

"You didn't think I could take care of myself." What really hurts is that Foster has never made me feel like I need adult supervision. All the times that he's helped me, I knew he was doing it because he wanted to, not because I needed saving.

Foster blanches as he blinks at me. "No, Beth–"

"It's fine," I sigh. "You're not alone. Everyone seems to think they know what I'm capable of and what's best for me. There are things I can't do. I can't complain at a restaurant, even if the food is awful or they get my order wrong. I can't sew. My mother has tried to teach me several times and it never goes well. I can't even skate, but you already know that and come the field trip, everyone at school will too." I run my hands roughly through my hair. "I can't do any of those things, but do you know what I can do? I can tell a guy I work with that I'm not interested in him, romantically."

"I'm really sorry, Beth." Genuine regret is written all over his face.

I pause before entering my temporary room. "Thank you. And thanks for making sure I got home safe. Good-night, Foster." With that, I close the door.

CHAPTER 16

FOSTER

Everyone fucks up, boys.

My mom worked two jobs when my brother and I were kids and as a result we spent a lot of time with our grandfather. He drove us to and from hockey practices and taught us to drive as soon as our legs were long enough to reach the pedals.

He also smoked like a chimney, swore like a sailor, and showed us R-rated movies that were far from age-appropriate.

But he made a mean mac and cheese and he taught Cody and me a lot about life, including accountability.

One day, we were taking shots in our driveway and I fired off a puck so hard it went through our living room window. My brother and I immediately went into damage control mode, trying to come up with a plausible lie that would prevent us from being punished.

When Gramps came out, it was Cody that had the genius idea to claim it was a bird. I watched my older brother swear that a bluejay broke the glass and then flew away.

Our grandfather was a lot of things, but an idiot was not one of them. He said nothing as he looked between our lying faces. Eventually, I cracked under the pressure like any nine-year-old would, crying and admitting that I'd been the one to break it.

He'd ruffled the hair on our sweaty heads and then helped us clean up the broken glass.

"Everyone fucks up, boys. It's how you handle the fuck up that counts," he'd said afterwards over ice cream.

Gramps died when I was sixteen, but his pearls of wisdom always seem to come back to me when I need them most.

Like right now. I fucked up with Beth and I am bound and determined to make things right.

Some people would tell me to approach the situation delicately. After all, we haven't known each other long and I don't want to come on too strong. But I'm too eager to repair the damage I caused last night to care what the sensible response is. So when she emerges from her bedroom at nine o'clock Saturday morning, I'm there ready to pounce.

"Good morning," I say as she pads into my kitchen in leggings and an oversized sweatshirt, looking surprised to see me.

"Good morning," she answers timidly. Weaving her fingers together and looking up at me through her long eyelashes she says, "I'm sorry for last night."

"You have nothing to be sorry for," I insist. "I was out of bounds."

"But I overreacted."

"Only because I overstepped."

She pushes her hair back from her face and gives me a sheepish smile. "So we were both out of bounds?"

I grin. "Sure. But me more so than you. You get off with a warning. I'm in the penalty box."

"Alright then," she rolls her eyes.

"So we're good?"

She regards me for a long moment before nodding. "We're good."

From her hesitation I get the distinct impression that we're not one hundred percent, but I'm not going to pull on that thread right now. "Good."

Beth takes a seat on a stool at the breakfast nook before asking, "What are you up to today?"

I glance at my watch before responding, "I've got ice time booked in less than an hour."

"Ah. Just you?"

"Just us."

"Hmmm?"

"You're coming with me."

Her head tilts to the side and she looks up at me like I'm speaking in foreign tongues. "Why would I go with you to your practice?"

"Because it's not my practice, it's yours. Beth Michaels, today you learn how to skate."

Her entire body freezes, with the exception of her face which contorts into an expression so horrified, it's almost comical.

"Oh...no. No. No. Thank you, but that's going to be a no."

"Beth–"

"Absolutely not, Foster."

"Why not?" I was expecting reluctance, not outright refusal.

"Ohhh, so many reasons," her laughter is forced as she hops off the stool and walks around me to pour herself some coffee.

"Such as?"

Turning on me with a stony look in her eyes she says, "I don't want to."

I don't buy it for a second.

"You said that you needed to learn for work."

"I'm sure I can think of a way to get out of Skate Day. And even if I can't, it's my problem to deal with, not yours."

I open my mouth to argue more, when the reality of the situation hits me: once again, I'm taking the decision out of her hands instead of letting her fight her own battles. Once again, I assumed that she wanted me to swoop in and solve her problems for her.

Gramps was right. Everyone fucks up and I am on a roll.

"Of course. I honestly thought I was helping. If you don't want to learn to skate, I'm not going to push the issue. I'm sorry, again."

Beth sets her mug down, rests her elbows on the counter, and buries her face in her hands. "No, I'm sorry for being an asshole. I do want to learn," she groans through her fingers. "But it's too late for me. I'm too old."

I let out a bark of laughter and she lifts her head to glare at me. "I'm sorry, but you're twenty-six years old. That's not too old."

"It's too old to learn basic things like skating, swimming, or how to ride a bike."

I shake my head. "One of my goalie coaches just learned how to swim last year. He's thirty-seven." When she gives me a dubious look, I continue, "I swear. He wanted to do a triathlon before he turned forty so he had to take swimming lessons."

She worries her bottom lip as she mulls this information over. I'm dying to sell her on this, but I hold my tongue not wanting to push her into something she doesn't want to do.

Beth studies her fingernails. "I'll probably fall down a lot."

I'll catch you every time.

"Probably," I say instead. "But I'll teach you how to get back up."

"Will you laugh at me when I fall?"

I step forward and stop her fidgeting by taking her hand in mine. When she looks up at me with those gorgeous brown eyes I hold her gaze and say, "Only if you look hilarious when it happens."

She shoves me away, giggling as she does.

"And I'll buy you hot chocolate after the lesson." I can't help but toss that in to sweeten the deal.

Beth squares her shoulders and rests her hands on her hips, causing her oversized sweater to bunch around her. "You really want to teach me to skate?"

God yes.

"If you want to learn, then yeah."

Her sigh is deeper than Lake Superior, but when it ends, she nods. "It had better be really good hot chocolate."

❄

"OH MY GOSH! Look at that one!" Beth points at another tall pine tree as I drive to the rink. It's the fourth "perfect" Christmas tree she's spotted.

"Yup," I confirm with a nod. "That's a tree, alright."

She rolls her eyes at me before looking out the window again. "Can I ask you a question?"

"Shoot."

"Why don't you like Christmas?"

I frown at the highway in front of me. "I don't dislike it," I answer with a shrug. "I liked it well enough when I was a kid. I guess I just associate it with family and I don't have one anymore, so..."

I focus on the road, drumming my fingers on the steering wheel and needlessly changing lanes for something to do. It feels like it's been years since anyone has asked about my family and I'm out of practice.

Feeling Beth's eyes on me, I turn my head in her direction. Those bottomless eyes I find myself thinking about so often, are brimming with sadness.

"I'm sorry," she sniffs. "I didn't know that."

"It's okay," I assure her. "My grandfather died when I was a teenager and I lost my mom a year later. I've got a brother, but..."

He hates my guts.

She's still looking at me intently so I clear my throat and offer, "We had a falling out."

"How long has it been since you talked to him?"

"Ten years."

She looks so gobsmacked that I have to smile. "I'm sorry, I just...can't imagine," she sputters. "If I don't text my sisters at least once a day, I'm pretty sure they'd file a missing persons report."

I would too, I think glancing over at her. She looks lost in thought, her gaze downcast as she fidgets with her fingers. I've noticed she does that when she's anxious—pressing on one fingernail, then moving to the next, over and over again.

"You miss them?" I ask.

She nods. "I know it probably sounds pathetic since I've only been here a few weeks, but I really do. I've never lived away from home before."

"It's not pathetic at all."

I pull into the parking lot of the complex we're skating at. There are three separate ices here and the parking lot is packed. I circle the lot as I look for a free spot to park.

"Exactly how many people are going to witness my downfall this morning?" Beth asks noting the number of cars.

"I prefer to call it your impending triumph." I find a free space and pull in. "And just me. I know the manager pretty well and have helped him out several times over the years. We've got one of the smaller rinks to ourselves for an hour."

Her head nods, but her lips remain sealed together.

"Hey," I prompt, softly. "We don't have to do this if you don't want to."

She appears to consider my offer for a moment before nodding again, this time with conviction. "No. I want to do this."

CHAPTER 17

BETH

I do not want to do this.

Foster walks us through what appears to be a staff entrance at the back of the complex. I follow him through a series of concrete hallways that he seems to know well. With a duffel bag slung over his shoulder, he looks even bigger than usual.

He pushes through a set of swinging doors, holding one open for me so I can walk through. The temperature drops several degrees as I enter the rink which is foreign and familiar all at once.

I spent a lot of time in rinks growing up. Not only was Ben a superstar on ice from the time I was in Kindergarten, but both my older sisters played hockey as well. The unmistakable scent of burnt coffee fills my nostrils and I drag my feet along the thick rubber-coated flooring towards the stands where several pairs of skates are lined up.

"I didn't know what size your feet were," Foster admits as he sets his bag down on the bench. "I asked the manager to leave a few pairs for you to try. If none of these work, I'll find a pair that does."

I run my fingers over the sleek black skates. They're all worn but in excellent condition. And they look freshly sharpened. "I think these ones should be fine."

He sits down and pulls his own skates out of his bag and I join him on the bench, sitting a few feet away. I watch him take off his boots and slip his feet into the skates. His long fingers tighten and pull at the laces like he's plucking a guitar. It's mesmerising how quickly he's laced up and ready to go, while I'm still pulling the skates on my feet.

I start to awkwardly pull at the laces with my gloved hands.

Foster settles in front of me, on his knees. "I've got you."

He slides my right foot between his legs to keep it steady and proceeds to tighten the skate with impressive dexterity. His hold feels intimate, which is utterly ridiculous given the layers of fabric and fibres keeping us from actually touching.

He ties them in a loopy bow before moving his hands to my ankle and giving it a gentle squeeze. "How does that feel?" His voice is husky.

Absolutely incredible.

"Good," I breathe. "Super good."

He smiles up at me. "Good."

Releasing my right foot, he repeats the same process with my left.

I know this should not be so stimulating, but Foster James on his knees in front of me is not a sight I'm going to get over any time soon. He's all business, focused on the task at hand. Unlike me, who can't help but notice how long his eyelashes are from this vantage point.

When he finishes, he leans back and looks up at me, a tenderness in his eyes. "Can I ask you something?"

I beat him to the punch by answering, "You want to know why I never learned to skate."

He nods, but adds, "Only if you want to tell me."

I pat the spot next to me and he joins me on the bench once again.

"The rule in my house was that everyone learned when 'the skates' fit." I make the finger quotes to emphasise "the skates." "We didn't have a lot of money growing up, so everyone in my family learned on the same pair of skates. 'The skates' fit me when I was five. I was so excited to learn so I could skate with my sisters. Up until then, I was only able to annoy them on non-frozen surfaces, which put me at a disadvantage every winter."

He chuckles and I continue.

"There was a pond just down the street that all the neighbourhood kids skated on every year. The dads would take turns clearing the snow from the ice so we could use it. One Saturday over Christmas vacation, the entire family walked down together. We carried our skates in buckets that doubled as seats to sit on as we got laced up. It was the first day the pond was deemed ready to be skated on and every kid from the area was there. I was waiting for my turn to have my skates tied when I heard one of the older boys yell something. To this day, I'm not sure what it was that he said, but after he said it, everything got really quiet. And then chaos."

I give myself a moment to take another breath before resuming the story. "All of a sudden every parent was screaming. Marcus, a boy a few years older than me, had skated out too far and fallen through the ice. He went under before anyone could get to him and his dad went in after him. I don't remember much, just being more frightened than ever before. I'd never seen my parents look scared. They got Marcus and his dad out pretty quickly and an ambulance arrived to take them to the hospital. Both of them were fine, by the way." I shift uncomfortably on the bench, remembering how it felt to walk home from the pond that day. Everyone was so quiet, which was a real novelty for my family.

"Everything went back to normal. The temperatures dropped and people were skating on the pond again within a couple of weeks. But the next time my dad asked me if I wanted to go, I told him I wasn't feeling well. The time after that, I feigned disinterest. I kept coming up with excuses and before we knew it spring had arrived. It wasn't obvious to my parents until the following winter that I'd developed a phobia, but by the time they did, I was adamant that I would not skate. Every time I thought about going out on the ice, I'd start to panic. I had several nightmares about being on thin ice and falling in."

"Did they try to get you to talk to anyone?"

I shrug. "I didn't want to and they didn't try to force me. Between raising four kids, their full-time jobs, and Ben's hockey schedule, it really wasn't high on their priority list."

"Are you still frightened?" he asks, glancing at the ice only metres away. "Because they drive a zamboni over this thing. There's no way we're going in."

"No," I laugh. "I got over the fear of falling through the ice when I was a teenager, but by that time the damage was done. All my friends knew how to skate. My brother was an NHL prospect, for God's sake. It was easier to lie and say I wasn't interested than risk looking like an idiot."

"You could never look like an idiot," he says solemnly, placing a hand on my knee. I feel the warmth of his fingers through my leggings.

"What about when you saw me dancing?" I raise an eyebrow at him.

"You didn't look like an idiot," he insists. "You looked like an uncoordinated person defending herself from a swarm of angry bees, but not an idiot."

I laugh hard and long, swatting at him as he grins down at me. Even though I'm about to do something I've dreaded for years, even though I'm sure I'm going to make an absolute fool of myself and potentially break something, I can't get over how good I feel when I'm around Foster. He makes me feel safe even when I'm about to do something scary.

He stands, offering me both hands and I tentatively put mine in them. I stand up, steadying myself after a small wobble.

"Ready?" His gaze penetrates all my defences. Forget the ice; I should be worried about drowning in his seafoam eyes.

"Ready," I say with a confidence I do not feel.

"We'll start slowly." He leads me to the ice entrance going slowly for my benefit. "Anytime you want to take a break, just let me know."

I nod and he lets go of my hands. I watch him step onto the ice like he's done it thousands of times before because, well, I'm sure he has.

"First things first," With a confident stance and a smile playing on his lips he offers his hand again and says, "Let's get you on the ice."

I nod, suddenly feeling very aware of my awkwardness. Foster towers over me, his dark hair peeking out from under his toque.

Placing my hand in his, I take a tentative step onto the ice, my legs shaking beneath me. He stays close, his presence reassuring as I concentrate on keeping my balance.

“How does that feel?” He assesses me to make sure I’m not panicking.

Well, my heart is fluttering a bit faster than I’m comfortable with, but otherwise I’m fine.

“Okay,” I answer, attempting to stay as still as humanly possible.

"You're doing great," he encourages. "Try to keep your knees slightly bent and your weight centred. It will help with your balance."

I nod, trying to follow his instructions. He starts skating backwards, effortlessly graceful, while I cling to his hands, like a newborn deer on ice. My only job is to remain upright and it’s a position I’m taking very seriously.

"Beautiful,” he praises and I stand a bit taller. “Okay, now we’re going to try to glide. You’re going to push off with one foot, then the other."

I take a deep breath and push off with my right foot, then my left. For one brief, glorious moment, I’m skating.

Holy shit! I’m doing it!

But the moment I think it, my balance falters and I feel myself tipping forward. Foster’s grip tightens, steadying me before I can fall.

"Whoa there," he says, eyes sparkling with amusement and patience. "You're doing amazing. It takes time."

His laughter forces me to relax, and I find myself giggling despite my nerves. We continue at a glacial pace with Foster guiding me and offering tips, his voice always calm and encouraging. As we move around the rink, I almost start to enjoy the sensation of gliding over the ice.

After about ten minutes of our pair's ice dancing routine, he slows to a stop. "You're ready to try it on your own," he says, releasing my hands and moving to stand beside me instead.

"Are you sure?"

"I'll be right here if you need me."

For a minute, I don't do anything but stand still and take up space. Foster remains at my side, as promised, not rushing me.

You can do this, Beth.

I take a tentative step, then another. The steps are so tiny, I'm not even sure if you can call them steps at all, but at least I'm moving forward.

My movements become smoother and to my surprise, I manage to stay upright, gliding slowly but steadily across the ice. I don't look at Foster out of fear of losing my balance, but I feel him beside me like a reassuring shadow.

I make my way from one side of the rink to the other completely unassisted. When I reach the boards, I place a hand on the glass to steady myself and finally look up to find his smile even bigger than my own.

Before I can say anything, he scoops me up like I weigh nothing and spins us around on the ice while I cling to him, giggling uncontrollably.

"I knew you could do it," he murmurs against my hair and I think this might be one of the best moments of my life. Setting me down, he beams at me with pride. “You didn’t fall once.”

Looking up at him, I’m not so sure.

Against all reason and self-preservation, I think I might be falling very hard.

CHAPTER 18

FOSTER

"Hang a picture on my boy cause he's a fucking wall!" Ben shouts, slapping my pads as he circles my net.

I stand in the crease, my eyes scanning the ice, taking in every detail. The roar of the crowd is a distant hum, my focus entirely on the game unfolding before me. The Habs have been relentless tonight, but I'm in the zone. Unbeatable.

I'm not normally this sure of myself, but since my skate with Beth this morning I've been riding a high like never before. Listening to her as she opened up to me and then watching her face her fears was inspiring. I can't remember the last time I felt that fucking good.

And it hasn't worn off. I walked into the arena feeling like I could take on Goliath and for the first two thirds of this game, that's exactly how I've been playing.

We're up by two goals eight minutes into the third period. When the puck drops the action is immediate. Players crash into each other, sticks clashing, the sounds echoing in the rink. I track the puck as it moves swiftly between skaters. The defence is holding strong, but I know it's only a matter of time before they break through.

A forward from the other team intercepts a pass at the far blueline, streaking down the ice, the puck dancing on his stick. I crouch lower, my eyes locked onto him. He dekes left, then right, trying to throw me off. But I stay with him, reading his movements, anticipating his shot.

Not today, asshole.

He shoots. I react instinctively, dropping into a butterfly stance, my pads meeting the ice. The puck slams into my right pad, and I quickly cover it with my glove before he can attempt a rebound. The whistle blows, and I rise, preparing for the faceoff to my right as the crowd cheers. I allow myself a brief moment of satisfaction, but there's no time to dwell.

The game isn't over yet.

Another faceoff, this time to my left. The Habs control the puck and set up in our zone. I stay sharp, my eyes darting between the puck carrier and the left wing waiting at the sideboard. A defenseman winds up for a slapshot from the point. I prepare myself, tracking the puck as it rockets toward me. I catch it cleanly in my glove, feeling the satisfying thud. I hold it high for a second, letting everyone know I've got it under control.

The game continues, a blur of fast-paced action. My teammates battle hard and I do my part, stopping shot after shot. There's a breakaway, a two-on-one, and a couple of scrambles in front of the net, but I stay alert, turning everything away.

With the clock ticking down, the tension rises. I know they're going to throw everything they have at us. They pull their goalie for an extra skater and the pressure mounts. The puck is everywhere, players crashing the net, sticks and skates tangled.

A shot from the point is deflected, changing direction at the last second. I push off my right skate, sliding across the crease, my glove hand flashing out. I feel the puck hit my glove, and I clamp down on it, freezing play. The roar of approval from the crowd is deafening, but I stay focused, not ready to celebrate yet.

The final seconds tick away, and with one last desperate attempt, the opposing team sends a flurry of shots my way. I block and deflect, my reflexes sharp, my mind clear. The buzzer sounds, and the game is over. We've won.

My teammates rush over, slapping my helmet, congratulating me. I pull off my mask, my breath coming in heavy puffs, sweat dripping down my face. The crowd is on their feet, cheering, and I allow myself a moment to soak it all in.

I am a fucking wall.

❄

AFTER A LONG CELEBRATORY SHOWER, I strut into the locker room feeling invincible. The moment I've cleared the doorway, music starts to blare and a chorus of whoops echo in the room.

I fight a grin as my teammates, all in various states of dress, gyrate to "Whatta Man." This haphazard dance party seems to be in my honour and if I'm not careful, I'll wind up getting a lap dance from Austin.

Again.

"Hear ye, hear ye, motherfuckers!" A shirtless Ben

jumps onto a bench and waits for everyone to quiet down before continuing. "Tonight, we toast to not only our fourth win in a row, but our second shutout in just eight days thanks to this beautiful monster."

Several teammates reach over to pat me on my bare shoulders and Will hands me a tall boy that I accept even though I know I won't drink it. Who needs alcohol when you're drunk on life?

While I genuinely appreciate the recognition of my efforts, I'm ready to throw some clothes on and get home.

Ben raises his beer can and continues, "To quote a great philosopher, 'The more you celebrate your life, the more in life there is to celebrate.'"

I eye him, sceptically. "What philosopher said that?"

"Oprah," he answers solemnly, causing the room to break out in laughter.

"Fuck, Michaels," Austin howls. "Read a lot of Oprah, do you?"

"Nah. Your mom talks about her a lot after we fuck and that quote just stuck with me. But this isn't about me and Austin's surprisingly flexible mother. This is about celebrating our team, as a team. Gentleman, we're going out."

Ah, Christ no.

Every other person in the room thinks it's a great idea, though. The music comes back on and the guys continue getting dressed as I stand here in my towel with an unopened beer and a bad feeling.

Ben hops off the bench and heads straight for me. "Don't try to get out of this, man. We're overdue for a night out. I need this."

He's not wrong. We haven't gone out as a team in a

while, but it doesn't make it any more appealing, especially when I had a very different evening in mind. And what does he mean that he *needs* this?

"Besides, what else are you going to do?" he asks, walking away.

Go home to your sister.

I told Beth I'd be home right after the game and after what she said earlier about missing her family, I don't really want to tell her I'm ditching her to go drinking with her brother. Not that I'd be drinking. I haven't gotten drunk in ten years. Watching your big brother descend into alcoholism really takes away the appeal.

Hurriedly, I throw on a long-sleeved t-shirt and a pair of jeans, all the while trying to brainstorm solutions to this unexpected turn of events.

An idea comes to me, both terrible and brilliant. Fuck it.

"Hey," I approach Ben as he's putting on deodorant at his locker and get right to the point. "I think you should invite Beth tonight."

He stares at me like I've sprouted a new head and started speaking with a German accent. "You want me to invite my baby sister out to party with a bunch of horned-up hockey players? Are you serious?"

I roll my eyes. "You know no one will actually try anything with her." Not if they don't want to die a slow and painful death at my hands, that is.

"You don't think so?"

I cock an eyebrow at him. "Would you actually fuck Austin's mom?"

"Fair enough."

"Look, I don't want to overstep, but I think Beth's pretty homesick."

"Really?" There's genuine concern on his face. "She seemed fine the last time I saw her."

I don't point out that he hasn't seen her in almost two weeks. "I mean, it makes sense. It's her first time being away from your family and it's so close to Christmas."

"I wish she'd have told me. I would have flown her home for the weekend."

Could he be any more obtuse?

"She doesn't need to go home every time she's lonely, man. Especially not when she has family *right here*."

I can see the actual moment my words sink into his thick skull. His eyes widen as he asks, "Am I the asshole?"

It's hard to keep a straight face because, honestly? Sometimes. Ben is a good guy. He's the first to step up when the team needs a volunteer for a children's charity event, never hesitating to give his time or energy. Whether he's signing autographs at a local school or helping a teammate move, he always shows up for those around him when asked. But sometimes people don't come out and ask for help.

"Nah, you've just had a lot going on lately." No need to hurt his feelings.

"I'm going to call her right now and invite her to the club," he says, reaching for his phone. Looking at the screen, he pauses before saying. "Shit. Valentina is calling. Can you call Beth for me?"

One step forward, two steps back.

"Sure."

"Thanks, Fozz," he says, already walking away. "I really appreciate you looking out for her."

Grabbing my coat from my locker, I slip out of the room without ceremony. It's way too loud to make a phone call there and I can't take two steps without someone congratulating me.

When I finally make it to my car I fish out my phone and bring up Beth's number. She picks up on the second ring.

"...hello?" The tremble in her voice stabs me through the heart.

"What's wrong? Are you okay?"

"I'm...fine..." she sobs on the other end.

I run my hand through my hair and grab my keys, ready to floor it all the way home. "Beth, you clearly aren't. Please talk to me. Tell me what's wrong."

My mind races like a greyhound on speed as I come up with plausible scenarios, each more terrible than the last. Did she fall? Break something? Did someone hurt her? I'll fucking kill them.

"This happens every time." Her voice is so heartbreakingly sad, I feel like I'm being pulled apart.

"What happened, Beth? Tell me what's happening?"

"He just signed to the little Deaf girl."

What?

"I don't know what that means." Who the hell is she talking about?

"In *Miracle On 34th Street,*" she sniffs. Her breathing has slowed and she's easier to understand. "Santa Claus signs to the little Deaf girl. It makes me ugly cry everytime."

A movie. She's crying over a Christmas movie. I'm so relieved that she's okay, I can't help but let out a laugh.

"Are you laughing at me?" She sounds offended, but I'd rather her mad than sad any day.

"I'm sorry," I manage to get out between chuckles. "I just thought it was something serious. Why do you keep watching a movie that makes you cry?"

"Because it makes me happy," she snaps back.

Clearly.

"Well, if you need a break from…being so happy, I have a proposition for you."

CHAPTER 19

BETH

I *have a proposition for you.*

There have been several times over the past couple of weeks where I have thought about my new roommate/friend in less than co-habitable, friendly ways. I don't feel badly for thinking these thoughts. After all, he's an attractive man who's been exceedingly good to me and as long as I keep these secret sexy thoughts locked up in the brain vault, no one will get embarrassed or hurt.

But hearing him say those words to me in that gravelly baritone sent a jolt of want between my thighs that made me forget all about timeless films with heartfelt messages.

Those words, spoken in that exact order, had my heart trying to flee my body by breaking itself out of my chest cavity. Suddenly I was wide awake and the farthest thing from weepy.

Foster James was propositioning me.

Okay, it was to go to a nightclub with him and twenty-two other men, one of whom is my brother, but still.

Leaping from the couch with a newfound eagerness, I jog to my bedroom.

My leggings and t-shirt are discarded in record speed, replaced by a simple cream-coloured, fitted sweater and a tight pair of jeans. My hair, freshly washed after my skating lesson, hardly needs any effort. I give it a quick comb through before pulling it back into a high ponytail.

It's my face that needs the most time and help. After several minutes of crying, I look like I'm having a severe allergic reaction. I run a facecloth under the freezing tap before ringing it out and draping it over my face. After a minute, I remove it and repeat the process again. In the end, I'm still a bit puffy, but it's a definite improvement.

Digging through my sparse makeup bag, I pull out my would-be saviours, the concealer and foundation.

"Don't fail me now, ladies," I say, applying liberal amounts of each to my face and blending them as best I can. I add a few swipes of mascara and give myself a final once over in the mirror.

Not bad, really. Hopefully, in a dimly lit bar, people won't be able to tell I was crying over a beloved holiday classic.

I grab my purse and rummage in it until I find the lipstick I bought on a whim this week. I don't usually wear bold colours on my lips, but the deep red hue made me feel festive. I wasn't brave enough to wear it to my staff party, but I'm feeling more courageous tonight. Maybe conquering my fear of skating has bolstered my confidence.

I'm fetching my coat from the hall closet when Foster comes through the door. His eyes light up when they meet mine. They lower then, taking in the rest of me, and when they return to my face again, I could swear they're three shades darker.

"I'm ready." I'm not sure how I manage to get the words past the lump that formed in my throat when he came in looking like an Adonis in his dark coat and jeans. I wonder briefly if he needs to get his clothes from retailers who specialise in outfitting men of his stature and girth.

Stop thinking about his girth.

"Yes," his words break me out of my internal monologue. "Yes, you are." With a final appreciative nod, he takes a step forward, relieving me of my coat. He holds it open for me and I turn and slip my arms in as he raises it up to my shoulders.

"Wow," I laugh as I nervously button it closed. "A chauffeur who helps you get dressed?"

I turn and find his heated gaze seemingly locked on my mouth. I don't know if I could breathe if I tried.

"It's a full-service operation," he states matter of factly. "Satisfaction guaranteed."

❄

You don't belong here.

That's what goes through my head as the valet opens my door for me. I think it as the bouncer takes one look at Foster and motions us towards a private entrance and as the gorgeous hostess leads us up a set of winding stairs to the VIP section of the club.

You don't belong here.

When we reach the top of the stairs, Foster reaches his hand back to me and I take it gratefully. Giving it a squeeze, he pulls me in front of him, forcing me to enter the roped off room first. His hand lightly touches the small of my back as I step through the entrance and I feel branded.

"Bug!" The room is noisy, but anyone within a kilometre of this bar can probably hear Ben calling out my childhood nickname. Every set of eyes in the room land on me, some more welcoming than others.

He weaves through the sea of bodies with a dumb grin on his face and scoops me up in a rib-fracturing hug.

"I'm so glad you came," he says over the bass-filled music as he sets me down. "I'm sorry I haven't seen you much since you got here. Do you want to hang out tomorrow? Catch up?"

Oh God, I think I'm going to start crying again.

I can count on one hand the number of times my brother has asked me to hang out with him. I've never resented him for this. He's been an elite athlete my entire life. But the combination of him wanting to spend time with me and me missing our parents and sisters has me choking up.

"I'd love that," I say with a watery smile, not even minding that he ruffles my hair with his hand.

Ben leads me around the room, introducing me to hockey players young and old as his "baby sister." The implication is clear: Do not attempt to sleep with her.

His teammates all seem friendly and in excellent moods. As well they should be. They're having a great season and had a positively stellar week on the ice.

Not to mention that many of them have gorgeous young women by their sides or, in some cases, in their laps. I thought I looked nice leaving the house, but now I feel somewhat dressed-down surrounded by model-like women in skimpy dresses.

Foster is nowhere to be seen when I scan the dimly lit room and I wonder if he's found a private corner to share with his own female companion. Not that it's any of my business what he does with whom, but I do wonder where he's gotten off to.

Not that I'm thinking about him getting off. Oh god. Now I am.

The sensible part of me knows that I'm being foolish. After all, Foster is so far out of my league, we're barely the same species. Still, the thought of him with another woman is almost too much to bear. It's like how I felt when I realised that I wasn't going to marry Uncle Jesse from *Full House* because he was thirty some years older than me and already married to a supermodel. Only take that disillusion and heartbreak and multiply it by ten.

Soon I find myself settled on a plush sofa with a forward named Alexei and his very pregnant wife, Kim. Ben, satisfied that I can't get into any trouble here, leaves to go to the restroom.

"How are you enjoying Ottawa?" Kim asks, leaning towards me to be heard over the noise. She pushes her long blonde hair over her shoulder with one hand as the other rests on her stomach.

"Good, so far. I've only been here for a few weeks."

She nods. "This is our second winter here. Alexei played in Florida for eight years before signing with the Otters."

I smile and nod like this is new information, but anyone who follows hockey knows Alexei Pavlov. He's been in the league for almost two decades and his career is the stuff of legends.

"I'm from Newfoundland, originally, but my family

moved to New Brunswick when I was fifteen," she continues. "I met him when he was in junior league. I've been following him around ever since." Her husband, though engaged in a conversation with a teammate, seems to sense his wife talking about him. When his eyes meet hers, his face softens and he winks before turning back to his conversation.

Such a brief look, but so much transpired between them.

"This is our fourth," she says, rubbing her larger-than-life belly. "Our oldest is twelve and our youngest is six, so she came as a bit of a surprise to both of us."

"When are you due?"

"December twenty-fifth," she answers with a smirk. "But I'm hoping she'll come a bit earlier."

Alexei stands and asks her "Can I get you something to drink, love?"

"Another sparkling water, please."

He nods at me, politely. "And you, Beth?"

I'm about to answer when a shadow falls over me.

"I've got her," Foster says, holding a tall frosted glass out to me. It's filled with liquid that's even brighter red than my lipstick. There are cranberries floating in the glass and the rim is coated in sparkling sugar crystals.

My eyes widen. "What on Earth is in this?"

He sits down dangerously close to me, draping an arm around the back of my seat. "No idea. But it's called a Holly Jolly, so I thought you'd like it."

I feel heat rush to my cheeks and pray to Santa and all his reindeers that no one can see me blushing in the low light of the club.

"Thank you." I bring the glass to my lips and take a small sip. Damn. That is jolly. And strong.

"How is it?" Foster asks.

"Brimming with Christmas cheer," I reply before taking another small drink. It goes down easier this time.

I look back up at Foster to find him once again staring at my mouth and immediately wonder if I've smudged my lipstick.

"You, uh... you have a bit of sugar on your lips," he says, his voice low.

Without thinking, I run my tongue over my top lip and his jaw immediately hardens. He's looking at me in a way I'm sure no one has ever before and it robs my body of breath. The heat from my cheeks spreads like wildfire through my entire body as though I'm being consumed.

He wants to kiss me, a tiny voice inside my head says.

It's completely illogical. So far-fetched that I dare not give the thought another moment of consideration except that Foster is staring at me like he wants me. Logic be damned.

I imagine what his lips would feel like on mine. Soft and tender or firm and demanding? Would he take my lower lip between his, marking me as his own? Would he pull me onto his lap? Place one strong hand on my hip, holding me to him while the other skated up my neck to get tangled up in my hair?

I feel myself getting wet, that dull and unmistakable throb of arousal pooling between my legs and I know that I'd only need the smallest amount of friction to come apart.

The song changes to something more upbeat and I'm

suddenly very aware of where we are. Not in a hidden corner far from prying eyes, but a crowded bar with Ben nearby.

"Good?" A voice that sounds remarkably like mine says, though I didn't intend to say it.

"Good." His response is strained.

With great difficulty, I tear my gaze from his, looking back at Kim. To be honest, I'd quite forgotten she was here.

Her mouth is slightly agape as her eyes bounce from me to Foster, and back to me again, blinking rapidly.

"I have to pee," she states bluntly, struggling to stand. "You know, pregnant bladder."

"Me too." I jump up to assist her, almost spilling my drink. "The peeing thing. Not the pregnancy part. I'm not pregnant." I laugh loudly, like an awkward person at a funeral. I stare into Kim's amused face with a look that I hope says "for the love of God, please take me with you."

"Right," she says, prying the drink from my hands and placing it on the table. "Follow me, not-pregnant new friend."

Without so much as a glance at Foster, I let her lead me away. Sweat prickles at the base of my scalp. My heart pounds so hard that I swear I hear it over the deafening club music. Kim parts the sea like Moses with her giant belly leading the way. People are practically diving in the opposite direction as though her water is breaking.

"Okay, folks. Out of the way. Sacred vessel, coming through," she says as we weave our way through the masses.

I see my brother talking to one of his teammates. Ben spots me and waves me over, but I shake my head and mouth "bathroom" as I point at Kim. He nods and gives me a thumbs up, completely unaware that I was moments from mounting his best friend twenty feet away.

What was I thinking?

You weren't, you horny little minx.

Finally, we make it into the ladies' room. When the two women scrutinising themselves in the mirror spot us, they promptly collect their purses and leave, giving us a wide berth on their way out.

"I swear, some of these girls think pregnancy is contagious," Kim sighs as she checks the stalls. When she's satisfied we're the only one's here, she asks, "What was that all about?"

"What do you mean?" I am a horrible liar, but I've got to at least try to deny it.

"Are you sleeping with Foster? Or are you just thinking about it? And does your brother know that you're sleeping/thinking about sleeping with Foster? I'm guessing not, seeing as he's still breathing. Forgive me if I'm out of line, but sweet Jesus, the sexual tension between the two of you nearly put me into labour." Her Newfoundland accent is much stronger than before.

"I don't...I mean, he wouldn't...we can't...it's just..." Panic takes over and every moment that's transpired between us over the last three weeks comes out of me like verbal lava.

I tell her about the airport, the non-existent apartment, and the offer to stay with him. The text messages, the winter tires, the run in with Jacob and the skating lessons. Kim gobbles it up like my life is a trashy soap opera, hanging on my every word until I get to tonight.

"I feel like you've just recapped the first half of a Hallmark movie," she sighs, resting her hands on her chest. "What are you going to do?"

"What am I going to do about what?"

"About the rising price of gasoline." She rolls her eyes. "About the fact that you and your new roommate want to play a lot more than tonsil hockey."

Forget what I wished for earlier, Santa. All I want for Christmas is a black hole to disappear into.

"We don't! Okay, maybe, under different circumstances, I might...but I assure you, he doesn't want that."

Kim puts her hands on where I assume her hips would be if she weren't more belly than woman and regards me through narrowed eyes. "Beth, I realise I don't know you. To be honest, I don't know Foster very well either. But I know what I saw and what I saw is a man who wants to rearrange your insides with his mini-stick."

As I open my mouth to protest, the bathroom door swings open and another long-legged stunner saunters in. Kim smiles at her and then waddles into the nearest stall as the woman goes into a separate one. I walk to the sink, turn the faucet to the coldest setting and hold my hands under the frigid water until they ache.

Closing my eyes, I replay all my recent interactions with Foster in my mind. The casual touches that felt less than casual. The long, appreciative looks I was so certain I was reading into. The fact that since I got off that plane, he has gone out of his way to make sure I'm happy, cared for, and safe.

What if he is interested in me? What exactly would he be interested in? A casual fling? A roommates with benefits situation? Something more?

My head spins with uncertainty and I close my eyes tightly in an attempt to quiet my racing thoughts.

When I can no longer feel my fingers, I remove them from the cold water and dry them with a paper towel. I take a long, deep breath and try to look at this thing logically.

What is it I always tell my students? The first step to finding answers is asking questions.

I need to have an honest conversation with Foster. The only way to know what he wants is to ask him. It might be embarrassing and I might get my feelings hurt, but we're both adults and we'll just have to deal.

I wait for Kim to emerge from the stall and watch as she washes her hands before leaving the bathroom with her. I don't get very far before I run into Ben.

"There you are," he says, wrapping me in a quick hug. "I'm heading out. Valentina wants me to meet her at some director's penthouse."

Am I imagining it, or does he seem less than enthused to leave his team party and join my supposed "future-sister-in-law"?

"I already talked to Fozz and he'll take you home. I'll see you tomorrow?"

"Of course." I give him an eager nod. "Tell Valentina that I'm really looking forward to meeting her."

His face clouds for a brief moment before clearing up again. "Will do."

I watch him leave, exchanging high-fives and one-armed hugs to almost every person he passes. He's always been the golden boy that everyone gravitates towards and I guess some things never change.

"Hey."

I turn and look up at Foster's expectant face. He looks as nervous as I feel.

"Did you want another drink? Or…" He trails off.

Shaking my head, I say, "No. I'm good."

He nods, solemnly. "I'm ready to go when you are. Just let me know when you want to leave."

"I'm ready." At least I hope I am.

CHAPTER 20

FOSTER

Whatever handle I thought I had on this situation has disappeared—if it ever existed in the first place.

Beth looks out the window silently as we drive home. Her long ponytail falls over one shoulder and even though I long to brush it back, I don't trust myself to touch her.

I'd been so close to kissing her. In public, no less.

I'd wanted to. Fuck, how could I not?

Even without the sugar stuck to her lips, I knew she'd be the sweetest thing I've ever tasted on my tongue. The urge to lean forward and capture her mouth, claiming it as my own in front of everyone there was almost more than I could take.

Thankfully, she'd had the sense to flee, giving me the opportunity to regain my sanity.

Once she had left, I took a moment to get my head straight. I was on my way to the bar to grab a tonic water when Ben intercepted me.

"Hey!" He'd thrown his arms around me. "Thanks for talking to me about Beth. I'm really glad she came tonight. I don't think you know how much it means to me, the way you've been looking out for her. Knowing she's got you helps me sleep at night."

The knowledge that my own sleep routine now includes fantasising about Beth tangled up in my bed sheets burns a hole through my psyche.

Suddenly, my escalating feelings for his sister feel like the ultimate betrayal of Ben's trust.

Ben, my friend and teammate and quite frankly the closest thing to family I have left.

Ben, who Beth is trying to build a stronger relationship with.

Ben, who is adamant that he doesn't want any of his teammates messing with her.

But I have no intention of messing with her. The moment we shared at the club was a momentary lapse in judgement. I can't risk pursuing her and jeopardise both of our relationships with her brother. No matter how badly I want her.

I pull into my driveway just after one in the morning. Beth hops out of the car and makes it to the house before me, entering the code in the door like she's done it a hundred times before.

We haven't spoken a single word since we left the club and I would give anything to know what's going on in that beautiful head of hers. She may say "goodnight" and act like this entire encounter never happened, or she may decide to call me on it.

At this point, I'm not sure which one would be worse. Pretending not to have strong feelings for her or being confronted by her about them.

She slips out of her boots and hangs her coat in the

closet before entering my living room and taking her favourite seat on my couch. At least I think it's her favourite seat. It's the place she seems to gravitate to most.

"Can I get you anything?" My voice comes out rusty, like I haven't spoken for days, not just the last thirty minutes. "Water, or…" I trail off, not even sure what else I'm able to offer her.

She plays with her ponytail nervously like she's thinking it over and when her big brown eyes finally look up at me, I know I'll give her whatever she wants or die trying.

"Do you like me, Foster?"

I freeze. Shut down completely.

My lack of response sends her into a panic and she backtracks. "Not that I think you do, or that you should, it's just something Kim said at the bar made me think that maybe you do. And sure, I've had those thoughts before, because there have been times where I've felt like you're flirting with me, but I told myself that you were just teasing me, not in a mean way, just in, you know, a friendly way, but then there was a moment tonight where I thought you might kiss me, but maybe that was just wishful thinking. Not that I'm wishing you'd kiss me or anything."

She covers her face in her hands and lets out the world's most adorably exasperated sigh. Desperate to ease her panicked state, I walk forward and sit down next to her, but she keeps her hands glued in place, hiding from me.

"Can we go back in time to where you asked if you could get me anything and this time I'll just say 'no thank you'?" Her words are muffled slightly because her palms are obstructing her mouth.

With a sense of calm I don't feel, I reach up and gently remove her hands from her face. My fingers brush against her wrist and I feel the rapid flutter of her pulse against my skin.

She looks up at me with a vulnerability that shreds my heart to pieces.

"I like you." I swallow. "A lot."

"Oh." Suddenly the attraction between us that's always been there is thrust into the light and the air around us changes.

I nod. "And I very much wanted to kiss the hell out of you tonight." And many other times.

She blinks several times like she may have misheard me. "Why didn't you?"

Her face is so close to mine. When did that happen?

"Aside from the fact that your brother was twenty feet away?" My lips twitch with amusement and she smiles, drawing my attention to her mouth. Her red lipstick has faded from her lips, but they're just as tempting as they were earlier. When I look back to her eyes, they appear to be focused on my lips.

I'm fucked.

"He's not here now," she whispers, her eyelashes lowering like a final curtain as she leans closer.

I should fight this. Slow things down until we're both sure what the other wants and fully aware of all possible outcomes and consequences.

I don't.

A small gasp escapes her as my mouth meets hers, like she didn't really believe I'd kiss her. I'm not sure I did either, to be honest. My hand finds the back of her neck as her head tilts to the side. She opens to me immediately and I'm instantly drunk on her taste.

Her full bottom lip fits so perfectly between mine, like it was designed just for me. I suck on it gently and she moans into my mouth. The sound heats my blood and turns my cock to granite.

She runs her fingers through my hair, and I groan as her nails rake against my scalp.

"I'm sorry," she breathes against my lips. "Was that too rough?"

I grip her chin, bringing her mouth to mine and kissing her deeply. "Don't be sorry and for God's sake, don't stop."

Feeling her smile against my mouth, she scratches my scalp again, using more pressure this time. I want to feel her nails on every part of my body. To be covered in her angry red scratches from head to toe.

Beth's mouth never leaves mine as she climbs onto my lap, straddling me. I grip her full hips and she presses against me, our bodies sealed together. She feels so fucking good on top of me, I can't think straight. I can't think at all.

Running my hand up her back and neck, I gently grip the ponytail that's been taunting me all fucking night. I give it a tug and her head falls back, giving me an all-access pass to her gorgeous neck. I let myself explore it with my lips, tongue, and teeth, noting which places are sensitive. As I lap at where her pulse is pounding she gasps and when I follow it by taking her earlobe between my teeth she squirms in my lap so much that I almost come in my jeans.

Christ. It really has been a while.

"Hey," I pant, holding her hips still on me before I embarrass myself. "We should maybe talk."

Her eyes are dazed and dark with need as she looks down at me. I feel her hurried breaths against my lips as her mouth hovers just above mine.

"Yes, we should." She nods, but makes no attempt to pull away. "I'm free later, if that works for you."

I can't help but grin up at her. I love when she's cheeky.

"Later is good."

"Good."

"Good."

She gives me a sly smile as she sits up and slowly grips the hem of her sweater through her fingers before pulling it off over her head to reveal smooth, pale skin. Her lacy emerald bra pushes her gorgeous tits up like they're on display, just for me. They rise and fall with her hurried breathing.

Tearing my eyes away from her cleavage, I meet her hooded eyes before leaning forward and placing a kiss between her breasts.

"Beautiful,' I murmur against her flushed skin, kissing it once more. "You're so beautiful, Beth."

She bites her lip to hide a smile as she runs her hands over my chest, her fingers playing with my shirt and my hands start their own exploration. Her skin feels so soft under my fingertips and she shivers as they glide over her body. Every inch of her is a delicate blend of softness and warmth. I feel like I could spend all night just touching her like this.

But Beth seems to be growing impatient, her nails

digging into my shirt like she needs me even closer. I lower her down onto the couch and reach behind my neck to remove my shirt.

She inhales sharply when she looks up at my bare chest.

"What?" I ask as her wide eyes stare at me.

"Your muscles have muscles."

"Occupational hazard," I chuckle as I kneel over her. Starting at her navel, I trail kisses up her abdomen, ribs, breasts, and collarbone until my face is nestled in her neck. I prop myself up and look down at her. With her swollen lips and bright eyes, she's absolutely ruining me.

"Anytime you want to take a break or stop all together, you'll tell me?"

"Stop?" Her eyes dance with laughter as she roughly runs her fingers over my scalp again. "Stopping sounds like a terrible decision."

Well, it won't be the first one I've made tonight.

Part of me knows that we're taking this too fast; every rational part of me screams it. There are several reasons why this is a bad idea, why I should put up boundaries and stick to them. But right now, all those reasons fade into the background and I can't deny what's right in front of me.

I want her. Plain and simple.

All I know is that it's been a long time since I've wanted anyone or anything and I'm allowing myself to be selfish, just this once.

I run my hand over the waist of her jeans. "Can I take these off? Don't get me wrong, your ass looks phenomenal in them, but at the moment, they're in my way."

She nods and my fingers make quick work of the

button and zipper as I continue to kiss every bit of her exposed skin I can reach.

"Lift your hips for me, darlin'," I murmur against her shoulder. She complies with a shiver and I work the pants down her legs, tossing them on the floor.

Damn.

"Absolutely beautiful," I marvel at the sight of her, wishing I could find more words to express what it's like, looking down at her, a vision in her bra and matching panties, but the word "beautiful" plays on repeat like my brain is caught in an infinite loop.

"You don't have to tell me that." Her arms drape across her stomach, self-consciously, causing me to freeze.

"Come again?"

She laughs a little but doesn't meet my eye. "I saw the kind of women you're usually around at the club, and I know I don't look like them. But it's okay. I know you want me, and that's all that matters. You don't have to pretend I'm something I'm not."

Unbelievable. Here I am unable to get my head around how fucking gorgeous she is and she doesn't even know.

"Beth, look at me."

Tentatively, her eyes meet mine and I hold her gaze firmly. "You are beautiful," I tell her, my voice steady and sincere as I slide down to my knees on the floor.

She sits up, confused by my change in positions and I grab her left leg, spinning her so I'm kneeling between her open legs.

"You need to know that your body is beautiful," I say, my voice filled with conviction. "And if you don't know, I'm going to have to show you." I run my hands up her trembling thighs and hook my thumbs in her panties. This time she lifts her hips without being asked and I slowly drag the lacy fabric down her long legs. She attempts to bring her knees together, but I hold them open. Leaning down, I start to kiss up the inside of her thighs. "Every curve." *Kiss*. "Every line." *Kiss*. "Every inch of you is perfection." *Kiss*. "A goddamn masterpiece."

Her whole body is shaking as my face hovers above where she wants me. Where she needs me. Her shallow breathing is making her chest rise and fall rapidly as she grips the couch cushions waiting for me to touch her.

I blow a stream of cool air on her sex and her head rolls back on the couch, a tortured moan escaping her lips.

I pull back, just to look at her again. Christ. She's the most beautiful sight I've ever seen and she doesn't even know it.

When my tongue finally tastes her centre her hips buck in response. I drape my arms across each of her thighs, holding her in place as I go down on her.

"Oh God, Foster," she cries, digging her nails into the upholstery and making me jealous of a piece of furniture. I reach out and grab her hand, moving it into my hair as I go back to work. If you can call it that. This feels like the best vacation I've ever had.

"Tell me what you like, beautiful girl."

"That," she answers immediately, making me grin.

"What about this?" I focus my efforts solely on her clit, circling it with the tip of my tongue.

"Yes…yes…that…"

Her other hand has made its way into my hair and she's using it as leverage as she rocks against my face.

"More? Or less?" My voice is thick. She hasn't even touched my cock and it's damn near ready to explode.

"More," she whines, her voice getting louder. "More, more, more."

I lean in using more pressure and stroking her faster and she writhes against me. Her cries get louder and shorter as she struggles to breathe until she comes apart hard on my mouth.

I stay with her as she comes down from her climax. When her grip on my hair lessens and her hands fall away, I sit back and admire her, relaxed and flushed from pleasure.

"Absolutely beautiful."

CHAPTER 21

BETH

I should buy him a present.

Wait, is that a weird post-orgasm thought?

Regardless of the answer to that question, my feelings remain the same. After the most intense climax of my life, my first impulse is to buy Foster James a fruit basket. Or maybe a house plant.

I've had men go down on me before, it always felt like an obligation on their part. With Foster, it felt like there was nothing else he'd rather be doing.

"Hey." Foster cups my cheek, gently guiding my gaze to meet his. Still kneeling in front of me, he looks me over, quietly assessing me. "You okay?"

I'm great. Never better. Just mentally shopping for a "thank you" present to give you for making me come so hard.

"Of course," I insist. My heart rate has returned to a regular rhythm and my body is cooling down rapidly. Which is fine except that my skin is damp with perspiration and, well, I'm almost completely naked. I start to shiver and I can't stop.

"Are you cold?" Foster doesn't wait for me to answer. He finds his long sleeve shirt on the floor and hands it to me. "Put this on."

"That's not necessary," I argue, pulling it on because I am in fact freezing. I'm not swimming in the shirt; I'm drowning in it.

Way to be sexy, Beth.

"Come on," he says, scooping me up into his arms and starting down the hall.

Wait, what? I don't want tonight, for whatever this is, to be over yet. The thought of Foster tucking me in like I'm a little one who's stayed up back their bedtime is humiliating and I'm about to protest, but he walks right by my room and into his.

I've gotten glimpses of his bedroom before while I walked by it, but I've never actually been inside. A king-sized bed, neatly made with crisp, charcoal-grey sheets and a heavy, navy-blue duvet, sits in the centre of the room. A pair of sleek, black nightstands flank the bed, each holding a minimalist lamp with warm, soft lighting. The walls are painted a deep slate grey, adding to the room's simple decor.

It's orderly and no-nonsense. In other words, it's Foster.

He pulls the comforter back and sets me down in the middle of the bed, climbing in after me and pulling the blanket over both of us. Gathering me against his bare chest, I snuggle against him, basking not only in his warmth but the mere feel of him.

His body is the definition of firm, yet his skin is so soft. I run my fingers over him, revelling in his reactions to my touch. They're subtle; the slight tensing of muscle or faint hitch in his breath but they're there. Part of me still can't believe that this is real. That I'm the one doing this to him.

"Better?" he asks as his hand slips inside my shirt to stroke my bare back and I almost purr.

The best.

"Much."

I continue to touch him because I need to. From the moment his lips touched mine, I've been all sensation and I can't seem to get enough.

When my hand slips under the waistband of the jeans he's still wearing, he groans against the top of my head.

"I think you should take these off," I say as I unbutton them and start on the zipper.

"Do you?" He chuckles, but it's strained. I think he's enjoying my teasing, but it's torture all the same.

"Absolutely," I press a soft kiss to his abdomen as I move my hands lower. "Circulation is very important when you sleep so loose clothing is better." Or none at all.

His lips quirk into a lopsided smile. "Is that what we're going to do, Beth? Sleep?"

"Eventually."

Before I can go further, he gently tugs my ponytail, pulling my face back to his. His kiss is deeper than before. Slower and yet, somehow, more urgent. His mouth moves on mine until I'm in some sort of a trance, unable to remember what I was attempting to do in the first place.

His hands push the shirt he draped me in above my waist before pausing. "Warm enough to take this off?"

My body is an inferno and this man is the source of the fire. I nod and he strips the shirt off of me in one swift motion, tossing it to the floor. The cute lacy bra I ordered online is the next to go, leaving me naked and trembling with anticipation.

But he makes me wait as he looks me over. He doesn't lay a finger or any other body part on me, much to my dismay.

And I let him look, not embarrassed or self-conscious about my nakedness. He made his feelings about how he sees me very clear on the couch.

You. Are. Beautiful.

It wasn't the first time a man told me I was beautiful, but it was the first time one made me believe it. I felt it when he looked at me. The sureness of the words as he spoke them matched with the sincerity shining in his eyes.

Those same eyes are even more hooded with lust, never leaving me as he stands and pushes his jeans and boxers briefs to the floor.

Now I'm the one gawking. Granted, I haven't seen that many penises in the flesh–literally and figuratively. But the sculpted God of a man that's crawling towards me on the bed appears to be larger than average...everywhere.

Laying back on the bed, he positions himself over me, bracing his weight on his forearms and my mind chooses this moment to fracture, a million thought fragments swirling around in my brain like a tornado of doubts.

Foster has already exceeded my expectations, but what if I don't meet his? What if this changes things between us? The effortless friendship we've spent the last month developing has meant a lot to me and after tonight it won't ever be the same.

Or what if it is? What if we wake up and act like nothing happened? Can I handle that? Hookups might be par for the course for Foster, but I don't think I'm going to pretend that I feel nothing after feeling so much.

Foster's green eyes almost glow in the dimly lit room. "I have a confession to make."

Here we go. He's got a wife in every NHL province and state. I fucking knew it.

"Oh?" I try to keep my tone neutral, which is difficult considering a large, naked man is on top of me about to tell me something I probably won't like.

He clears his throat. "It's, uh, it's been a while."

I narrow my eyes as if seeing him clearer will make me understand.

"What's been a while?"

"Since I've...since I've been with anyone."

I stare up at him, not sure how to react. He's a professional athlete. I'm sure his idea of a drought is a lot different than the rest of the population. "How long?"

He swallows. "Eight months."

"Bullshit."

"I swear."

I search his face for deception and find none. Not that he'd have a reason to lie to me, but still. He's Foster James. There are Tik Tok thirst trap reels of him that have gone beyond viral. I've got a couple saved on my phone. Given the man's options, why would he abstain for so long?

He looks nervous as he awaits my response.

"Foster," I hedge, attempting my best deadpan. "Are you bad at sex?"

His face breaks into the most beautiful grin as he lets out a bark of laughter.

"It's okay if you are," I fight to keep a straight face as

he buries his face in my neck. "You're good at lots of other things."

When he finally manages to stop shaking with laughter, he speaks again. "I hooked up plenty during the first few years of my career. I just got tired."

"Of sex?"

"Of the scene. Forcing conversations with women I didn't care about. Women who didn't care about me. There were no feelings involved. No trust."

"Why are you telling me this?"

His intense gaze holds mine and I can't look away. "I care about you, Beth. A lot. I need you to know that before we go any further."

My heart pounds in my chest and it's beating only for him. He's made me feel beautiful and now so special and cared for.

"I care about you, too," I breathe. "And I trust you."

"I trust you, too. Completely."

"I promise not to tell anyone you're bad at sex."

His low growl rumbles in his chest as he pushes himself off of me. I miss the warmth and pressure of his body immediately.

"What are you doing?" I ask as I watch him disappear into the ensuite bathroom. He doesn't leave me waiting long, reappearing a moment later, a square, foil wrapper in his hand.

"Helping you get your facts straight." He opens the packet, rolling the condom onto himself with quick precision.

Clasping my ankles, he drags me closer to him and then kneels on the bed between my spread legs. I'm almost vibrating with need as he strokes the inside of my thighs, my hips attempting to levitate up to meet him.

"Eager looks good on you, Baby," he chuckles, leaning his large frame over me, pinning me down.

I'm holding my breath as he lines himself up with my slick entrance, waiting for him to fill me. Instead, he takes one of my nipples in his mouth and sucks, causing a wave of pleasure to race down my spine. I'm downright writhing beneath him as he continues to kiss and lick at my aching breasts.

My arousal is all-consuming. I've never felt a need like this before. It doesn't matter that I had an orgasm a half hour ago; I'm desperate to come again.

"Foster," I pant, trembling underneath him. "Foster, please."

At my pleading tone, his mouth releases me and his head snaps up. He gives me a look that my sex-starved mind can only interpret as complete adoration before sliding into me.

"Ohhhhh God, Foster."

Full. I am so full.

Foster's strong jaw flexes and his neck muscles strain, but he holds himself perfectly still. If I didn't know better, I'd think he was in pain, but I know he's just as far gone as I am.

On an exhale, he rocks his hips tentatively against mine, causing me to moan loudly.

"I know, Baby." He takes one of my knees and hooks it around him. "I've got you."

And then he starts to move in sure, steady thrusts as I grip his shoulders tightly.

I barely recognize my own voice or the unintelligible

words streaming from my mouth. They intertwine with Foster's groans in the hottest harmony I've ever heard.

Before long, I feel myself tightening around him.

"Beth," he rasps, quickening his pace. "Your perfect little pussy is fucking ruining me."

My climax crests so suddenly, it takes me by surprise. I let out a strangled cry as I'm wracked by uncontrollable shudders.

"Jesus, Beth, that was…so…fucking–" Foster's sentence is cut off by his own shattering release. We cling to each other, a couple of shivering messes, as he buries his face in my neck.

"Fucking ruined," he murmurs against my damp skin.

That makes two of us.

CHAPTER 22

FOSTER

Soft light filters in through my curtains, casting a warm glow across the room. My eyes slowly adjust, and I turn to see Beth lying beside me, her hair splayed out across the pillow like a dark halo. She looks peaceful, serene, her lips slightly parted in sleep. The curve of her cheek catches the light just so, and I can't help but appreciate just how lovely she is.

Waking up next to her, my arm around her, with her body nestled against mine feels right.

It was after four o'clock before we finally detangled from one another and went to sleep. Still, when I look at my watch I'm shocked to see that it's past ten.

Careful not to wake her, I creep out of the bed. It's a challenge, but lucky for me, I'm pretty agile.

I pull on a pair of joggers and silently slip into the hall, then turn to look at her one more time. I don't know what's going to happen next, but I do know if this is the only time Beth Michaels sleeps in my bed, I want to remember it forever.

Don't think like that, I scold myself. Last night was

incredible, and I refuse to believe it was just a one-time thing. I can't.

We're going to have to talk about last night at some point. Part of me knows that she may not want more and if that's the case, I'll respect her decision. But after last night, there's no question in my mind what I want and it's Beth.

I step into the kitchen, the cool tile floor a sharp contrast to the warmth of the morning sun streaming through the large bay window. I reach for my favourite cast iron pan, placing it on the stove, and turn the burner to medium heat.

While the pan heats up, I grind the coffee beans and start the percolator. Before long, the scent of freshly brewing coffee fills the air. I grab the bacon from the fridge, laying the strips in the hot pan.

I've got a big day planned and a big day needs a big breakfast.

First, I'm taking Beth for another skating lesson. She made so much progress yesterday and I want to keep building on those gains. If we leave it too long, she may lose some of her confidence.

After that, I figure we'd get lunch at the market. There are lots of really cool food stands and shops I think she'll like. Then I thought I'd take her shopping for her own pair of skates.

I flip the bacon and as I'm watching it sizzle in the cast iron pan, I realise I'm humming to myself. Just a warm-up song they play almost every game night, but still; I don't hum. What is this girl doing to me? Next thing you know, I'll be singing in the shower and dancing in the rain.

The coffee finishes brewing, and I'm pouring myself a steaming cup when there's a knock at the door.

Confused, I walk to answer it as I try to remember if I've ordered anything recently that requires a signature.

"Morning," a dishevelled Ben greets me when I open the door and he pushes past me.

Well, shit. My stomach drops like I just let in an overtime goal.

"Good morning." I manage to keep my tone casual. It's not uncommon for Ben to show up unannounced, but today it's an unwelcome surprise.

He kicks his boots off while shrugging out of his coat, so I guess he plans on staying.

"Come on in," I mutter, closing the door.

"Smells good in here."

I trail him to the kitchen and watch as he takes a mug from the cupboard and helps himself to the coffee, offering no explanation for his presence.

"Where's Beth?" he asks, sitting down at the island so he's facing me as I tend to the bacon.

Naked in my bed.

"Not awake yet, I guess."

"You have fun last night?"

Best night of my life, thanks for asking.

"It was fine. Kind of crowded."

My best friend smirks. "I know. Sorry I forced you to be social. But it meant a lot to me and the guys that you came."

You have no idea how hard I came. I nod, focusing on the food in front of me as I struggle to silence my inner monologue.

"Speaking of the boys, did anyone try anything with Beth?"

The piece of bacon I'm flipping drops into the pan, hot grease splashing up and hitting my stomach.

"Fuck." I drop the tongs and step away from the stove.

"That's what shirts are for, Fozzie Bear," Ben laughs into his coffee. "Put some clothes on before my sister sees you."

No sooner are the words out of his mouth than Beth appears behind him dressed in one of my t-shirts.

This is bad. Every muscle in my body tenses at her ill-timed arrival.

I know Ben well enough that I am absolutely certain if he turns around to see his sister scantily clad and looking freshly fucked, this is not going to end well for anyone involved.

She freezes, a look of sheer horror on her face, and I force myself to keep my focus on Ben in the hopes he won't turn around.

"Fair point," I say as Beth backs herself up around the corner and out of sight. "Do me a favour and make sure nothing catches on fire while I'm gone. I'll be right back."

I catch up to Beth just as she's entering her bedroom. The one she definitely did not sleep in last night.

We very narrowly avoided a disaster just now. Hell, if Ben had walked in a minute later, I'd have been lucky to escape with my life.

Worth it. No one has ever looked better than Beth right now. She's all legs and messy hair, my t-shirt barely covering her ass. Even though her brother is only a few walls away, all I want to do is throw her over my shoulder and put her back in my bed where she belongs.

Beth is visibly flustered as she silently motions to the kitchen. Her movements are over the top, like she's in a silent comedy.

Fuck, she's cute.

"Sleep well?" I whisper, unable to stop myself from grinning at her.

"What are we going to do?" she hisses. I understand why she's on edge. Ben's surprise appearance is inconvenient, but not a complete disaster. He already knows she's staying here. We just need to act naturally and he'll be none the wiser.

"Go get dressed and then come to the kitchen."

"That's it?"

"That's it."

She nods and turns to follow my instructions, but I catch her hand before she can disappear and pull her into my arms for a quick kiss.

Okay, maybe not that quick. Once my lips meet hers, it's hard to let her go.

She giggles as I release her and I want nothing more than to follow her as she enters her room. She's about to close the door, but just before she does, she pauses. With a wicked smile that hits me straight in my stomach, she pulls my t-shirt off and tosses it at my head.

I'm treated to a brief view of her naked body before she closes the door in my face.

Pulling the shirt on as I head back to the kitchen, I stifle a groan as I realise it smells like her. That's not going to help me get rid of this hard on.

Ben's removing the bacon from the pan as I return to the kitchen. I grab a carton of eggs from the fridge and a bowl from the cupboard, avoiding making eye contact with him as I join him at the counter.

"How's Valentina?" I don't know why I didn't think of asking him sooner. There is nothing that distracts him like talking about his supermodel girlfriend.

"She's fine, I guess." He grabs forks from the drawer and walks back to the island.

I wait for him to continue as I start cracking eggs into the bowl, but he doesn't. I study him as he sinks onto the chair looking exhausted.

"Everything okay?"

"It's fine." His tone is clipped. "She's pissed at me. She wanted me to go to brunch with her and her friends this morning, but I feel like that's all we fucking do."

"Get brunch with her friends?"

"Or get cocktails with her friends, or go to art galleries with her friends." He sighs and rakes his hands through his hair. "She never wants to do anything with my friends. I asked her to come to the club last night because I wanted her to meet Beth and she said she would, but then she called and said she needed me to meet her at some condo downtown instead. And when I got there, guess what? It was just the same boring people talking about the same boring shit. I care about her, but everything is always on her terms. I'm sick of it."

"Sick of what?" A fully-clothed Beth walks into the kitchen looking bright and chipper causing my heart rate to increase.

"Morning, Bug." Ben's funk over his relationship woes seems to fade. He stands and ruffles her hair before grabbing his coffee mug and heading for a refill. "Late night?"

She shoots me a nervous glance before shrugging. "Not especially."

I have to turn away to hide my grin. I plate the food and say nothing.

"Really?" Ben asks. "You were always up at six a.m. on weekends."

I catch her eye roll as I bring the plates to the table.

"When I was ten, dumbass." She sits down at the table across from me. "I had to get up early to maximise watching Saturday morning cartoons."

Ben sits down next to her, elbowing her in the side. "Well, in my head you're still ten. And don't call me a dumbass or I'll tell Mom." He takes his phone out of his pocket and when he glances at the screen he frowns before setting it down next to him, face down.

Beth seems to notice as well, but doesn't dwell on it. "Alright. So, what do you want to do today, dumbass?"

He laughs and I smile watching the two of them bicker back and forth even though the sight stings. Cody and I used to give each other shit all the time.

He was always there to keep my ego in check when we were kids. People started raving about my skills in the net at an early age and Cody could always be counted on to remind me that he could still beat me in an arm wrestling match. As we got older, the good-natured teasing gradually morphed into resentment and we were never the same.

"We could go shopping," Ben suggests. "Do you need anything for your new place? Or do you have any Christmas gifts to buy?" He pauses, a forkful of eggs hovering in front of his mouth before asking, "Speaking of which, what are we getting Mom and Dad?"

"We're getting them matching handcrafted rocking chairs made from the reclaimed wood of the two big oak trees they lost in Hurricane Fiona."

"Nice." He nods appreciatively. "That is incredibly thoughtful of us."

"I agree." She grins at him.

Ben's phone buzzes and then buzzes again a few seconds later. I see his shoulders stiffen, but he doesn't move to look at his phone.

"Shopping sounds fun." Beth glances at his phone as it buzzes again. "I was also planning to test drive a car later."

"You were?" Ben and I ask at the exact same time making her shift in her seat. This is the first time she's mentioned it. I assumed she'd continue driving my Lexus while she was staying here.

"Yes." She sips from her mug before continuing. "I need to find something in the next few weeks so I can drive home for Christmas."

"You think you're *driving* home?" Ben almost spits his coffee out.

I watch her stiffen at his tone. "I *am* driving home."

"Beth, that's a fourteen-hour drive."

"I'm aware of that, Ben."

"Well then, you should know that you can't make that drive on your own. Book a flight."

As much as I hate the idea of her travelling that far by herself, I don't appreciate the way Ben's speaking to her and from the way Beth is glaring at him, I can tell I'm not alone.

"Flight prices are insane this time of year." She says with a surprisingly calm voice.

"So?"

"So, we're not all professional athletes, Benjamin. I can't afford to spend two thousand dollars right now."

I picture her using this voice on particularly exasperating students and Ben, the dumb bastard, is not reading the room at all.

"I'll buy you the plane ticket, Bug. You're not getting a used car and driving it across the country in December." He says it in a way that suggests the discussion is over. "Are you still driving Foster's Lexus?"

Beth's lips are pressed so tightly together they've turned white and I'm genuinely concerned if she opens them that fire might stream out.

"Yes," I answer for her.

Ben raises an eyebrow, then slowly looks from me to his sister who is barely controlling her rage.

"I've got three cars," I add with a shrug. "It's not like I could drive them all at the same time."

He still looks suspicious, but luckily, his phone starts to ring, distracting him from whatever he's thinking.

He picks up the phone and sighs before pushing himself away from the table. "Hey," he says into it as he walks into the other room.

Beth is staring at her mostly untouched plate of food and my brain scrambles to form a sentence that isn't going to piss her off.

I can't lie; I fucking hate the idea of her driving that far in the winter by herself. But she's a grown woman who can make her own decisions and the last thing she needs right now is another person telling her what to do.

"Are you okay?" Is all I come up with.

She doesn't look up from her plate. "I hate being spoken to like I'm a child."

"I know."

"What do you think I should do?"

I let out a long breath as I sit back in my chair feeling like I'm walking into a trap. "Do you really want my opinion?"

Her lips twitch. "Probably not, but tell me anyway?"

I chuckle. "Alright. Let him buy you the plane ticket. Road conditions are unpredictable this time of year; it will be one less thing to worry about. Plus, flying will save you a day of travel meaning you get more time with your family."

She takes a bite of her bacon, appearing to consider my argument as she chews.

"Fine." Ben's voice carries from the other room.

"What's up his ass?" Beth asks.

Before I can answer, her brother's heavy footsteps draw closer.

"Yes," Ben says into the phone as he reenters the kitchen. "I said 'fine'. I'm on my way." He ends the call looking utterly defeated. "I'm sorry Beth. I gotta go."

"Is everything okay?" At least she doesn't look like she's about to stab him with a fork again.

"Yeah," he says as he shoves the rest of his bacon into his mouth. "Everything's fine. Look, about the flight–"

"I'll think about it," she says, cutting him off.

"Thank you. Maybe we can do something later in the week?" He looks so downtrodden that I actually feel bad for the big idiot.

"Of course." She gives him a small smile. "I'll text you."

"Great." He turns to me, offering me his fist, which I bump with my own. "Thanks for breakfast, Fozz. I'll see you tomorrow."

"Anytime. Take care, man."

We don't say anything until we hear the front door close.

"Do you think he's okay?"

I frown. "He's been better. I think he and Valentina aren't getting along at the moment."

She nods. "I still find it hard to believe he's in a relationship. After he and Maddy broke up, I've never seen him with a girl more than once."

I don't recognize that name, but I'm sure Ben's never mentioned a girlfriend to me before. Whatever he and Valentina are going through, I hope they work through it soon.

"So," I say, glancing at my watch and seeing we still have time to make it to the rink. "Feeling up for another skating lesson? Unless, that is, you're too tired?"

Her ponytail falls across her shoulder as she tilts her head to the side and gives me an innocent smile. "Why would I be tired?"

I grin, eager to play along. "I worked you pretty hard yesterday." I bite my lip as her cheeks turn pink. "On the ice, that is. I wasn't sure if you'd be up for another round."

"Absolutely," she answers without hesitation. "I can take more."

I'm so fucked.

CHAPTER 23

BETH

"Look at me! Foster, are you looking at me?"

I know I sound like a little kid insisting that their mom watch their fiftieth consecutive cartwheel, but I don't care. I'm skating!

I'm sure I still look like an old lady out here, but I feel like Tessa Virtue. I'm gliding across the ice with a rhythm that feels almost natural. My feet are aching a bit in these skates that don't fit perfectly, but I don't even mind the burn as I reach one side of the rink and start another lap.

I am graceful. I am powerful. I am alive.

"I haven't been able to stop looking at you." Foster skates backwards past me giving my body a look of frank appreciation. His movements are so smooth. He doesn't even look where he's going; his body just knows. It's beautiful to watch.

"Have you been trying, though?"

"Not at all."

I roll my eyes at him and he grins.

"How do you feel?" he asks, skating alongside me. "About the skating," he adds hurriedly.

Aside from a few vague references, we still haven't discussed last night and I'm hesitant to initiate the conversation. Not that I don't have a lot of say on the matter; I could write a dissertation on the events that took place for future generations to study.

"I feel great. Maybe a little sad that I didn't make myself learn a long time ago. I missed a lot of class trips and birthday parties. Oh, and this one time this huge winter carnival came to Charlottetown when I was nine. They turned a soccer field into an outdoor rink where there were games and balloon animals and cotton candy. I stayed home with my mom and was so sad when my sister told me about everything they'd done that I promised myself that if they had it again, I would learn to skate. But it never came back."

Foster takes my hand in his and gives it a squeeze and the disappointment I was feeling melts away.

Last night was a huge deal to me. Not only because it was the best sex I've ever had, but because I initiated it. I told Foster he could kiss me.

And, damn, did he ever kiss me.

It was so much more than physical pleasure, though. I've never felt so desired and it gave me the confidence to ask for what I wanted. And he gave it to me.

But the reality of the morning after came hard and swift. Having to act like nothing happened for Ben's sake sucked. And Foster played his part well.

I think back to him telling me how long it had been since he'd been with anyone and while it's just as hard a concept to wrap my head around today, I have no reason to doubt him.

Foster likes me. He cares about me, he said so himself

and I believe him. But what does that mean going forward?

I make a sudden, and perhaps rash decision. Directness worked last night, right?

"How are you feeling?" I ask in a conversational tone. "About the sex?"

Foster almost loses his footing, but recovers quickly. He runs his hands roughly over his face. "Great…The sex was great. I thought so, anyway…so I feel great about it?"

It's so hard not to laugh watching this giant of a man stumble over his words.

He clears his throat. "And you?"

"It was okay, I guess." I manage to say with a straight face before skating away from him towards the glass as fast as I can. I don't get very far; Foster skates up behind me, catching me around the waist and lifting me off the ice as I squeal.

"Okay?" His voice is a low growl, but I can feel him smiling against my ear.

"Yup," I gasp, struggling to breathe and not laugh. "Solid six out of ten."

He sets me down against the boards and spins me to face him, cupping my face. I tilt forward hoping he'll kiss me, but he doesn't. His eyes study mine, looking from one to the other, his expression grave.

"What are you doing?" I sound as breathless as I feel.

"Looking for signs of a concussion. You may have gotten one by hitting your head on my headboard so many times last night. Or maybe it happened during round three in my shower. You said you couldn't remember your own name after that."

My jaw goes slack and before I can respond, he kisses

me, hard and fast. My hands find his back, grasping at his sweater. I'm trying to pull him closer to me and, at the same time, holding on for dear life.

His lips are firm and sure as he makes a meal out of my willing mouth. I whimper as he runs his tongue over mine.

"Did you have something to say?" He hovers just above my desperate lips.

"Umm…I don't remember." I try to stand on my tip toes, but it's impossible on skates.

"Mmm…Might be more serious than a concussion. Maybe you've got amnesia. Can you remember anything?"

I'm running purely on lust and endorphins, but if he wants to play the teasing game, that's fine by me.

I place my hand on his stomach and let it travel south. "I remember you liking this." I press against his growing erection, cupping him through his jeans.

"Jesus, Beth," he groans against my mouth. "You win. I'll cancel the CAT scan."

There's no more talking. Just taste and touch and feel.

Someone bangs on the glass and I scream as Foster hugs me to him protectively.

"Sorry, Foster." A middle-aged man stands on the other side on the glass looking anywhere but us. "I'm about to open the doors for the family skate. And I figured you'd probably want to…anyway, sorry."

"Thanks, Danny. We appreciate it." Foster's hold tightens on me like he thinks I might run away and the moment Danny turns around, he presses his lips to the top of my head, shaking with amusement. "You good?"

I nod. "Good." I start to skate towards the exit.

"Look at you." He's positively beaming at me. "You're skating like a pro. I must be a great teacher."

"Solid six out of ten."

He laughs and looks like he might chase me again, but dozens of people are starting to fill the ice that was our private skating pond just moments ago. We're almost to the exit when I hear my name.

"Ms. Michaels! Ms. Michaels!"

A pink blur comes barreling towards me on the ice. I realise too late that she's not slowing down and is going to crash into me or the boards. On instinct, I widen my stance and prepare to take the blow, when Foster steps forward and catches her.

"Whoa, Speed Racer," he laughs, steadying my student on her feet.

"Sorry!" The girl looks up at me with a grin that's missing both incisors.

"Amelia!" I exclaim. "You're so fast!"

"I know!" She beams. Her head looks impossibly big in her pink helmet. "My dad says I need to learn to stop, though."

"That might be a good idea." I look up to find Foster studying her with an unreadable expression.

"Dad! Daaaaaad! It's Ms. Michaels!"

A tall man skates over to us slowly, but he's not looking at me or even Amelia; he's staring at Foster, whose eyes are fixed right back at him.

"Ms. Michaels, this is my Dad!"

"It's nice to meet you," I say as I look nervously between the two men.

"Same." Her father nods at me before returning to his staring match with Foster. "Hey, Foster."

Foster looks like he's seen a ghost. He swallows hard. "Cody."

CHAPTER 24

FOSTER

My brother's name sounds foreign as it leaves my mouth. Cody's voice sounds different, too.

Maybe it's because I haven't heard it in a decade, or maybe it's because this time he's not telling me to fuck off.

Lose my number. I never want to see your face again.

Those were the last words my brother said to me before he actually pushed me out of our childhood home and slammed the door in my face.

All I can do is stand here and stare at him. In my mind, I always picture him how he looked that day. Red-rimmed eyes filled with hatred. Bloated face and wiry frame.

It's almost like I'm looking at another version of my brother. He's got a full beard, which is funny because he was never able to grow one. Flecks of grey pepper it along with the rest of his hair.

He's put on at least forty pounds since I've seen him. Cody's always been a couple inches shorter than me, but he's standing tall, looking healthy, maybe even a little soft around the middle.

"Hi!"

I find the young girl staring up at me. The girl with my brother's eyes and my mother's name.

"Hi," I manage, my voice thick. "I'm Foster."

"Like the goalie?"

"That's me."

"No way! I've got your jersey! My dad does, too. Our last name is James too!"

It's too much. It's all just too fucking much.

"That's great." My smile is forced as I look at Beth pleadingly. "We should get going."

"How do you know Ms. Michaels?" Amelia asks, seemingly oblivious to the tension between the adults around her.

"I'm a friend of her brother's." My eyes involuntarily meet Cody's as I say the word "brother" and he flinches.

"Cool! I don't have any brothers."

Good to know.

"I'll see you at school tomorrow, Amelia." Beth says before nodding at my brother. "It was nice to meet you, Mr. James."

"Cody, please," he tells her.

I walk off the ice not knowing where I'm going, just needing to get away. I feel Beth at my side, her concern palpable.

"Foster, wait."

I turn to face my brother who's followed me off the ice. Beth gives me a questioning look and I nod at her. She squeezes my arm before returning to keep Amelia company while she waits for her dad.

Her dad. Cody is a dad.

My brother stands a few feet in front of me looking torn.

"I don't know what to say," he admits.

"That makes two of us." What do you say to the man who disappeared from your life a decade ago without looking back?

"Look, Foster, I know a lot has happened, but this isn't how I wanted the family reunion to go, believe me. I mean, Christ, it's been ten years."

Does he think I don't know how long it's been?

"Who's fault is that?" The acid of my tone burns on my tongue.

His shoulders sag and I know that my words hit their mark. "Mine. It's my fault."

"Daddy!" Amelia calls. "You can get his autograph later. I wanna skate!"

I can't help but laugh without humour at the idea of my brother wanting my autograph.

"I'll be right there, Sweetie." He sighs, looking up at me. "I have to go. Can I…would it be okay if I reached out sometime? There are a lot of things I want to tell you."

My head aches and I clench my fists to keep from screaming.

"I'm not the one who changed my number." I glare at him. "But yeah, sure. Give me a call."

"Okay. Thanks. I'll talk to you soon…little brother."

My throat stings as he walks away from me. I haven't been anyone's little brother in a long time and I feel like my chest is going to cave from the sudden grief.

Beth joins me on the bench and we change out of our skates quickly. We don't speak as I lead her through the back hallways of the rink to the rear exit.

My hands grip the steering wheel, my eyes focusing on the road ahead as light snowflakes drift lazily down from the sky. The windshield wipers flick back and forth as the highway stretches out before us, a ribbon of asphalt dusted with white. The hum of the tires against the cold pavement provides a steady rhythm to my scattered thoughts.

I turn the heat off entirely. I want to be cold. To be numb. Despite everything that just happened, I feel a sense of calm driving through this quiet, snowy world. I feel in control, if only of this car.

"Are you okay?"

I've been so absorbed by thoughts of Cody, I almost forgot Beth was here. We've driven almost the entire trip in silence.

"Not really." It's the truth.

"That's okay." Her tone is soft as she rests a warm hand on my knee. "It's okay to not be okay."

A new thought occurs to me. I have a niece, and Beth knows her better than I do. I feel angry. Not towards Beth of course, but at Cody. It's his fault. How could he not tell me he had a child?

"What's she like?"

Beth frowns at me. "Amelia?"

Hearing my mother's name hurts more than it should. I simply nod.

"Well, I've only taught her for a few weeks." The corners of her mouth turn up. "You know, as an educator I'm not supposed to have favourites, but if I did, she would be one of them. She's very kind towards all of her classmates. She has a wonderful sense of humour, but finds it hard to reign it in sometimes. She's very strong in math, so much so that she seems almost bored during lessons."

I shake my head slowly. Unbelievable.

"What?"

"You just described my brother." I clear my throat, gripping the steering wheel. "He was great at math and he hated it. Thought it made him a nerd."

Cody was a gifted student. His grades were excellent, despite him putting in very little effort. He even won a scholarship to Waterloo, but didn't take it saying university wasn't for him.

"What happened between you two?" Beth asks hesitantly.

I blow out a breath as I pull into my driveway and park the car. I don't want to have this conversation, but if I have to talk to anyone, it might as well be Beth.

"It wasn't one big fight; more like a gradual falling out. I moved away for hockey at fifteen. We talked a lot at first, but over time he got more and more distant. I came home for the summer that first year and he was hanging around with new guys he'd met at work. I was still training everyday of the off season and all he wanted to do was drink or get high. We grew apart. My mom had told me it was just a phase that he'd grow out of and to focus on hockey. So I did."

"I went back to my junior team in Quebec in September." I swallow the lump in my throat. "My grandfather died the next month. When I came home from the funeral, Cody wouldn't even talk to me. Acted like it was my fault. Again, my mom just said to give it time. Focus on hockey. I didn't know at that point that she was sick."

Beth puts a gentle hand on my leg, and the words

continue to tumble out of me. "She was gone a year later. I kept trying to talk to Cody, but there was this wall between us. Anytime I brought up Mom or Gramps, he'd get angry, so I stopped trying. It was okay, for a while. We fell into this routine of talking to each other as long as it wasn't about anything that mattered. I invited him to come visit me for his birthday. When we went to a bar with a few of my teammates, he just kind of lost it. Got really drunk really fucking fast. And angry. Wound up punching a guy at the bar and then tried to fight one of the bouncers. I had to bail him out of jail."

I'd never felt so hopeless. I was only twenty; I didn't know how to take care of myself, let alone someone else. "My coach got wind of what happened and he wasn't happy. Sat me down and gave me a long talk about addiction. When I told Cody that I think he should get some help, he told me he hated me and never wanted to see my face again. And until today, he got his wish."

"I'm so sorry."

I look up to find tears streaking down Beth's beautiful face.

"It's okay, really."

"It's not," she insists.

"Okay. It's not. I just never expected to run into him like that. He looks so…different. Says he wants to talk."

"Do you want to talk to him?"

"I don't know what I want." My jaw aches from clenching my teeth. "I want the last ten years of my life back."

She squeezes my hand in hers. "You can't get the time you lost with him back, but you might get the next ten years."

I don't know what I'm going to do, but one thing I do know is that I'm grateful Beth's here with me.

"You may be right. You're very smart." I raise her hand to my face and kiss the back of it. "And so attractive."

She laughs and tries to pull her hand away, but I hold it tight. "I don't want to talk about my brother anymore. I want to talk about you and me."

Her mouth forms a little "o" making me want to kiss it. "You and me?

"Yeah." I search her eyes before just going for it. "I like you, Beth. So much. I think you like me, too."

"So much."

That statement alone is enough to mend the fractured heart in my chest.

I push a stray lock of hair off of her forehead and say, "Good. So…do you want to date me?"

"Like, out loud?"

I burst into laughter and she swats me on the arm. I adore this woman and I don't want to fight it anymore.

"I wasn't going to alert the team publicist or anything. I don't want to keep this a secret, but we can take it slowly and tell people, if and when you want to."

"I want to," she insists, pushing the hair back from her face. "I think quiet is a good idea, for now, at least. Especially until we get Ben used to the idea."

Knowing her brother, that could take a while. Ben has made it clear that he does not want any of his teammates pursuing his sister. Given how much stress his current relationship woes are causing him, now is not the time to tell him. We're better off to ask forgiveness than permission.

"So, we'll date quietly." I smile at her as I lean across the seat. I stroke her cheek, tilting her face up.

"Quietly," she agrees as she closes the distance between us, her mouth meeting mine.

I pull away, resting my forehead against hers."You'll have to be quieter than you were last night or everyone's going to know."

She blushes, but says "I don't remember it quite that way. Maybe my amnesia's back?"

"If that's your way of asking me to refresh your memory, I accept."

CHAPTER 25

BETH

"Beth! I was just talking about you!" Meredith, a teacher who didn't know my name until last week, catches up to me in the hall.

I bet you were.

Any doubts I had on whether Jacob was going to tell people about Foster evaporated when I walked into school Monday morning. Heads swivelled in my direction. Some people waved excitedly like I was a celebrity or public figure, while others just stared.

I located Tamara as quickly as I could and asked for a damage report. She informed me that Jacob had told several of my coworkers that he dropped me off at Foster James's house after the party on Friday night. One of them must have remembered that I mentioned I was staying with my brother's friend, and a quick Google search confirmed that the Otters' best defenseman did indeed have a sister named Beth.

It's now Wednesday and I haven't been able to leave the safety of my classroom without being sought out by someone with questions about hockey, Ben, or, worst of all, Foster.

"I still can't believe your brother plays for the Otters," she says again, giving my arm a light slap like we were the oldest of friends. I was only introduced to her at the Christmas party where she gave me a courtesy smile,then left to find someone better to talk to.

Meredith is perhaps my least favourite kind of hanger-on. She reminds me of the popular girls in highschool who used to ask me to introduce them to Ben, like he wasn't a grown man with better things to do than rebuke the advances of teenage girls.

It appears she's tired of beating around the bush, jumping right in with "I would love to meet your brother sometime. I've been a huge Otters fan my entire life."

The team was only established sixteen years ago, I think. I would bet my meagre life savings that she is more a fan of the players than the game itself.

"Gosh," I say, trying to hide my annoyance. "I'd love to, but he's pretty busy with the team and his girlfriend."

Her face falls and I decide to put a final nail in the coffin. "She's a supermodel."

Momentarily crestfallen, she quickly rallies to try another angle. "Maybe we could go to a game sometime? You probably get the VIP treatment. Do you get to go backstage?"

I'm fairly certain at this point of the conversation that Meredith has never been to a hockey game.

Thankfully, the bell rings, saving me from responding.

I say goodbye and beeline to my classroom before my students make it inside from recess. Tamara stands in the doorway eating an apple and smirking as she watches Meredith walk away.

"Look at you, becoming best friends with the cool girls."

I snort. "Hardly. Just another person who wants to rub elbows with my brother."

"Knowing Meredith, it's something else altogether she wants to rub with him."

"Please, not you, too," I beg.

"No," she laughs. "Your brother is not my type. He's too pretty. Now, that Norwegian forward with the crooked nose that's missing half his teeth? That's a face I'd like to sit on."

We're cackling as the kids come back in, rosy-cheeked from the cold and hair sweaty and matted under their toques.

Amelia waves at me on her way to her desk near the back of my classroom. Unlike the adults who work here, she hasn't told anyone about seeing me with Foster on the weekend. Instead, she's been giving me conspiratorial little smiles, almost like we're sharing a secret.

I've never been great with secrets. My sister can tell by the pitch of my voice or the number of times I blink if I'm hiding something.

But Foster and I aren't a secret. The word secret implies that we're doing something wrong, and that's not how I feel at all.

Every moment I spend with Foster, whether we're in his kitchen, in the rink, or in his bed, feels overwhelmingly right. Being around him is the most natural thing in the world.

It's almost dizzying at times, though. Like whatever

this is between us is a walking paradox. How can someone make my heart race and my head swim, yet make me feel so centred and grounded at the same time?

We've been in constant contact since he left on Monday. He Facetimed me when he got back to the hotel after the team beat Philly last night and we talked for more than an hour before I fell asleep on him. When my alarm went off this morning, it woke him up, too, as he'd stayed on the call all night.

"Why didn't you hang up after I fell asleep?" I'd asked, feeling horrible for waking him.

"I like waking up next to you. Almost as much as I like falling asleep next to you."

I'm not even sure how I've been functioning all day, seeing as at that moment my heart exploded in my chest.

The rest of the day goes by without incident. Well, Tamal got his second nosebleed this week and had to go to the office, and Daisy pretended to feel woozy from the sight of blood and said she needed to go to the office, but that's it. Tamal was fine and Daisy just has a crush on him and insists on following him everywhere.

As I'm leaving for the day, I run into Jacob. It seems that Tamara was right about him orchestrating all our chance encounters last week; this is the first time I've seen him since Friday.

"Hi, Beth."

"Hi, Jacob." I don't want to be mad at the guy, but I am. I miss the anonymity of last week when I was Beth, the new teacher from Prince Edward Island, instead of my typical role of being Beth, Ben Michaels' sister.

"How's your week going?" he asks cautiously.

I'm the talk of the town, thanks to you.

"It's been fine, thanks."

He moves ahead of me to the double doors to hold one open, but I side step and push open the other one for myself then hurry down the steps.

Jacob catches up to me. "Look, I'm sorry everyone found out who your brother is."

"They didn't find out, Jacob. You told them."

"Well, technically I just told Marcus that you were staying with Foster James. He was the one who figured the rest out and told everyone."

"Ah. So you set the rumour mill in motion, but didn't stick around to supervise what it produced. Great. I feel better." I reach Foster's car and throw my bag in the backseat.

Jacob stands with his hands in his coat pocket looking abashed. "I'm sorry. I was just so surprised. I mean, I was working up the nerve to ask you out when Foster freaking James opens the door. But I shouldn't have told anyone."

I sigh. Like it or not, this is my life. It's not like I would have kept my family a secret from the people I work with forever, though I would have appreciated telling them on my own terms.

People will always see me as Ben's sister.

Until, that is, they find out I'm dating Foster. After that, they'll see me as his girlfriend.

I've seen how athletes' girlfriends are scrutinised in the media and online. Picked apart and judged to see if they measure up. Am I going to be okay with that?

"It's okay," I tell him. He didn't do it to be malicious and he was one of the first people here to actually try to get to know me.

"Really?"

"Really."

He's visibly relieved, his face breaking into a broad grin. "I promise, the next time I see you with a pro-athlete, I'll just keep it to myself."

"Much appreciated."

He hesitates, unsure of himself. "Maybe we could still go to a game sometime? My treat," he asks hopefully.

"I'd like that—as friends."

He seems a bit disappointed, but not surprised by my gentle let down. We say our goodbyes and I hop in the car. I can see him in the rear view mirror watching as I drive away.

CHAPTER 26

FOSTER

"Jingle balls...deck those halls...winter wonderland," Will sings loudly and proudly in the showers, much to the dismay of everyone within earshot.

"Does he seriously not know the words to Jingle Bells?" Austin mutters as he rinses himself off.

"How is he flat and sharp at the same time?" Ben asks when our tone deaf songbird hits a particularly nasty high note.

Will loves Christmas more than any grown man I've ever met. He's a normal person eleven months of the year, but as soon as December hits, he's insufferable.

"Give it a rest, Prancer!" Austin hollers over his shoulder as he towels himself off. We're all in the locker room after getting our asses handed to us by the Red Wings. I should be disappointed, and I am, but mostly I'm just excited to get home.

Talking to Beth on Facetime is better than nothing, but it isn't enough. I'm aching to see her in person, to hold her in my arms.

Will, completely unphased by the team's unfavourable response to his serenading, smiles at the jeers.

"I can't help that I've got the Christmas spirit," he says as he's lacing up his boots.

"Anyone want to crowd fund for an exorcism?" Ben asks.

Will's grin only gets bigger. "Only three more weeks, boys! You can take it."

"That's what I told your mom the last time I filled her stocking," Austin retorts. If he'd said that to anyone else, a brawl would start, but Will just laughs before launching into a jazzy rendition of God Rest Ye Merry Santa Claus.

I choose the seat next to Will on the flight back. This is partly because I'm the only one willing to sit next to him as there is a very good chance he'll break into song again. It also means I won't be stuck next to Ben for the next few hours, while I'm thinking about going home to his sister.

"Check it out," Will grins, showing me his phone. A video is playing of a house with a display of Christmas lights that cover every inch of its exterior. Strings of multicoloured bulbs wrap around the eaves, tracing the roofline in a vibrant cascade of reds, greens, and blues. The windows twinkle with lights in the shape of stars, wreaths, and candy canes, creating a festive glow that spills into the night. A giant inflatable snowman waves from the lawn, illuminated from within, while glowing reindeer graze nearby. The front door is adorned with a lit-up wreath. It's giving major Griswald family vibes.

"Is that your place?" I ask, recognizing the bright red door as I squint at the screen.

"Sure is," he answers proudly. "The company I hired just finished setting it up. Isn't it sick?"

That's one way of describing it. I should take Beth to see it. She'd probably lose her mind.

"My entire family would spend a weekend getting our place set up back home when I was younger. I wish I had the time to do it myself, but the company I use is great." He's still staring at his phone with a dumb grin on his face.

"Wait, aren't you going home for Christmas?"

"Of course."

"So why get your place done if you're spending the holidays with your folks?"

He puts his phone away and leans back in his seat. "I miss my family a lot this time of year. All my siblings are in Nova Scotia and they're always hanging out together, posting pics on Instagram. I guess that's why I get so into Christmas. When I sing the songs and see the lights, it reminds me that I'll be home soon."

We chat a bit more about his family before Will crosses his arms and closes his eyes. He's snoring within minutes.

I take out my own phone and pull up the message I received a few days ago from Cody.

> Cody: Hey Foster. I'm sorry we ran into each other the way we did, but not sorry it happened. I've been wanting to reach out for some time, just kept losing my nerve. I'd love to meet up and talk. I take full responsibility for what happened between us. I hope I hear back from you. I miss you.

I've lost track of how many times I've read it. If it were

a physical note, the paper would be bent and creased from being opened, read, and refolded.

A couple of times I even typed out a response, but each time hit the backspace button over and over until each word of my message disappeared.

Of course I want to see my brother again, but I'm scared. What if he hasn't gotten the help he needs and I lose him again? Or what if he has and there isn't a place for me in his life anymore? What if I can't form a connection with my niece because I've been absent her entire life?

There are a lot of possibilities I'm not ready to face right now.

After closing Cody's text window, I bring up Beth's. The last thing she sent me was a selfie of herself in her classroom wearing a pair of antlers and a bright red nose captioning it "this is what you're coming home to."

All I could think was: "I can't wait."

Even now, I'm grinning at the screen as I think about seeing her in a couple of hours.

"Hey," Ben says as he approaches my seat, crouching down in the aisle.

The phone slips out of my hands and I panic, attempting to retrieve it. Jesus. You'd think I was looking at naked pictures of her, judging by my reaction.

As usual, Ben doesn't notice anything that doesn't directly involve himself. I tuck the phone into my jeans and ask, "What's up?"

"Are you bringing a plus one to the Christmas party?" The annual Otters holiday gala is less than two weeks away. The owners throw it every year in one of the nicer hotels in downtown Ottawa.

"Wasn't planning on it." I want to take Beth, obviously, but I feel like that would set off even Ben's warning bells. Still, I wish I could invite her. Being forced to be social would be easier to endure with her by my side.

"I figured. Can I have your extra ticket for Beth?"

Well, that worked out nicely.

"Of course."

"Thanks, man." He gives my arm a thump with his hand. "I feel bad for ditching her on Sunday. Plus, she'll finally get to meet Valentina."

"How are things going with you two?" He's been acting a bit off this week, less obnoxious than usual.

"Better, I think? She wants me to go to St. Bart's with her for the holidays."

I stare at him. "But you're going home for Christmas to see your family."

He shrugs. "I know that was the plan. But maybe I can fly them all up for a long weekend in the New Year instead."

My face must not be doing a good job at hiding what I'm thinking because he starts to get defensive.

"Relationships are about compromise," he says, sounding more like a self-help book than my best friend.

"Sure," I hedge, treading carefully. "But what compromises has she made for you?"

"That's not the point–"

"Well, maybe it should be. Don't compromises require effort from both parties? A certain amount of give and take? I don't know much about relationships–"

"You're right, you don't," he snaps coldly.

His words hit like a physical blow, causing me to sit up straighter in my seat. I take a second to recover before giving him a curt nod. "Alright, man. Forget I said anything."

"Fozz, I'm sorry. I'm really tired and in a shitty mood cause we lost. I don't mean to be an asshole."

It occurs to me that Ben is apologising for being an asshole a lot lately. He may claim that Valentina is the best thing that's ever happened to him, but I'm far from convinced.

"It's fine. The ticket is yours. I hope everything works out." When he doesn't move to leave I add, "Get some rest, man." Then I close my eyes and wait for him to leave.

I don't open them until I hear him stand and go back to his seat. I take my phone out again and look at the picture of Beth, letting her impish smile soothe the sting left by Ben's words. Maybe I don't know much about relationships, but for her, I'm ready to learn.

She's talked about missing her family a few times since she got here and I know how excited she is to have everyone home for Christmas. She'll be gutted if Ben ditches them for his girlfriend.

My thoughts are interrupted when Will snores so loud he actually wakes himself up.

"What?" he asks sleepily, rubbing his eyes. "Are we home?"

I shake my head. "Another half hour or so, buddy.'

He pulls out his phone and I think about the decorations he showed me. It gives me an idea.

"Can I get the contact for the company you used for your house?"

CHAPTER 27

BETH

Foster: Figured out what we're doing tonight yet?

Beth: How can I figure it out if you refuse to give me any hints?

Foster: No hints

Beth: Three hints would be fair

Beth: Two hints would barely be civil

Beth: FINE. I will accept one hint. Final offer.

Foster: Zero hints. See you soon.

"Is this a kinky sex thing?"

Foster's deep laugh fills the air as he tightens my blindfold.

"I'm not objecting if it is; I'm just curious," I add for clarity.

"Beth's up for kinky sex. Noted." I hear his grin even though I can't see it. I can't see anything.

When Foster said he had a surprise for tonight, I had a few guesses, but none of them included him picking me up at work and blindfolding me. I texted, begging for hints, but he gave me nothing.

The man is an impenetrable fortress.

Fort Foster buckles my seatbelt for me before starting the car, and away we go.

At first, I try to pay attention to our direction, noting how long we drive and any turns we make, but I don't know the area well enough and I'm hopelessly lost within minutes.

"Having fun yet?"

"No," I sulk. I don't like surprises. I read the last pages of books to make sure the ending isn't dumb. I read the Wikipedia page on movies to make sure I'll like them. I like to know where I stand and what to expect at all times.

"You will be," he assures me. "How was your day?"

"Fine. A few of the boys got sent to the office for stealing the girls' toques and filling them with snow."

"Was Amelia one of the girls?"

I don't miss the slight change in his tone when he asks about his niece. "She was. But she didn't take it lying down."

"What did she do?"

"Caught up with the boy who did it to her and shoved snow down his back."

I hear him chuckle beside me.

"We don't encourage retaliation at school, Foster."

"Of course." He clears his throat. "That was very wrong of her."

"I can still hear you snickering." I shake my head. "Have you replied to Cody yet?"

He's silent for a beat. "Not yet."

His answer doesn't surprise me. Foster's lost so much and been on his own for so long, it seems perfectly natural for him to be hesitant about letting his brother back in his life.

"He waited ten years to reach out. I figure I can give myself a week to reply. Right?"

"Of course." I reach my hand in his direction blindly and he takes it, kissing it before intertwining our fingers.

"I missed you."

I'm aglow from within. I missed him, too, more than I would have thought possible. "You should have woken me when you got in last night."

"Nah. You had to work this morning. Plus, you looked so peaceful when I looked in on you."

"You looked in on me? Really?" I debated sleeping in his bed last night in the hopes that I'd wake up when he got home. In the end, I decided not to. This thing between us is so new and I didn't want to overstep.

"I did. Your hair was a disaster and you were face down in your pillow, ass up in the air. I should have taken a picture because you were a sight to be seen."

I try to wrench my hand away, but he holds on to it with ease, pulling it back up to his mouth to kiss it again.

"You're awful," I tell him, even though I can't stop smiling.

"You're perfect."

I'm not sure how long we've been driving when he stops the car and kills the engine. He instructs me to keep my blindfold in place and I obey. As much as I hate surprises, he's put the effort in and I'm invested now.

He opens the car door and lifts me straight out of my seat.

"Foster!" I squeal as he cradles me against his chest. "I can walk!"

"Where's the fun in that?"

I hear a door open and then I'm guessing we're inside given it's much warmer now. He sets me down and starts to unbutton my coat.

I'm getting nervous. Where exactly are we and what are we doing here? What if there are people here ready to jump out and scare the bejesus out of me?

"Ready?" he asks and I nod, unsure. He undoes the blind fold and I blink several times to focus my eyes as I take in my surroundings.

What the hell?

"We're…we're at your house?" We're standing in his foyer.

"Surprise," he smirks and he kicks off his boots and walks away.

"I…what?" I slip off my boots and follow him into the living room. "What was the point of all of…oh."

Foster is standing in the middle of his living room looking expectantly at me. Behind him is the most beautiful fir tree I've ever seen. It's at least nine feet tall, branches gracefully sweeping downward in a symmetrical cascade. It's huge, taking up a third of the room. I take in its dark green needles and breathe in its fresh, fragrant scent.

Stacked on the floor and coffee table are brand new boxes of Christmas decorations and lights.

My vision clouds and I blink several times in an attempt to clear my eyes. My mind reels and my thoughts are a jumbled mess. I can't speak, only stare and blink.

"I thought you could help me liven the place up a bit." He runs a hand over his face before crossing his arms over his chest. "I tried to pick a tree like the ones you've pointed out. And I didn't know what kind of decorations you liked, so I pretty much bought out the entire store. I might have gone a bit overboard."

I shake my head, still unable to speak.

"Beth?" His brow furrows with concern. "Is this okay? I just thought it might make you feel more at home, but we don't have to do this if you don't want to. I can return all of this stuff; it's not a problem."

My legs start to move towards him. At least one part of my body is still accepting instructions from my broken brain. I close the distance between us taking the last couple steps as a run and leap into him. He catches me easily and I wrap my arms around his neck as I bury my face in his neck.

I never expected this, not from anyone. My eyes can't hold back their tears and my voice wavers. "Thank you." My words are almost a whisper.

"Beth, Baby," he says into my hair as he strokes my back. "Please don't cry."

The more he rubs my back, the harder I sob. It's overwhelming, the thoughtfulness, the effort he put into something so personal, so perfect. Every detail, every moment he spent on this, it all speaks volumes.

"Sorry," I sniff, wiping at my eyes. "This is the nicest thing anyone's ever done for me. I'm not used to romantic gestures."

His face softens as he gently sweeps my hair back from my forehead. "Get used to them."

His lips touch mine, and the world falls away. My heart races, pounding in my chest as if trying to match the rhythm of our kiss. I can't think, can't breathe; all I know is the warmth of his embrace and the softness of his mouth. Gentle at first, tentative, as if he's testing the waters, but then deepens, sending a shiver down my spine.

All week, I've felt like I'm falling for him, completely and utterly, and this kiss is further confirmation for me. My hands find their way to his shoulders, pulling him closer, not wanting this moment to end.

When he pulls back, we're both breathing heavily. He rests his forehead on mine.

"I have a confession to make." His breath dances on my lips.

"Another one?" I tease.

"Afraid so. I've never decorated a tree before."

My eyes widen. "Are you serious?"

"Very. It was sort of my mom's thing. She worked a lot of late nights when we were kids and would decorate when Cody and I were asleep. I'd go to bed with the house looking normal and wake up to find everything covered in tinsel. I think she liked surprising us."

Just like he surprised me. I'm still so overcome with emotion that he went to all this trouble for me and I want this to be fun for him, too.

"Well, I'm glad you told me. Since it's your first time, I'll be gentle."

He chuckles as he releases me. "Christ, you're as bad as my teammates."

"First things first." I move to the centre of the room and assess my surroundings. "We need music."

Foster fishes his phone from his pocket and swipes a few times before handing it to me. A music app is open on the screen and I spend a couple minutes searching for the perfect playlist while he disappears into the kitchen.

I make my selection, and moments later the room is filled with Dolly Parton and Kenny Rogers' sweet harmonies. Foster returns holding a glass of red wine. One dark eyebrow raises at my song selection.

"I will accept no criticism of Dolly," I warn. There are few things I will defend to the death and the Queen of Country is one of them.

"Wouldn't dream of it."

Sipping my wine, I start to look through what I have to work with. He bought enough to decorate an entire forest.

I glance over at Foster, who's standing with a strand of twinkling lights in his hands, looking a bit lost but eager.

"Here, let me show you," I say, taking one end of the lights and guiding him to the base of the tree. "We start at the bottom and work our way up."

He follows my lead, wrapping the lights around the branches, and I can't help but smile at his concentration.

"You're doing great," I encourage, my heart warming at the sight of him trying so hard.

Periodically, I back up and squint at the tree, trying to find branches that need more lights.

"Move that strand slightly higher," I instruct and he follows my directions. "A bit higher…too high. Right there! Now pull them slightly more to the front."

He smirks at me over his shoulder and I allow myself a moment to enjoy the view.

"Am I being too bossy?" I ask.

"Not at all. Besides, I plan on being the one in charge later tonight." He winks at me and my thighs clench.

I know I can be strong-minded, but so far I have thoroughly enjoyed his domineering side in the bedroom.

We hang the ornaments next. I've selected the navy and silver ones because they suit the colours of the room better than the red and gold. I try not to laugh watching Foster handle dainty glass ornaments in his massive paws.

"Like this?" he asks as he places a larger ornament on a sturdy branch.

"Perfect," I reply, stepping back to admire our work. The tree is starting to come alive with colour and light and I'm having more fun than I have in ages.

Eventually, the ornaments are all hung and the tree looks spectacular.

"She is breathtaking," I say as I gaze at it.

"She certainly is." He's not looking at the tree though.

I blush. "It just needs something for the top." I glance around at the boxes strewn across the room wondering if I missed it.

"Will this one do?" Foster hands me a beautiful crystal star.

I hold the star in my hands, turning it slowly to catch the light. It's stunning. More intricate than any tree topper

I've ever seen. The delicate details glisten, casting tiny rainbows around the room. I run my fingers over its smooth, cool surface.

"Foster, it's beautiful. You do the honours." I try to hand it back to him, but he shakes his head.

"Together."

He places his hands on my waist and lifts me so high, I'm almost sitting on his shoulder. His arms around my thighs hold me steady as I lean forward and place the star in its rightful place.

He sets me down, and we stand back to admire our handiwork. I think I might cry again. The music, the lights, and most of all the company all making the night so magical.

"One last thing," Foster says, grabbing a blanket and then my hand, leading me back to the foyer.

I slip on my boots without asking questions–it's not like he'll tell me where we're going.

He wraps the blanket around my shoulders and guides me outside onto his front yard. The sun set hours ago and there isn't much to see aside from the glittering snow.

Foster stands behind me with his hands on my shoulders. "Ready?"

"Ready for wha–"

Everything goes blindingly white. I gasp as the entire house lights up in a brilliant Christmas display. It's mesmerising, a winter wonderland. Every corner of Foster's house is adorned with twinkling lights; there must be thousands of them.

It's absolutely incredible.

I don't say anything. At this point there's nothing left

to say. The man has spent the last several hours making an amazing night more and more memorable.

I start to giggle. I've got so much joy in me and it's the only release I'm capable of.

Foster grins as he pulls me into his chest. "Too much?"

"Never. Exactly the right amount."

CHAPTER 28

BETH

"Everyone thinks that when you're pregnant you can eat whatever you want." Kim sets her hot dog down on her stomach and wipes her mouth with a napkin. "What they don't tell you is that almost everything gives you heartburn. Everything I want to eat and everything I don't want to eat. Bananas give me heartburn. BA-NA-NAS, for Christ's sake." She picks up the hot dog again, scowling at it. "I probably won't get any sleep tonight because of this."

I tear my eyes away from the action on the ice to give her a sideways glance. "But you're still eating it?"

"I'm no quitter, Beth."

Laughing, I turn back to the ice. Our seats are phenomenal, right behind the Otters' bench. When Kim invited me to join her at the game, I assumed we'd be in the VIP box with the rest of the WAGs, but apparently my super pregnant friend prefers to be closer to the action. Her exact words were that she likes to watch the sweat roll off her husband.

Live hockey hits different. The energy in the arena is palpable; the roar of the crowd vibrates through my entire body, making every cheer and groan feel more intense. I can feel the chill of the ice, see the players' eyes tracking the puck, and hear the skates slicing through the rink. .

Everything comes together to create this larger-than-life immersive experience.

It's like comparing watching a movie on your phone or viewing it in a huge theatre in 4k with surround sound.

I've been on the edge of my seat since the puck dropped. The first time a player was slammed into the boards, I jumped a foot into the air, spilling my oversized bag of popcorn. It sits untouched by my feet, safe from further spillage. Three minutes into the second period and the Otters are up by two, the tension sky high. It's always been a surreal experience watching my brother play at this level, but he's not the only person I'm focused on now.

Foster is playing another great game. I watch his every move as he guards his net. He crouches low, shifting from side to side as he follows the play, ready to block any shot that comes his way. Each time an opposing player winds up for a shot, he reacts with lightning speed. It's as if he can sense the trajectory of the puck before the player sends it to him.

He's a living, breathing fortress of calm amid the chaos of everything else happening on the ice, and when I look at him, I can't help but feel awe.

And so turned on.

I thought I was attracted to Foster before we started dating, but this past week I've really levelled up. Is it normal to crush this hard on someone you're actually seeing? It's swoon city over here.

As though reading my thoughts, Kim tugs on the sleeve of my jersey. I bought it to support Ben when he signed with the Otters.

"I wasn't sure whose jersey you'd be wearing tonight," she drops casually before taking a sip from her sparkling water.

I chew on the inside of my lip and watch the shift change. "I don't know what you're talking about."

"After I saw the two of you barely refrain from eating one another's faces, I thought you might be wearing a different number."

The truth is, I'm dying to talk to someone about Foster. But I can't. The more people who know, the more likely something will get back to Ben and my life is complicated enough right now.

Shrugging my shoulders I say, "This is the only jersey I own."

I really like Kim and I feel like I can trust her, but this thing with Foster is too new and we're trying to keep it quiet. We need to keep it quiet.

Ben has been off his game lately, both literally and figuratively. I've texted him a few times this week to check in, but he left me on read. He couldn't even be bothered to send me his signature thumbs up emoji.

His behaviour on the ice has been concerning me, too. He's stopped making his usual outlet passes, isn't clearing the puck like he used to, and has racked up more penalties than normal for slashing or cross-checking.

I'm worried about him and all the more convinced I need to keep what's going on with Foster and me to myself.

"It must have been someone else ogling him," Kim

adds as she leans forward to rub her lower back. "Matter of fact, it could have been her."

I follow her gaze to a young woman several rows over from us in the stands. She's wearing Foster's jersey, tied up to expose her midriff and low cut jeans. Over her head, she holds a sign that says "FUTURE MRS. JAMES" in huge red letters.

A tight knot of jealousy twists in my stomach. It's irrational and I hate it. Foster probably has legions of women who would love to be with him. It's not like this is the first time I've seen someone holding a sign with his name on it.

But it's the first time since he's been mine.

The realisation hits me like a locomotive.

Foster James is mine.

He hasn't said the words, but he's been showing me all week. Longer, even.

It's not just the big gestures like our tree decorating date last night. It's the way he remembers the little things, like how I like my coffee in the morning, or my favourite type of wine in the evening. When we're out together, he instinctively puts himself between me and other people. Even the way he texts me through the day, sometimes with a question or sometimes just to make me smile. He wants me to know he's thinking about me.

I've never been with someone who is so interested in my thoughts and feelings.

He makes me feel important and valued and as someone who is used to feeling like a background singer in the musical of her own life, it feels great.

I don't want to lose that.

The period is winding down, and suddenly the crowd

is on its feet. One of the Panther's forwards gets a breakaway and guns for our net as our defence scrambles to catch up.

I hold my breath as he winds up, but Foster stops the slapshot easily. Before we can celebrate, the player crashes into him. Foster goes down hard and all hell breaks loose. Ben and his teammates react instantly as gloves are thrown off and fists start flying. My heart races as the drama unfolds, players grappling and throwing punches. The refs rush in, trying to pull them apart, but the fight has taken on a life of its own.

"I hate when they fight." I groan into my hands, barely able to make myself watch.

"I love when they fight," Kim sits up as straight as her eight-month-pregnant belly will allow and eagerly watches. "Alexei does too. A good brawl always makes him extra…affectionate."

"Really?" The refs have finally broken up the fighting and the players are on their way to their dressing rooms. I can't believe they have to play another period after that.

"Mmmm. I think the only thing that makes him more…affectionate, is when I wear his jersey to bed."

Interesting. As I watch Foster leave the ice, I find myself wondering if that's something he would enjoy. After all the effort he put into planning our romantic decorating night yesterday, I'm eager to return the gesture.

I won't lie—the thought of doing something like that for Foster sends an exciting little thrill through me.

When I turn to tell Kim that I'll be right back, she beats me to the punch.

"Need me to hold your popcorn while you run to the merch shop?" Her lips curve in a smug smile.

It's positively criminal how well my new friend reads me.

CHAPTER 29

FOSTER

I needed to do press after the game because of the fight. I'm not a fan of talking to reporters to begin with, but I especially dislike it after a fight.

I've always believed that fighting is a part of the sport. We don't fight merely for the sake of violence. In-game combat acts as a powerful deterrent, protecting star athletes from harm. Aggressors know that any cheap shot or reckless play will be met with swift retribution. It's an unwritten code that ensures that everyone thinks twice before targeting key players, maintaining a level of respect and safety on the ice.

What I don't like is having to justify that aspect of the game every time someone drops their gloves. If a player takes out another team's goalie, that team will retaliate. It's not malicious and rarely personal; it's just the way it is.

I'm not sure what reporters want to hear from me: No, the forward didn't hurt my feelings when he skated into me. Yes, I trust my defensemen to have my back. Yes, I'm tired of answering your stupid questions.

People might think that games are the most stressful part of my job, but they'd be wrong. I feel most at ease when I'm on the ice. There's something about being in the crease, locked in, everything else just fades. I know what to do out there; my instincts take over. But put me in front of a bunch of reporters and it's a different story. I don't have the same control. The spotlight feels sharper, and every word has weight. I'd much rather face a breakaway than answer questions about a bad game. On the ice, it's all reaction. In front of the media, it feels like I'm second-guessing myself the whole time and it's exhausting.

Being exhausted could also be due to the fact that one gets less sleep when they stay up all night having sex with their beautiful girlfriend.

I regret nothing.

Beth being in the stands tonight, watching me play gave me rookie level energy. Just knowing she was in the building gave me a rush. I'm glad that I played well, though I know it wouldn't matter to her if I didn't.

The house is dark when I enter, with the exception of the warm glow from the Christmas tree. The place really does feel more like a home than ever and it's not just the decorations; it's Beth.

The girl who was only supposed to be here for a few days went and weaved herself into my thoughts, my dreams, and now she's taking up permanent residence in my heart.

After our late night yesterday, I expect to find her asleep on the couch, but it's empty.

Maybe she's gone to bed already?

I feel a stab of disappointment, not that I really blame

her for wanting to get some rest before the start of another school week.

I'm just greedy when it comes to her.

Just as I'm about to head down the hall Beth appears in front of me like my very own manifestation.

"Hi," she says shyly. Her hair is pulled up in a high ponytail and she's still wearing the jersey she wore to the game. The black tights are gone and I'm treated to an eyeful of her long smooth legs.

"Hi."

"Great game tonight. Did you get hurt in the fight?"

It didn't even occur to me that the fight would have upset her. When was the last time someone cared enough about me to be worried?

"Nah," I answer, my eyes still taking her in. "My defensemen were all over it."

She plays with one of her sleeves and that's when I notice that it's not the jersey she wore earlier. That one was a few years old. The one she's wearing now is the newer style, with the team logo on the right upper arm.

I go very still. Every muscle in my body tenses as I hold my breath. The world around me fades until all I can see is Beth's coy smile as she stares up at me.

"Beth."

"Hmm?"

"Whose jersey are you wearing?"

Those whiskey eyes blink up at me, her expression all innocence. "Mine."

I run my tongue over my now dry lips and take a step towards her. "Whose name is on it?"

Slowly, she turns around, sweeping her ponytail over her shoulder as she does so it doesn't obstruct my view.

JAMES. 33.

My name.

My number.

My girl.

I hear my heart as it pounds in my chest, each beat echoing loudly in my head as I stare at her; my real-life fantasy.

When I take another step closer, she shivers and I know she wants my hands on her almost as badly as I want to touch her.

"Are you cold, Baby? 'Cause if you are, I'm going to have to insist that you keep this on. Can you do that for me?"

She nods her head quickly.

"Good girl." I press a kiss to the nape of her neck and trail my hands down her, starting at her shoulders. When I reach her lower back, she arches it pushing her round ass against me.

I grab her by the hips and pull her to me, her back flush against my front and she gasps when she feels my hard cock pressing into her.

"Did you have any idea what wearing this would do to me?"

"I thought you...might like it." Her breathing is shallow as I snake my arms around her. I can feel her heart beating wildly through the jersey.

Like. It's far too flimsy a word for what I'm feeling. I like a lot of things. Coffee, dogs, long drives on clear days. I try and fail to explain to myself this rush of emotion that swells inside me everytime I'm with her. How do I even begin to describe the way my heart races when she's near or the way my thoughts spin when she's gone?

I'm about to throw her over my shoulder and sprint to my bedroom, but she looks so gorgeous in the soft glow coming from the tree. Instead, I pivot and walk further into the living room. When we reach the couch I spin her around to face me, pick her up at the waist, then set her down on the back edge. She holds onto my shoulders for balance as I step between her spread thighs. Leaning down, I angle my head and capture her lips as she sighs into my mouth.

I love kissing this woman. I've kissed a lot of women and the mechanics are mostly the same, but something about Beth elevates the experience. The softness of her lips, her taste, her touch—I could kiss her for hours on end.

But not tonight. I'm so wound up that if I don't get inside of her soon, my heart might give out on me.

Beth rolls her hips, rocking herself against me and I groan at the feel of the wet heat at her core.

I break the kiss and press my forehead to hers. I'm practically panting and she hasn't even touched me yet.

"It's going to be a struggle to go slow right now," I say, our breaths mingling.

"I don't want slow." She starts to unbuckle my belt and I strip off my shirt, tossing it across the room. I allow her to slide herself off the couch so she can continue undressing me and soon my jeans and boxers are on the floor as well.

I drop to my knees and pull her panties down, pausing a moment to taste her.

"Foster," she whimpers as my tongue parts her. "Please."

She doesn't need to finish the sentence. As much as she loves it, she wants more than my mouth tonight.

I stand and kiss her roughly, letting her taste herself on my lips before turning her around and bending her over the couch.

I'm so desperate to get inside her that I almost forget a key player.

Swearing under my breath, I say, "Don't move, Baby. I'll be right back."

But she shoots me a flirtatious smile over her shoulder before producing a condom from somewhere on the couch.

Thank fuck.

"Your attention to detail is so hot." I pluck the condom from her hand and tear it open, almost dropping it in my eagerness to put it on.

She giggles. "Hotter than me wearing this?"

I stare at my name stitched across her shoulders as I align myself at her entrance. "Nothing is hotter than that." We both cry out as I slam into her. At this angle, her pussy is the tightest thing I've ever felt, gripping me like a vice and making me see stars.

My fingers grip her hips through the jersey as I set a steady rhythm. It feels fucking unreal. It always does. Every time with Beth is the best sex of my life.

"Faster...please," she begs as she bucks against me and my balls throb.

Without pulling out of her, I straighten her up so her back is against my chest, then hook her outside knee up to rest on the top of the couch. I continue to move, deeper than before and it's like nothing I've ever experienced.

"What do you need, Beth?" My heart is beating faster than it ever has on the ice.

"This...you. Just you," she cries as her inner walls begin to tighten even more around me.

Fuck. I need her too. Like I've never needed anyone. My head swims with the realisation and I'm dangerously close to coming.

"You have me," I tell her as I reach my hand between her thighs. "Now show me how beautiful you are when you come." My finger circles her clit once and then presses down hard and she shatters like glass against me.

So fucking gorgeous.

I manage only a few more strokes before I join her, burying my face in her neck on a long, shuddering groan.

Life altering. Every fucking time.

When we've regained our senses, we straighten on wobbly legs. Beth smirks up at me as she slumps against my chest, her now off-centred ponytail tickling my chin.

"So, you do like the jersey?"

There's that word again. *Like.*

"Mmmm," is all I'm capable of as I cup her face and gently guide her mouth to mine.

No, "like" isn't enough, not even close. This is something deeper, something I'm not ready to name, but I know it's real, and it's everything.

CHAPTER 30

BETH

"What if she doesn't like me?"

I will myself to stop playing with my seatbelt as we drive to Ben's penthouse in the city. I just spent eighty dollars on this manicure and I'm hoping if I'm careful it will last me through the holidays.

"That's literally impossible," Foster answers, not taking his eyes off the road. He reaches over and takes my hand which had already started picking at the seatbelt again.

"It's entirely possible. I have flaws, like everyone."

He frowns as his eyes scan me up and down in appraisal. He shakes his head. "Nope. I've studied every inch of you and you're perfect." He kisses my hand before locking his eyes on mine. "Every. Inch." He winks and I swat at him, making him laugh.

I missed him while he was away last week. His laugh, his smell, his presence. Yes, we texted constantly and Facetimed almost every day, but still; I missed having him at home. Knowing that Foster's house is only going to be "home" for another week made his absence even more difficult. I leave for my parents' in nine days and when I return, I'll be moving into my own place.

But my complicated feelings about leaving Foster's house is a problem for another day. Today I am focused on not making a terrible first impression with Valentina.

I know I shouldn't be so nervous about meeting my brother's girlfriend, but I can't help it. She's a supermodel. Her job title has the word "super" in it. The idea of being around someone who seems to live in a world of luxury and sophistication is intimidating. Her work must be so glamorous and thrilling.

The most exciting thing that happened to me today was that my class won the school door decorating contest and we got ice cream sandwiches.

They were really good ice cream sandwiches.

"What if we have absolutely nothing in common? What are we going to talk about?"

Foster shrugs. "Both of your boyfriends are hockey players."

A small squeak escapes me, startling him.

"What?" he asks, looking curiously between me and the highway in front of us.

"Nothing. You just said that you're my boyfriend."

"I am your boyfriend."

My boyfriend. My heart flutters, and I bite back a grin, attempting to play it cool, but inside, I'm squealing.

"So, if you're my boyfriend, then by using deductive reasoning, would you consider me your girlfriend?"

The corner of his mouth turns up ever so slightly. The subtle movement might have gone unnoticed, but I know his face well enough to know when he's fighting a grin, and right now it looks like it's taking everything in him not to laugh at me.

"Yes. I consider you my girlfriend."

"Oh."

"Oh?" He cocks an eyebrow at me as he stops at a red light. "Do you not consider me your boyfriend?"

I do. Is that crazy? It's only been two and half weeks since we first spent the night together and Foster's been on the road half of that time. But I feel more for him already than I ever did for any other guy I've dated, and it's getting harder to keep it a secret. I almost let it slip while talking to my sisters over the weekend. I don't know how much longer I can hold it in.

Realising that he's still waiting for me to answer, I say, "I would be open to considering it."

Foster smirks. "You're considering considering it?"

"Yes. I am taking it under consideration."

"Well, let me know when you've considered it."

"I will."

"I wouldn't want to rush your consideration."

"That's very considerate of you."

Foster's deep, rich laughter fills the small space. It's infectious, and I find myself grinning just listening to him. I love making him laugh. I love the way his eyes crinkle at the corners, the way his whole face lights up.

As his laughter fades, he looks at me with a smile that makes my heart skip a beat.

There's something so pure, so unguarded about him when it's just the two of us. I don't think he shares this side of himself with many people and that makes me happy.

I want him all to myself.

❄

"YOU MADE IT!" Ben greets us as he opens the door, welcoming us into his condo.

He pulls me in for a quick hug and even from the brief contact, I can tell that he's tense.

"I'm so glad you're here." Ben takes Foster's coat and waits while I unbutton mine. "Seriously, you have no fucking idea how glad I am." His tone is upbeat, but there's a strain in his smile. This is not like him at all.

On that ominous note, I shrug off my coat and instantly feel Foster's gaze on me. More specifically, on my dress.

I spotted the dress in the window of a consignment store while I was window shopping downtown over the weekend. It's a deep red sheath dress with cap sleeves, a square neckline, and a skirt that falls just to my knees. It's unlike anything I've ever worn, but it called to me. Wearing it makes me feel like Grace Kelly—timelessly elegant, effortlessly poised.

As Ben disappears with our coats, Foster approaches me from behind.

"That dress..." His mouth hovers just above my ear; not touching me, but affecting me all the same.

My pulse quickens. "What about it?" I made sure to slip my coat on before he could catch a glimpse of me in the dress, knowing full well that if he saw me in it, we probably wouldn't have made it out of the house on time.

"It needs to be on my fucking floor," he growls before stepping away, putting some much-needed distance between us.

Ben appears again and motions us to follow him into

the living room. I still remember the first time I visited, how awestruck I was by the space. The décor had been simple back then, but the floor-to-ceiling windows offered a stunning panoramic view of the city that left me speechless.

Today, the interior is almost unrecognisable. The room is dimly lit, with overhead lights casting dramatic spotlights on different areas. The living space, once open and minimalist, now features three long, plush white sofas arranged around a sleek glass coffee table. Bold, vibrant abstract paintings dominate three of the four walls, adding a burst of colour to the otherwise washed-out space.

It's about as inviting as a roped-off art exhibit.

And the occupants appear to be just as welcoming.

Four people in the living room are deeply engaged in conversation and fail to acknowledge Foster and me.

I recognize Valentina from her pictures online, but I have no idea who her friends are. My first thought is they must be models too—how could they not be, looking like that?

I've never struggled with body image issues, but I've always seen myself as more cute than striking. These three women and their male companion possess a kind of beauty that feels surreal. Perfectly symmetrical features, flawless skin, and makeup so polished it's as if they don't exist in this world, but instead stepped straight out of a magazine into the condo.

"Babe," Ben says, attracting the group's attention. "Beth is here."

"Hi," I beam at her. "It's so nice to meet you."

She stands, stepping around the coffee table as she walks towards me. She's almost as tall as Ben.

Do I hug her? Shake her hand? I have no idea what the proper etiquette is.

When she reaches me, she places her hands on my shoulders as she leans down and gives me a quick air kiss next to my cheek.

"Hey." She turns and with an effortlessly graceful hand motion gestures to the beautiful creatures sitting on the sofa. "This is Gwen, Dante, and Xan." Even her voice is elegant. Soft but captivating as she introduces her friends.

I give the group an awkward little wave. The first two return my greeting with warm smiles. The third, Xan, I presume, stares straight past me and locks her gaze on Foster. Her long black hair is slicked back in a high, sleek ponytail. She's like a cat, eyes on her target, ready to prowl.

"And you are?" she purrs at him. The sound makes my eye twitch.

I can sense his discomfort at being the centre of attention. My instinct is to close the distance between us and reassure him, but my feet stay firmly planted in place.

"This is my best friend, Foster," Ben supplies. "I'll grab you a drink, Bug."

"I'll help," Foster says, giving me an intense look as he follows Ben into the kitchen. Foster is not a fan of crowds, or meeting new people.

Still. He's gone and now I'm alone with not one but four strangers.

I glance nervously up at Valentina. Her blonde hair falls in soft, golden waves that catch the light perfectly. Her skin is flawless, glowing with a natural radiance I could never achieve no matter how much money I spend on serums from Sephora. The silence between us has stretched on too long, and I'm pretty sure she doesn't know what to say to me either.

"Ben says you were travelling for work last week?"

She nods. "There was a show in Paris."

"Paris? That sounds amazing. I've heard it's really beautiful there."

"You've never been?" Gwen asks from her spot on the couch. Her posh British accent combined with her platinum bob make her impossibly chic. But there is no trace of malice in her question.

"Me? No, I've actually never left North America."

Xan scoffs and I feel myself shrink inwardly. When I was younger, our family vacations were mostly road trips. The rare times we flew, it was usually to watch Ben play hockey. I'd love to spend a summer travelling just for the fun of it someday, but that hasn't happened yet.

Valentina ignores her friend's rude reaction. "If you go, go in spring. It's dreary this time of year."

The others murmur their agreement.

"Are you all models?" I ask, tittering with nervous laughter. Xan laughs too, but I feel she's laughing at me, not with me.

"Do you hear that, Dante?" Xan's tone was mocking. "She thinks you're a model."

She irritated me earlier when she eye-fucked my boyfriend, but now I'm actually starting to loathe this woman.

"I'm prettier than you are," Dante tells her before turning to me. "I'm a designer. It was my show they walked in last week."

"Oh, that's incredible."

"So is your dress," he remarks as he casts his eyes downward. "Where ever did you get it?"

I feel myself flush under the sudden interest in my clothing. Smoothing my hands down the front of my skirt, I answer, "Well, to be honest, I found it in a thrift shop this weekend."

I expect him to judge me for wearing second-hand clothing, but he surprises me by coming in for a better look.

He's only slightly taller than me, but his presence feels much larger. Dressed in a tailored blazer and slim-fit trousers, he moves with a natural elegance, like it's effortless. His light hair, perfectly styled, frames his sharp features, and his glasses highlight his intense, thoughtful eyes.

"Look at this stitching…" He gives the dress a thorough examination before declaring. "It's vintage Chanel. I'd stake my reputation on it."

Suddenly everyone in the room is a lot more interested in me, or my garment at least.

"It fits you perfectly," Dante adds. "You look like Rita Hayworth."

There is no suggestion in his tone or leer in his gaze. He strikes me as a man who appreciates beautiful things and he finds my dress beautiful.

Should I tell him I paid eighteen dollars for it?

No, Beth. That's an inside thought.

My new friend is inspecting one of my sleeves as Foster steps out of the kitchen, a glass of champagne in hand. He freezes when he notices Dante's hand on my shoulder, his usual stoic expression tightening into a deep scowl.

CHAPTER 31

FOSTER

It was just supposed to be the four of us.

Ben assured me it was going to be the four of us.

Surprise, surprise—it's not just the four of us.

This is so on-brand for Ben; I shouldn't be surprised. How many times has he told me one thing then delivered another?

I didn't even have to say anything. Once we were alone in the ultra-modern kitchen, he started to apologise.

"They weren't supposed to fucking be here," he whined before taking a long pull from his beer. "I specifically told Valentina that I didn't want her friends around tonight, but when I got home from the gym, they were already here. They're always fucking here. And it's not always those three, sometimes it's stylists or other models, but it's always someone. We haven't spent a night alone in two weeks. Tell me that's not fucked up."

He looked so miserable that I didn't want to make him feel worse. I let him continue to vent in hushed tones while grabbing extra champagne glasses.

I may be miffed at the unwanted company tonight, but Ben is absolutely livid.

Eager to get back to Beth, I told him it was fine. We'd be leaving soon enough for the Christmas party. Still, my concern is Beth. I'm used to being forced into unwanted social situations, but she's not, and she's alone out there. She was nervous enough about meeting Valentina and I'm hoping a drink might take the edge off.

She seems to be doing fine, however.

The guy with the perfect haircut and unnaturally white teeth is standing far too close to her, his hand on her arm.

I hate it.

I step in and hand Beth the flute of champagne, trying to steady my nerves. I'm so tense it's a wonder I don't shatter the delicate glass in my grip. Standing closer to her than necessary, I slip my hands into my pockets and give Dante a slow, measured look. His eyes widen, and he takes a step back before returning to his seat on the couch. Message received.

I might not be much of a conversationalist, but my methods of non-verbal communication are just fine.

Beth raises her glass and takes a slow sip of champagne. Her eyes flash with surprise at my possessive display, but the slight curve of her lips says she enjoyed it. The red lipstick she's wearing is a perfect match to the vibrant shade of her dress and I can't take my eyes off of her.

That fucking dress. The moment I saw her in it, my heart stopped altogether and my brain followed suit. Unfortunately, my dick was alive and kicking, which was less than ideal considering our host's proximity. It clings to her like a second skin, outlining every graceful curve, and all I can think about is holding her just as close. She seems more relaxed now, the tension from earlier gone. Watching her socialise with this new crowd, I make a decision. If she can get along with these people, then so can I.

For her. I'll do anything for her.

"I could use a refill." The dark-haired alpha-predator rises from her seat and saunters over to me. "Join me? What's your poison?"

Correction: I can't get along with this one.

"Foster doesn't drink, Xan," Ben says as he joins us. He holds the open champagne bottle in his hands. Xan pouts at me like I've disappointed her before holding out her glass to Ben. He pretends not to notice, filling everyone else's glasses before hers.

I see Ben enjoys her company as much as I do.

My eyes look everywhere but her, though I can still feel her watching me. Subtlety is an artform this woman doesn't possess.

As a pro athlete I've had my fair share of women pursue me. It only bothers me when they refuse to respect when I'm not interested.

This is one of those times.

What's worse is that I can sense Beth's discomfort returning as the conversation resumes around us. Her eyes keep shifting nervously to Xan, like she expects her to pounce on me.

If we were anywhere else, surrounded by strangers, I'd pull Beth against me. Drape my arm around her shoulder and keep her glued to me all night so there would be no doubt in anyone's mind that we belonged to each other.

But in this condo with her already upset brother,

there's nothing I can do but ignore Xan and hope she gets the hint sooner rather than later.

"Babe, do you want to open another bottle of bubbles?" Valentina phrases this as if it's a question, but there is only one clear answer.

"We'll have to leave for dinner soon," Ben responds, a pointed gaze fixed on Valentina.

"We can be late," she responds, a slight annoyance in her tone as she stares at the swirling alcohol in her glass.

"Yeah, Benny," Xan adds, like an idiot who just found a hornet's nest and pokes it with a stick. "It's rude to invite us here only to tell us to leave."

He glares at her. "Now that you bring it up, I don't remember inviting you in the first place."

I stifle a laugh. Something tells me that will only make matters worse. Everyone stands in uncomfortable silence.

"Ben, I need your help with something in the bedroom," Valentina says flatly and heads towards the hallway. Ben rolls his eyes and turns to follow. He's not even trying to hide his irritation anymore.

"Well, that was awkward," Xan sniffs before draining her glass.

Dante gives her a look of pure disdain but says nothing.

The English woman, whose name I've forgotten, doesn't hold back. "For fuck's sake, Xan. Why do you always have to remind us what a slag you are? Do us all a favour and seek professional help."

Xan doesn't look chagrined in the least. In fact, she looks extremely pleased at the chaos she's created. "Whatever, Gwen. I need a cigarette." Her cold eyes slide back to me. "Join me?"

"No, thanks."

She sidles up to me, placing her hand on my arm and running it over my bicep. "You don't drink. You don't smoke. Maybe we should get out of here and I can figure out what your vice is."

Even through the layers of clothing, her touch makes my skin crawl.

"Maybe you shouldn't touch people without their consent."

Beth's words are followed by a stunned silence. Her voice is gentle, almost sweet, like she's talking to one of her students.

"Is that so?" Xan's mouth twists into a cruel smile.

"It is. Personal boundaries are very important and should always be respected. It's a lesson that children are taught in Kindergarten. I can teach you a song to help you remember, if you'd like." Beth's complete lack of aggression is pissing Xan off, much to her friends' amusement.

"I'd like to hear the song," the English woman apparently named Gwen says, raising her hand in the air and barely holding back her laughter.

"I would also like to hear this song," Dante agrees.

"Fuck you both." Xan spits out before turning on Beth. "As for you, Second-Hand Sue, if Foster doesn't want me to touch him, he can–"

"I don't want you to touch me."

She turns at me, and slides her hand further up my arm. "You don't mean that," her voice dripping with flirtation, like this is part of the chase. I'm guessing she hasn't been turned down before.

"I've never meant anything more in my life. Ever."

Xan removes her hand and drops the sex kitten act, her expression souring.

Beth claps. She actually claps. "Thank you for using your listening ears, Xan. Now, as my brother said, we have another event to go to."

Gwen and Dante exchange delighted looks before setting down their glasses and starting for the front door.

"It was an absolute pleasure," Gwen tells Beth, giving her a peck on the cheek before she leaves. "You have no idea."

"Take care of that dress, my dear," Dante adds with a wink. "Hold on to that one," he says in a low voice as he walks past me. Maybe I judged this guy too quickly.

Xan, who seems less than thrilled by this turn of events, starts dragging her heels when she reaches the door. "I have a coat!"

Beth reaches into the closet and pulls out what appears to be a purple fur coat. "Is this it?"

Xan scowls and snatches the monstrosity from her hand. Beth grins.

"Oh good. I just grabbed the tackiest one and hoped for the best."

I can hear Gwen's howl of laughter from the hallway.

"You miserable cu–"

"Bye, Xan! Don't trip over your cloven hooves on your way out!" Beth slams the door in her face.

She takes a few deep breaths before turning to face me. We stare at one another for a few beats before I erupt into laughter.

I laugh long and hard, the kind of laughter that makes your stomach ache and your lungs burn. Beth joins in which only makes me laugh harder. She covers her mouth and I'm not sure if it's because she's trying to quiet herself or she can't believe the things she just said.

Eventually, we get control of ourselves and calm down.

The urge to hold her is so strong, but I remind myself where we are. I settle for looking at her like she's the most incredible thing I've ever seen, because that's exactly what she is.

She smoothes her hands over her hair and straightens her dress before saying, "I think that went well." And the laughter begins again.

CHAPTER 32

BETH

"The salmon is delicious."

I make the statement not to proclaim my appreciation for the fish I'm eating, but to break the awkward silence at our table.

The ballroom at Chateau Laurier is tastefully decorated with green and gold, the team's colours. The high ceilings are adorned with elegant crystal chandeliers that twinkle in the dimly lit room. The tables, covered in pristine white linen cloths, are set with fine china and crystal glassware. Each place setting is accented with a festive napkin, folded into intricate designs, and a sprig of holly. A string quartet plays Christmas songs from the small stage at the front of the room.

The rest of the tables seem to be having a great time. Animated conversation and laughter swells around us. And while I'm happy to see others enjoying the all-out splendour of the evening, I wish that my own party were feeling a bit more festive.

Ben and Valentina are barely speaking. When they

emerged from the bedroom to find everyone gone, things appeared to be better. Strained still, but better.

I'd worried that I overstepped by asking her friends to leave. But watching Xan be so disrespectful to Ben in his own home set me off in a way I wasn't expecting.

Seeing her put her nasty little hands on my boyfriend was the straw that broke the camel's back.

My brother seemed almost gleeful when he realised they were gone so I didn't let myself feel too bad for kicking them out.

But now we're having dinner and the tension is building once again. Valentina said little on our way here and has spent most of dinner on her phone, hardly touching her food. Ben, on the other hand, made friends with one of the servers who has been bringing him a fresh drink every twenty minutes.

On the other side of the table, Kim and Alexei appear to be in their own private bubble. I can't help but watch as they communicate through glances and gestures. Alexei can barely tear his gaze away from the mother of his children. He's usually so reserved and stoic on the ice, but he transforms into someone else entirely around his wife, completely tuned in to her every mood and movement. Kim looks radiant in a shimmering gown, even as she's forced to sit farther away from the table to accommodate her almost comically large belly. Alexei's hand is gently resting on the back of her chair, his thumb lazily stroking her shoulder as we eat. He leans in close to whisper something and she laughs, her face lighting up while he gazes at her like she's his entire world.

And then there's Foster who, true to form, is quieter with so many people around. He can't hold my hand or put his arms around me because of where we are and who we're with, but I've appreciated each time he's brushed his leg against mine under the table tonight.

One unhappy couple, one obnoxiously in love couple, and one very happy couple who can't tell anyone they're a couple makes for strained conversation.

After dinner, there are speeches from the owners celebrating the achievements of the team. Arthur Stetson, the team's head coach, also addresses the room, thanking his players for putting in countless hours, going above and beyond, making the team what it is. When he's done thanking them for their passion, perseverance, and exceptional teamwork, a lot of us are left dabbing our eyes.

They open the dance floor in the adjacent ballroom and people rise from their tables and begin to mingle. Valentina walks away from the table without a word and Ben heads in the direction of the bar. I stare after him, concern eating away at me.

Foster stands and says, "I'll go check on him."

"Thank you." As I squeeze his arm, his face softens the way it always does right before he's about to kiss me and I wish more than anything that he could. Instead, he gives me a quick nod before walking away. I follow him with my eyes until he's lost to the crowd. Turning back, I realise it's just Kim and I left. "Where's Alexei?"

"He wanted to talk to Arthur about something." She strokes her stomach, her eyes trained on my face. "Are you okay?"

"Of course."

"Beth…"

"I'm just tired." Tired of worrying about my brother who seems to be on a path of self-destruction. Tired of keeping things from him and my family because I'm worried about how they'll react. But mostly I'm tired of hiding my feelings for Foster when other people are around.

Kim's eyes are sympathetic as she twists the rings around on her finger. She moves them, slowly and thoughtfully. As she plays with them, the diamonds catch the light from the lit candles, making the little reflections dance across the white tablecloth.

"You know," she gives me a tiny smile when she looks up at me, "Alexei's parents were not at all happy when we started dating."

I'm not sure how she reads my mind so well, but right now I'm grateful for her psychic abilities.

"Really?" It's hard to imagine that anyone could look at the two of them and not see they're perfect together.

"Hard to believe, right? I mean, imagine not liking me," she laughs. "They thought I was a distraction, that I would hold him back. And according to his mother, the way I smiled all the time was 'unnerving.' They actually stopped talking to him at one point."

"What made them come around?"

She ponders my question. "Time, mostly. And seeing how happy I made their son. They warmed to me eventually, especially when I gave them the world's most gorgeous grandbabies. What I'm trying to say is that a good family will stand by you, no matter what path you choose. It's not about whether they understand every decision you make; it's about wanting you to be happy. They'll celebrate your wins and pick you up when things fall apart. Even if what makes you happy is completely different from what they imagined, they'll get behind you. So, hang in there, kid. It's going to be okay."

Just then Alexei appears at her side with her coat.

"You're leaving already?"

"My parents are home with the kids, so we've got a wild date night planned," she says, grinning. "We're going to eat junk food and watch *Only Murders In The Building* in our hotel room."

I hug her goodbye, barely able to get my arms around her. She vows to keep me up-to-date on the little one's arrival and I promise to visit as soon as I'm back in the city.

"Merry Christmas, Beth."

"Merry Christmas, Kim. And thanks for the talk."

"Any time," Kim says. "I mean it. I love talking."

"She really does," Alexei confirms, smirking down at her.

As I watch them walk away, hand in hand, I feel someone approach from my left.

"Beth Michaels," a young man says as he draws close to me. "I've been trying to talk to you all night.

"Austin Crawford." I've only met him once before, but he has the kind of cocky grin you're not likely to forget. "Here I am."

"Here you are, indeed. Looking absolutely radiant, I might add."

Austin strikes me as a bit of a man-child. Used to getting whatever he wants as long as he asks nicely enough. I'm sure his boyish charm and the fact that he's prettier than most girls don't hurt his cause either.

"Why exactly were you trying to talk to me?"

"To ask you to dance, of course." He motions to the almost empty dance floor.

"That is a very kind offer, but I was just going to find my brother."

"I just saw him talking to Foster. Seemed like a serious conversation; the kind I like to avoid at all costs. I said I'd keep you company." He extends his hand. "Shall we?"

I'm really not in the mood to dance, but I can't bring myself to refuse the offer. I nod and place my hand in his. As he leads me to the dance floor my thoughts drift back to Ben, wondering if he's alright. I try to catch a glimpse of them at the bar, but there are too many people blocking my view.

Foster will take care of him, I remind myself.

Austin works the room like he owns it and everyone inside it. By the time we make it to the dance floor, the tempo's changed and a slower song has started.

I place my hands on his shoulders as he rests his on my hips and we start to move in time to the music. Well, Austin moves in time. I'm just trying not to step on his feet.

"How are you liking Ottawa?" He leans in close, to be heard above the song.

"I love it," I answer honestly. My heart will always belong to the Island, but I'm so glad I took this chance and moved here.

"You know," he scans the room coyly. "I offered to get you at the airport."

"Did you, now?"

"Damn straight. I practically begged for the job, in fact. Not that it would have been a chore at all. But your big brother made Foster go."

I wobble on my heels and nearly twist my ankle. It's a slow song and I'm still struggling.

"I'm sure you would have been a perfect chauffeur."

"A better roommate, too." When he pumps his eyebrows up and down, I can't help but laugh.

Austin is a natural-born flirt, but he seems perfectly harmless. He's the sort of guy who enjoys the chase more than the catch.

He leads us into a turn. I try to keep up but step the wrong way and ram my knee into his leg. His arms wrap around me to keep me from falling over. "I'm so sorry!" It probably hurt me more than the trunk he calls a limb, but I feel bad nonetheless.

"It's fine," he laughs.

"I'm a horrible dancer," I admit.

"You just need practice," he insists.

"Or a better partner."

Foster's unexpected voice startles us both, causing Austin to tighten his grip on me which results in Foster's frown to become an outright scowl.

And that is what we call a vicious cycle.

"Hey, buddy," Austin smirks at him, his arms still encircling me. "Just keeping her company, like I said I would."

"You never said that." Foster's glare turns downright murderous.

"Sure I did. Just not loud enough for you or Ben to hear me."

Oh, he is an outright scamp. He grins at Foster, almost daring him to say something, but Foster refuses to take the bait.

"Well, my work here is done. Thank you for the dance,

Beth." Austin brings my hand up to his and kisses it. "I look forward to our next one." He gives me a wink and then makes a quick exit.

I expect Foster's mood to improve once he's gone, but it doesn't. "Are you ready to go?" His tone is clipped.

"Where's Ben?"

"I got him and Valentina a car service; they're headed home."

"Is he okay?"

"No, but he's going to be. They've got a lot to talk about."

The walk to the underground parking garage is a quiet one. I keep glancing up at Foster's controlled expression wondering what's wrong.

Is there something he's not telling me about Ben? Or maybe he's just overstimulated from being around so many people. Could he be angry at me?

By the time we reach the car, my brain is spinning with scenarios, none of them good.

"Did I do something?"

Foster pauses, his hands resting on the keys in the ignition. His green eyes are as stormy as his mood. "What?"

"You seem upset and I just want to know if it's something I've done, or..."

His hands are in my hair, pulling my mouth to his in a deep, claiming kiss. When we pull apart, he rests his forehead against mine. "I don't like crowds. I'm irritated with your brother for repeatedly charging us admission to the shitshow he calls a relationship. But mostly, I'm upset because so many men got to touch you tonight and I didn't."

My lips turn up in a smirk. "It was two men."

"That's two too many," he growls. "Especially when all I've wanted to do is touch you. I should have been the one who got to kiss you on the hand and tell you how gorgeous you look. I should have been the one dancing with you."

"I kept kicking him."

"Not hard enough," he grumbles.

I run my fingers through his hair, scraping my nails against his scalp the way he likes and he groans appreciatively.

"I've gotten pretty good at masking my feelings over the years, but I don't want to have to do that with you. Hiding how I feel about you is hard," he admits.

It is hard; like carrying a weight that grows heavier every day. Constantly worrying that I'll reach for his hand when someone is looking or that our gazes will linger too long and it won't go unnoticed.

Suddenly it all seems unfair that Foster and I are the ones going out of our way to make others, namely my brother, happy. When would Ben ever show a fragment of that kind of consideration to me?

I bring my mouth to Foster's again, pouring everything I'm feeling into the kiss. When I suck on his lower lip, he practically purrs.

"I need to get you home." His voice is low and urgent.

"I can't wait."

He pulls away and reaches for the ignition again, but I stop him.

"I mean it. I can't wait."

CHAPTER 33

BETH

"What are you doing?" Foster asks as I'm awkwardly climbing over the console. I manage to simultaneously hit my head on the roof and smack my knee on the cup holder before tumbling over in a heap into the backseat.

"Seducing you, obviously."

Righting myself with as much dignity as possible, I motion to a stunned-looking Foster to join me. When he tries to follow, he gets stuck—He's too damn big. I can't stop myself from giggling as he curses, trying to dislodge himself from between the front seats. He hops out of the car, quickly scans the abandoned parking garage, and climbs through the rear door.

He's barely settled on the leather interior before I'm in his lap. The skirt of my dress rides up as I straddle him and his hands are running up my thighs. I shamelessly grind against him, feeling every inch of him hardening underneath me.

"Not feeling patient tonight, Baby?" he teases, gripping my ass.

I shake my head as I hastily undo his belt and start on his pants. "Fresh out of patience."

Chuckling, he squeezes me hard over my panties while I continue to maul him. I've been looking forward to being with him all night, but sex in a semi-public setting was not on the agenda. At this point, though, if Foster isn't inside me in the next sixty seconds, I'm going to lose what's left of my mind.

I tug at his pants and he helps me push them down past his hips. His cock springs out, beads of pre-cum already forming at its tip.

I reach for him, almost frantically, but with one hand Foster captures my wrists and pins them to his chest as his other hand continues to palm my ass.

"We'll have to be quick. And quiet." His voice is low and authoritative. "Anyone could walk by."

I take a quick glance around my surroundings as my heart pounds in my chest.

"Can you do that, Beth?"

I nod quickly.

"Say it." He kisses my neck, his lips pressing against my thundering pulse.

"I can be quick and quiet."

"I know you can." Then he slides my panties to the side, too eager to be inside me to take them off.

I slide down onto him and immediately break the quiet rule as my body adjusts to his size. I'm beyond wet and desperate with need.

"Sweet Christ, Beth. You feel incredible." Foster groans as his hands squeeze my thighs. I start to move, but he stops me with a startled grunt. "Fuck. Condom."

Jesus. I've never had unprotected sex and I'm startled

that the thought didn't even cross my lust-fueled mind. But as Foster attempts to pull out, I cling to him like a vice. "I'm…I'm on the pill. And I don't, I don't have anything."

It's insane to be embarrassed talking about sexual health to a man that's literally inside me, but here we are.

His hold on me tightens. "They test us regularly," he promises, making me meet his eyes, his breathing laboured. "Are you sure? We can stop."

"Please don't stop," I plead. "I'm sure. I want you. All of you."

"Beth, Baby, you have all of me. I'll give you anything you want."

He grips my hips as I start to ride him. There's no hesitation, no slow build-up. I am taking what I need from him and he gives it willingly.

My hands fist his shirt, clinging to him as I use his broad shoulders for support. My back arches, pressing my chest forward and my head falls back as I move. My thighs tremble against him as I rock. I lean forward, needing to be closer to him, but it's still not enough. I want to erase any space between us, to melt into him until we're one.

Foster watches me like I'm the greatest thing he's ever seen.

"You're doing so well," he praises. "Being so quiet for me. When I get you home you can make all the noise you want, I promise. Wake up the whole neighbourhood." His hand comes between us to stroke my clit.

My vision blurs and I can't hold back my moan as I ride him faster and harder. I'm close. So close and Foster knows it. He increases the pressure right where I need him.

"Oh God—"

"That's it, sweet girl. Come for me."

I do, surrendering myself to the feeling of pure ecstasy as wave after wave of pleasure crashes through me. Foster pulls me into a rough kiss that absorbs our mingled cries as he shudders beneath me.

He holds me against him, kissing me with increasing softness until we're both breathless and boneless and sated in one another's arms.

Eventually I pull away and look down at him. His tousled hair and rumpled suit make him look sexier than ever. He's gazing up at me with such devotion, like he can't believe I'm real.

The sound of a nearby car unlocking sends me scrambling off his lap like a startled deer. Foster fumbles to do up his pants, his eyes darting around, searching for anyone who might have seen us. We sit there in tense silence for a moment before he finally exhales, shoulders relaxing. I release the breath I've been holding, my heart still racing. That was a little too close for comfort.

"Take me home?"

He smiles as he reaches up to push a loose tendril of hair behind my ear. "There is nothing I'd rather do."

CHAPTER 34

FOSTER

It's after ten when I arrive at my hotel room in Chicago. I drop my bags the moment I'm through the door and collapse onto the bed. The worst thing about away games isn't the travel or the ever-changing schedule; it's not being able to sleep in your own bed whenever you want to.

Especially now that I have someone to share it with.

I pull up Beth's contact on my phone and Facetime her, as promised. She picks up on the second ring and my chest swells the moment her sleepy face comes into focus. I've only been gone for a few hours, but it feels like ages.

"Hey," she says snuggling into my pillow. I know it's mine by the colour of the pillow case her brown hair is fanned out on. I'd told her she could sleep in my room while I was away and I'm pleased she decided to.

The fact that I'm not there with her is a grave injustice.

"Hey. How was your evening?"

"It was good. I corrected spelling tests. Gold stars all around."

"Nice."

"Are you ready for tomorrow?"

Chicago's a tough team, but we're evenly matched. As of right now, we're set to head into Christmas break as the top team in the Atlantic division and that feels amazing.

"I think so, yeah. We're meeting to discuss strategy in the morning."

She nods as her mouth turns downwards. "How is Ben?"

I blow out a breath, not sure how to answer that question. How is Ben? I hadn't seen him since the Christmas party, but he texted me the day after to tell me he and Valentina broke up. I offered to meet up, but he said he wanted to be alone.

Then I asked if he wanted to talk about it on the plane today. He immediately said "no," pulled out his headphones and ignored me for the rest of the trip.

"I'm not really sure," I tell her, honestly. "He's moody as hell and not saying much. I'm sure he'll talk when he's ready. Ben loves talking about himself."

The worry on her face eases a microscopic amount. "He does. Speaking of brothers and talking..."

I walked right into that one. I did end up responding to Cody's initial message last week. I thanked him for reaching out and told him I'd let him know when I'm ready to meet up.

He texted back right away and said he understood and to take all the time I needed.

Part of me wishes that he'd be an asshole about it or try to guilt me into seeing him. I've held on to this hurt and resentment for so long, I want a reason to cling to it.

"I was thinking I'd message him next week. Try to meet up for coffee after you leave to go home?"

As much as I hate the idea of Beth leaving for two weeks, I know how excited she is to spend time with her family. She's been talking about their annual cookie baking and outdoor Christmas lights tour; family traditions I hope to be a part of, someday.

"Well, I for one think reconnecting with your family over Christmas sounds lovely. Besides, if you're hanging with your brother, you won't have time to attract puck bunnies."

I let out a bark of laughter as she pretends to glare at me through the screen. "Baby, there were no puck bunnies before you and there sure as hell won't be any after. You're the only puck bunny I want."

Her mouth drops open and there's fire in those whiskey eyes. "Foster James, I am not a puck bunny!"

I give her a lazy smile. "You sure about that? What are you wearing?"

The pink in her cheeks is visible through the phone. "A jersey."

"Mmmhmm. You're wearing a hockey jersey in a hockey player's bed. Sounds like a puck bunny's natural habitat to me."

"You're the worst."

"Aww, I'm not complaining. My jersey looks so good on you."

"Who says it's yours? Maybe I picked up Austin's."

I know she's kidding, but I scowl anyway. "Don't even joke about that. I'd burn it. And the bedsheets."

She beams at me, clearly pleased to have gotten the upper hand. She can have it and anything else she wants.

"It's your jersey."

"Damn right it is. Show me? Not that I don't trust you, I'll just sleep better knowing for sure. It might be hard for me to see my name with you wearing it, so just slip it off real quick."

Her laughter is silenced by a loud knock on my door.

"What was that?" Beth asks in a panicked voice and damned if I know the answer. I sit up in bed just as another three loud bangs shake the room.

"Fozzie! Open up!"

Fuck.

"It's your brother. I better find out what he wants before he breaks the door down, okay? I– I'll talk to you tomorrow." I almost said "I love you." It was on the tip of my tongue, ready to roll off.

"Okay…text me if something's wrong?"

"I'm sure everything is fine, but I will. I promise."

I almost told Beth that I love her. The implications make me light-headed as I stand and make my way to the door.

Am I in love with Beth? Yes. Is it too soon to tell her? Also yes.

Is her brother pounding on my door because he found out about us and has come to beat me to death with a pillowcase full of pucks?

Possibly.

"Alright, alright," I say, throwing open the door.

Outside my room stand Ben, Will, and Austin in almost identical outfits of jeans and long sleeved shirts.

"Did we interrupt your beauty sleep? It's okay. I'm pretty enough for the both of us." Austin's smug face is looking especially punchable at this moment. Ever since the Christmas party, he's been goading me more than usual. Smiling at me for too long. Making snide comments under his breath. He grates on my nerves at the best of times, but this is starting to become intolerable. I'm sure it doesn't help that my girlfriend just joked about wearing his jersey in bed.

"What is going on? Other than you assholes waking everyone on the goddamn floor."

"We're going out." Ben states plainly.

"Okay. Have fun." I start to close the door. A hand swings out, slamming onto the wood.

"You're coming. Get dressed."

Irritation prickles at the base of my skull and I cross my arms as I lean against the doorframe. "I'm not going out."

"Come on, Fozzie. I need this." Ben rubs at his temples. He looks like he hasn't slept in days. "When do I ever ask you for anything?"

A chorus of "Constantly," "Always," and "All the damn time," is his response.

Ben glares at Austin and Will before continuing. "Please, man? I just survived a breakup and need to fuck someone new to get her out of my system. It's Friday night, we're in the city of love–"

"The city of love is Paris. We're in Chicago," Will pipes up, but Ben ignores him.

"I need to go out and I need you there looking out for me."

How did I become the adopted mother to this lost baby bird of a man? The last thing I want is to be dragged to some dive bar with these idiots, but what choice do I have? He's my best friend and Beth's brother, and I don't want his judgement, or lack thereof, getting him in trouble.

"Give me five minutes. I'll meet you in the lobby."

"I knew I could count on you, Fozz." Ben is already walking away, leaving before I can change my mind. "That's why you're the best."

I hope he still feels that way when he finds out I'm in love with his sister.

❄

HAVE you ever found yourself in a situation that makes you question all of the choices you've made in your life? Really made you want to sit down and pour over memories of the roads you took to get to where you are at this exact moment in time?

Standing against this wall, observing the room around me, all I can think is how the fuck did I get here.

Ben Michaels is how I got here. He walked into the living room of my life, made himself comfortable, and never left. Not only has he been the best friend I've ever had, but he also brought Beth into my life.

And as miserable as I am in this very moment, and I'm really fucking miserable, I know I wouldn't change a damn thing.

This club is everything I hate. The shitty music is too loud and there are not enough places to sit, so people are forced to stand around as they pretend to want to be here.

We were identified as hockey players almost immediately. It's hard to say if anyone recognized us outright or just saw four big guys walk in and put two and two together.

I'm sure the shiner Will's sporting thanks to a hit earlier this week didn't help.

I've been keeping an eye on Ben since we got here. He's spent the last ten minutes on a stool at the bar. A pretty blonde stands between his legs, her hands resting on his forearms. Part of me wishes he'd just take her back to the hotel already so I can get the hell out of here.

The other guys seem to be just fine. Will is doing what he does best; making friends. He's talking to a large group that managed to acquire seats and appears to be reenacting how he got his black eye. The guy has more personality than he knows what to do with and people always gravitate to him.

Austin is surrounded by three women at a nearby pool table. I'm not sure if he plans to leave with all of them, but, to be honest, it wouldn't surprise me. He's done it before. It's like he's got something to prove, chasing women with the same relentless energy he brings to the ice every game.

Suddenly, Ben appears in front of me, alone. God, he looks like shit. Bloodshot, glassy eyes with dark circles underneath.

"Hey," he says, his voice raw from whatever he's been drinking. "You ready to go?"

Since the moment I walked in the joint.

"Definitely."

"Great. Got a surprise for you." His words slur, just enough for me to notice.

"I don't think I can handle any more of your surprises tonight, thanks."

He grins. "You'll like this one. Kristen has a friend." He nods at two women at the bar. One is the blonde he's been talking to, the other a petite redhead. They're both smiling at me.

Ah, fuck no.

I blink at him. "Not interested."

"C'mon, man. She's cute."

I don't care if she's Helen of fucking Troy; she's not Beth.

"It's not going to happen, Ben."

"What's not going to happen?" Austin joins in, throwing an arm around each of us.

Ben ignores him. "Just take her back to your room. You don't have to fuck her. Kirsten doesn't want to leave her here by herself."

"I thought you said her name was Kristen."

"It doesn't matter what her name is. Can we just go?"

This selfish son-of-a-bitch. "No. I am not taking some random woman back to my hotel room, Ben. Not fucking happening."

"I'll take her," Austin volunteers. "Wait, who are we talking about?"

"No one was fucking talking to you, Austin." Ben shoves him away.

"What the fuck, man?" Austin seethes.

I've had enough. Enough of Ben, enough of Austin, and everyone else here. I push off the wall to leave, but Ben blocks me.

"I'm going back to the hotel, Ben. Alone."

"Come on, Fozz. What is the big deal? She's ready and willing. And you haven't gotten laid in ages."

"I wouldn't be so sure about that," Austin chuckles darkly.

I stiffen, glaring at him, but he's too busy staring daggers at Ben to even notice.

"What is he talking about?" Ben asks. When I don't say anything, he turns to Austin. "What are you talking about?"

"I'm just saying, I'm pretty sure our boy Fozzie has been doing just fine lately. If I had to guess, I'd say he's off the market altogether."

Ben looks between the two of us, not comprehending. I could fucking strangle Austin.

"What?" Ben is waiting for someone to fill him in. "Do you have a girlfriend I don't know about?"

Words evade me. I can't lie to his face, but I also don't want him to find out about me and Beth like this. If Austin would just shut his fucking mouth–

"Either that, or your sister's been finding creative ways to repay his hospitality. Maybe in the backseat of his Lexus?"

The fucker saw us.

Ben freezes where he stands. It's as though someone threw a bucket of ice water on him, sobering him immediately. For a minute nothing happens; the three of us stand there, motionless, waiting for someone to react.

Then Ben's fist connects to Austin's cheek. I hear the impact over the music and watch Austin's head snap back at an unnatural angle. Ben lunges for him again, shaking me out of my stupor as I throw myself between them.

"Ben! Enough!" I hold him around the waist as he attempts to throw another punch at a staggering Austin.

"What the fuck is happening?" Will yells, arriving on scene. He stands in front of Austin, who's got a hand up over his injured eye.

"Take it back!" Ben shouts, still trying to get his hands on him. I'm taking elbows to the ribs as I attempt to hold him back. "He said Foster was fucking my little sister. Take. It. Back."

Will's eyebrows shoot up as his eyes round on me. "Are you?"

Fuck.

Still attempting to wrestle Ben away, I look around to see we're attracting attention. There are a couple of people taking videos with their phones, including the girl that Ben wanted me to take home. Perfect.

I need to get everyone out of here before someone calls the cops. If Ben gets arrested, this could go from bad to catastrophic.

"Of course he's not," Ben spits. He's still furious, but no longer struggling against me. "Tell them, Fozz."

My throat feels tight as I scan the room for the nearest exit. "We need to get out of here," I say calmly. "People are filming us. If the cops show up, we're fucked."

Ben blinks at me, looking so lost and confused. "Are you fucking her?"

I stare back at him, swallowing hard. "It's not like that."

Four words. Four single syllable words are all it takes to end our friendship.

My best friend of four years looks at me like he doesn't even know me.

"Foster's right. We need to get out of here. Now." Will leads Austin towards the exit and Ben and I follow without a word.

We find a cab immediately. A small miracle. The night air is freezing, but nothing compared to the cold shoulder

Ben gives me on the ride back to the hotel. I check on Austin, who doesn't appear to have a concussion, but is still in rough shape.

Will attempts to make conversation, but gives up when no one responds.

It's late when we get to the hotel; we file through the empty lobby in silence. Will and Austin make it to the elevator first.

"We'll get the next one," I tell them when the doors open. Will looks hesitant to leave us alone, but nods and leaves with Austin.

The moment the doors close, Ben turns on me. "I fucking trusted you."

"Ben–"

"You're going to end it." He pushes the elevator button, not looking at me. "You're going to end it now. Do you understand me?"

"No."

His eyes swing to mine. "What did you just say?"

"I'm not going to do that." He's talked me into a lot of things over the years, but this one is non-negotiable. "I'm not giving up Beth."

He stares at me with more contempt than I ever thought he was capable of, and memories of Cody from years ago seep in, making me feel sick.

The next elevator arrives silently and Ben stalks on. "Then I'll end it for you. From now on, you only talk to me when we're on the ice. I don't want you near me or my family. I don't know you and I don't fucking want to."

The doors close, and I'm once again alone.

CHAPTER 35

FOSTER

Time flies when you're having fun.

That would explain why the last two days have crawled by. Every miserable minute dragged out as long as possible.

We were supposed to fly out of Chicago last night, heading home after the game, but a snowstorm had other plans. Thick flakes started falling in the afternoon as the winds picked up, and by the time we were ready to leave, the city was blanketed in white. All flights grounded indefinitely. We were storm-stayed, forced to hunker down in the hotel for another night.

Will tried to get a game of poker going, but no one was in the mood. Ben didn't want to see me, Austin didn't want to see Ben, and the only person I wanted to see was eight hundred miles away.

Twenty-four hours later, when the worst of the storm passed, we finally boarded our flight and made it out of the snow-covered city.

True to his word, Ben hasn't spoken to me. I'm trying

to give him his space and let him process the idea of Beth and I, but it's hard.

It's like I've lost a brother all over again.

I've been in constant contact with Beth. She says she's okay, but I can tell Ben's reaction to learning about us is stressing her out. Her voice sounds strained when we talk.

What if he never gets on board with it? Never accepts the two of us together?

The thought of causing a rift in Beth's close-knit family has been keeping me awake at night.

It's after midnight when the car drops me off at home. I enter the house quietly, even though I don't think for a minute she'll be asleep.

My suspicions are confirmed when she barrels into my chest before I even take off my coat. I wrap my arms around her and bury my face in her hair, savouring the feel of her.

"I missed you," she mumbles into my chest. Despite how warm she feels in my arms, she's trembling like a leaf.

"I missed you, too."

She pulls away just enough to give me a smile, but I don't miss the sadness on her face. Worry lines etch her forehead and her tired eyes tell me I'm not the only one losing sleep.

And I feel responsible. For all of it. Her sadness, her worry, her exhaustion.

I thought everything would become clear once I saw her, but seeing the toll this has taken on her makes me more confused than ever.

"Let's get some sleep." I smooth her hair away from

her face and bring my lips to her forehead. "You've got work in the morning."

She nods sleepily, and we walk hand in hand to my bedroom. Once in bed, she curls into me, and within minutes she's fast asleep in my arms. I hold her like I'm scared I might lose her.

Because I am.

❄

I WAKE to find myself alone. Beth's side of the bed is cold and I'm scrambling before I'm even fully conscious.

A dozen worst case scenarios swirl through my mind as I stumble through the house in search of her. They all end with her being gone. When I find her getting ready for work in the kitchen, I breathe a huge sigh of relief.

She's still here.

"Morning," she says as she crosses the room towards me. She gives me a kiss that's not nearly long enough to calm my frazzled nerves before going back to packing her lunch.

"Morning," I collapse into a stool and attempt to get my heart rate under control. "I didn't hear you get up."

"I tried not to wake you," she admits. "You looked like you were dead on your feet when you got home."

So did you, I want to say but don't.

"It's been a rough few days," I admit. "Have you heard from your family again?"

Beth winces as she pours coffee into her travel mug. The last time we spoke, she'd been flooded by calls and texts from her parents and sisters. Ben, of course, alerted them of our situation and didn't hold back voicing his disapproval.

"I have." She doesn't meet my eyes.

"And?"

An entire war is happening on her face as she finds her words. "And everyone is upset. Tara is hurt that I didn't tell them about you. It's not that I didn't want to, of course, but she can't keep anything to herself. Ally's not taking sides, she's just upset that everyone isn't getting along. Mom and Dad seem more concerned about Ben than anything else, like usual. They're disappointed that I upset him. They said he's got so much on his plate, he doesn't need to be worrying about me on top of everything. My dad even went so far as to suggest that I should move back home. Because it would be better for Ben."

The wobble in her voice has me on my feet and moving towards her. I wrap my arms around her protectively, wishing I could shield her from everything.

"They want me to stay with him until Christmas."

I expected as much, but it's still a hard pill to swallow.

"What did you say?"

She laughs but there's no humour in it. "I told them 'Maybe I just shouldn't come home at all.'"

I think about the years I've been on my own. About the family I lost to circumstances outside of my control, and the brother I might not have lost if I'd done things differently. Beth shouldn't have to choose between me and her family.

But if her family can't see that right now, I don't want to be the reason she loses them. If I put a wedge between her and the people she loves most, she'll eventually start to resent me for it.

I squeeze her tighter to me and say the words I don't want to.

"Maybe they're right."

Her head snaps up, confusion on her face.

"What?"

"Not about everything, obviously. Just about staying with Ben."

"You want me to leave?"

"Beth, I promise that is the last thing that I want." I cup her chin and stroke her cheek. "I haven't had a family for a long time and I don't want to be the reason yours falls apart. You're leaving for home in less than a week. Maybe if you stay with him, he'll calm down enough for you to be able to get through to him."

She doesn't meet my eyes as she slips out of my embrace. Her arms cross over her chest as she keeps her gaze on the floor. "Maybe."

Shit. She's second-guessing herself and it's because of me.

"You know I want you to stay, right?" I take her hand, desperate to hold on to her.

She nods and gives me an unconvincing "Of course," before pulling away. "I'd better get to work."

Panic builds in my chest as I start to worry that I'm losing her.

"I've got practice with the team this afternoon, but we can talk more tonight, okay?"

More nodding. "Sure."

I walk her to the door, more and more convinced that I've said the wrong thing as she takes off her ridiculous pompom slippers and slips on her winter boots. She puts on her coat before pressing her lips to mine and I watch her go, praying it's not the last time.

❄

PRACTICE IS BRUTAL. We've lost the last two games and morale is low. Coach heard about what happened at the bar in Chicago and has been particularly harsh on the four of us.

Beth has been quiet in our texts and I'm trying not to read too much into it. It's the last week of school before Christmas break and I'm sure she's run off her feet keeping the kids in line.

Still, when I pull into an empty driveway my heart sinks. She should have gotten home from school an hour ago.

My spirits lift as I hear a car pulling in behind me as I'm hopping out of my truck, but the moment is quickly gone.

Ben's ostentatious sports car is driving towards me.

Perfect.

Shaking my head, I start for the door. It's been a shitty day and I expect it's about to get a lot worse. I pull my phone out to text Beth.

> Foster: Hey. I just got home. Are you on your way?

I decide I had better give her a warning that we're not alone.

> Foster: Your brother is here.

Unlocking the door I walk into the quiet house. I sense Ben on my heels and fight the urge to close the door in his stubborn face.

The higher road sucks sometimes.

"I'm here to get Beth," he says, standing imposingly in the doorway.

"Does she know that?"

He glares at me. "I texted her earlier to say I was picking her up."

I extend my arms and look around my empty foyer. "Well, she's clearly not here, so close the door. You're letting out all the heat."

"Where the fuck is she?" He steps in and slams the door shut.

"I don't know, she probably–"

That's when I notice that her fuzzy pompom slippers aren't by the door where she left them this morning.

I try to remain calm as I take my phone out again and call Beth. It goes to voicemail.

Ben follows me into the house, lamenting about something, but I'm not listening. I'm looking for further signs to confirm my theory.

The thick paperback she's been reading in the evenings is no longer on the coffee table.

Her navy Canada Games hoodie is missing from the back of the kitchen chair.

I drag myself down the hallway and look into her room, finding exactly what I was both expecting and dreading.

A neatly made bed and vacant room.

No suitcase. No clothes in the closet. No Beth.

The silence weighs heavily on me as I walk back into the living room to find Ben looking unimpressed.

"Well?"

"She's gone."

"What do you mean 'gone?'"

I run my hands through my hair, pulling at the roots in frustration. "I mean, all of her stuff is no longer here. She must have come home after school and packed up everything."

"Where did she go?"

Where *did* she go? She doesn't know many people in the area yet and the rental she secured isn't available until the New Year. I remember that she's hung out with Kim a couple of times and am about to text Alexei when something in the kitchen snags my eye.

On the island countertop rests a piece of light blue snowflake paper and I snap it up, my eyes recognizing Beth's handwriting.

Foster,

I've decided to stay with Tamara for a few nights. I'm sorry for not talking to you about it first, but I was afraid you would try to talk me out of it. It's still a compromise, but at least it's on my terms.

Just like you don't want to come between me and my family, I don't want to come between you and your team. So you focus on hockey, I'll focus on my family, and we'll figure out everything else together.

I hope this doesn't read like a goodbye letter, because that's not what this is. Despite the fact I'm leaving, I promise you're not losing me.

Good luck in Tampa. I'll be wearing your number and cheering you on.

Love, Beth

I read the note three times, the pressure in my chest easing but not disappearing entirely.

I promise you're not losing me.

Then why does it feel like exactly that? I'm proud of Beth for standing up to her family and choosing her own path. But at the same time, I can't help feeling frustrated with myself for ever suggesting she leave. I want her here —with me.

Ben stalks into the kitchen. "Well?"

"She's staying with her coworker, Tamara."

He doesn't hide his irritation. "But I told her I'd pick her up and she could stay with me."

I shake my head, my patience officially spent. "Yeah. You told her, Ben. Maybe if you'd asked her, she'd have told you she didn't want to do that."

"Fine," he scoffs. "As long as she's not staying here, with you." He turns to leave but stops and turns back. "Just to be clear, you're going to stay away from her."

"Absolutely not."

"You listen to–"

"No, you listen to me." I push away from the island, facing him head on. "Your friendship has meant a lot to me over the years. It made me feel less alone and I never meant to take it for granted. I didn't mean to fall for your sister, but it happened and I'm not sorry. Beth healed a part of me that I thought would always be broken. As long as she wants me, I'm going to be here. Because I'm hers. I'm sorry if that upsets you, but at the end of the day, it's not about you."

I stand there, half expecting him to take a swing at me. I don't care if he hits me. If he does, the pain probably won't even register.

He swallows hard, then turns and walks toward the front door. As soon as the door closes, I pull out my phone and text Beth.

Foster: I got your note. Take as much time as you need, love. I'm not going anywhere.

CHAPTER 36

BETH

I sit in the cosy corner of the cafe, cradling a warm mug of hot chocolate in my hands. The rich scent of cocoa with a hint of cinnamon fills the air and it's making my stomach growl. I haven't eaten much over the past few days. My insides have been tying themselves in elaborate knots and I haven't had much of an appetite.

Through the large window beside me, I watch a family glide across an outdoor skating rink. The evening sky is a deep, velvety blue, and the twinkling lights strung around the rink make the ice glow. The parents skate hand in hand, their laughter carrying softly through the crisp air while their children dart ahead, their cheeks flushed with joy.

I take a sip of my hot chocolate, but my taste buds, like my appetite, seem to be on vacation.

Packing up and leaving the house I've called a home for the past month was harder than I ever would have imagined. But I need to sort this mess out with my family and I don't want Foster to be dragged into it.

A bell chimes from the doorway and I look up to see Ben entering. He scans the room before spotting me.

"Hey," he says as he approaches the table, warily.

"Hey."

I'd ignored his calls earlier today. I didn't have the energy to fight with him. But the text that followed caught me completely off guard.

Ben: I'm sorry, Bug. Can we talk? Please?

We agreed to meet at a cafe close to Tamara's apartment. I'm honestly not sure what I expect him to say at this point, but I've never known my brother to use the words "please" and "sorry" in the same message, so I decided to hear him out.

He slides into the booth across from me looking as tired and dishevelled as I've ever seen him.

"I'm a shitty brother."

I don't know how to respond to that statement, so I don't.

"Ouch," he winces. "Not disagreeing."

"Sorry. You're the only brother I have, so I don't have anything to compare you to."

"That's fair, I guess. I know I haven't made any time for you since you moved here. I've been completely self-absorbed and I've been making everything about me."

My fingers tap against the white mug in my hands. "Well, everything has always been about you."

Hurt registers on his face and I rush to continue. "It's not really your fault. It's just sort of the way it's always been. Mom and Dad put so much focus on you and your hockey career that you became the main family focus.

You're used to everyone listening to you and doing what you want. And I'm sorry, Ben, but that's just not going to work for me anymore."

"I still think of you as a kid, I guess."

"But I'm an adult now. I have been for a long time. I'm going to make mistakes and learn from them as I go. And that's on me. I'm going to buy the car I want, live where I want, and date who I want. You can't protect me from getting my heart broken."

"Foster won't break your heart," he states with absolute certainty, surprising me. "Not on purpose, at least. He's the best person I know. I should have noticed that you two were catching feelings, but I was too absorbed in my own issues. And I definitely shouldn't have reacted the way I did when I found out. It's just," he sighs, running a hand through his hair. "I've had my heart broken. I didn't want that for either of you."

My brother, usually so full of confidence and swagger, looks like someone drained all the life out of him. "Did you really love Valentina?"

He shakes his head. "No."

"Then…"

"Madelyn got engaged." His expression softens when he says her name. "We haven't talked in years, but I still keep an eye on her socials. Her boyfriend…fiance posted a picture and tagged her in it. I saw it and…I just shut down. I went out to get drunk and that's when I met Valentina. I told myself that if Maddy could find someone, then I could, too."

I reach across the table and rest my hand on his. "I didn't realise you still had feelings for Maddy."

He smiles sadly. "I never stopped loving her. We were

so young when we broke up. I always thought our paths would cross again and I'd win her back. But that's not going to happen now. That's why I tried so hard to make things work with Valentina. I wanted to prove I could be a good partner. Someone that actually deserves Maddy."

"Hey. From my vantage point, you were doing more than your share in your relationship with Valentina. But regardless of what you do or how much you give, you can't make something work if you're not with the right person."

"What if Maddy was my person? What if I don't get another one?" He huffs out a laugh. "I'm making this about me again, aren't I?"

I laugh, because he's not wrong. "A little bit. But that's okay."

"No, it's not. Let's talk about something less depressing than my love life. How is work?"

"Hectic. We were supposed to have a skate day on Friday, but the principal just announced that the rink we had booked cancelled. Something about a peewee tournament taking priority. The kids are crushed."

I spent most of my day consoling my students and brainstorming with other teachers on what we can do to make the last day of school special for the kids. So far, we haven't come up with anything.

"That sucks."

"It does. The kids were really looking forward to it. So was I, to be honest. I haven't had a chance to break in my new skates yet."

The gleaming white hockey skates Foster surprised me with are still in the box, freshly sharpened and ready to go. I was excited to try them out with my students.

"Since when do you know how to skate?" He looks amazed with this new information.

"Since Foster taught me." Saying his name soothes the ache in my chest.

Ben shakes his head, apparently speechless and we take a minute to watch the family wrap up their skate.

"I'm sorry if I messed things up with you two."

"You didn't," I insist. "Despite your best efforts. I'm going to continue seeing Foster, regardless of how you or anyone else feels about it. And I'm going to have a very frank conversation with Mom and Dad about how I feel. You all don't need to agree with my decisions, but you need to respect them. I'm an adult and I will do what I want."

"I understand. And I'm going to be better at listening to you. If you want me to cancel your plane ticket so you can drive home, I won't fight you on it."

"I appreciate that," I grin. "But please don't. It's such a long drive and I really don't want to do it."

He laughs, looking lighter than I've seen him in a long time. "Maybe I should let you start making my decisions for me. I'm unqualified, apparently."

I clap my hands, excitedly. "I'd love to, thank you for asking. For starters, stop thinking with your dick. You'll find someone who's right for you in your own time; you don't need to force it."

"That's fair."

"And stop being a dick to your goalie. He's a good man who's done a lot for both of us."

"He really is. Anything else?"

"Call Mom more. Not just when you want something. That's all I can think of right now."

"I will. Can I ask for one thing in return?"

"Shoot."

"Tell me Foster's wifi password?"

"Never going to happen."

CHAPTER 37

FOSTER

It's minus twenty-five outside and I'm still managing to sweat as I walk up the freshly shovelled cobblestone path. The bungalow is decorated with colourful lights and a partially deflated Rudolph leans against the white porch. It looks like a family lives here.

When Beth called me last night to tell me about her talk with Ben, I realised right then and there that I was ready to talk to my own brother. I texted Cody and he wrote back immediately inviting me over for coffee this morning.

He appears in the doorway as I'm wiping my snow-covered boots on the outdoor mat. His face lights up with a smile I haven't seen in so many years, I'd almost forgotten it. The same smile he'd give me when we were kids and had just gotten away with one scheme or another.

"You're here," he says, extending his hand to me.

I take it in mine, almost certain that this is the first time I've shaken my brother's hand. If we embraced as kids, it was either a hug or a headlock.

I clear my throat. "Thanks for having me."

He welcomes me into the house, a wreath jingling on the door as it closes. Removing my boots, I line them up neatly with the other footwear. I smile at the smallest pair.

He takes my coat and hangs it from a hook by the door. "Would you like a coffee?"

"I'd love one."

Cody leads me through a hallway with framed pictures on the wall. I slow as I pass them, desperate for a glimpse into the last ten years of his life. He notices me lingering and backtracks to me.

"This was taken on Amelia's first day of Kindergarten," he says, pointing to the family portrait. Amelia sits between Cody and a blonde woman with glasses, her hopeful smile almost identical to the little girl.

"You all look really happy."

"We were," he chuckles. "Although, Amelia threw up about fifteen minutes after it was taken and all three of us were sick for a solid week with a stomach bug."

I follow him into the kitchen and he pours me a cup of coffee. "Still take it black?"

"Yeah."

He smiles. "Black coffee gives me heartburn now. Jenna got me on to oat milk and it's not half bad."

"Is Jenna your wife?" I'm almost embarrassed that I have to ask.

"Yeah. We got married when Amelia was four. She'd really like to meet you, sometime. She's been after this reunion for years."

I don't say anything, because I don't know what to say.

I look around the kitchen. "This is a nice place." A lot nicer than the house we grew up in.

"Thanks. We've been here for almost two years. We were in Markham, but moved here when the bank Jenna works for opened a new branch. We really like the area. It's a young neighbourhood and there are a lot of kids around Amelia's age."

"And what do you do for work?"

He hesitates for the briefest moment. "I'm an accountant."

I laugh without thinking and once I start, I can't stop.

"I know, I know," Cody smirks. "Get it out of your system."

"I'm sorry." I cover my mouth, trying to contain myself. "The guy who said math was for nerds became an accountant."

"Numbers are my first language. I stopped fighting it years ago."

"Do you like it?"

"I really do. It's less stressful than hockey and a lot easier on the body. I mostly work from home, which is great for me. I get to be here when Amelia gets off the bus." That's something we definitely didn't have when we were kids.

He motions to a small, oval dining room table. I take a seat across from him and we continue to drink our coffees. Even though it's nice just sitting here, being with my brother in his peaceful home, it's not why I came.

"You said you had some things to say?" I hope it doesn't come out blunt, but I need Cody to start talking. We spent years avoiding it and look how that ended for us.

He clears his throat and rests his forearms on the table between us. "I take full responsibility for what happened between us, Foster. God, there's so much to say I don't even know where to start."

"Start from the beginning. When I came home that first summer after being away all year."

He nods and I sense he's preparing himself to be vulnerable.

"I was so proud of you when you went to the junior league. We all were. But I missed you. I had just stopped playing hockey and your career was just beginning. I didn't want to be jealous of you, but I was a little. I lost touch with my old hockey friends and the new ones I made weren't the best guys."

Douchebags, if I remember correctly. I say nothing.

"By the time you came home, I'd kind of gotten used to you not being there."

His words stings, but I understand where he's coming from.

"And then Gramps was gone so fast. You came home for the funeral and went back right away."

"I had to." I was under contract and only had so many days off.

"I know that, I do. But I was seventeen and I didn't have anyone to talk to about it. I felt really alone. And because I'd always had the two of you, I didn't know how to handle it. I started getting high every day. It helped keep me numb."

Memories of how he'd acted back then resurface. How he seemed not to care about anyone or anything. And I'd been too focused on hockey to notice what was really happening.

"Mom getting sick was the final straw. I was so angry. From the time I woke up until I went to sleep at night, this anger just ate away at me. I was angry at everyone, including Mom because she insisted on not telling you. And that just made me resent you even more. You were off playing hockey and being a sixteen-year-old and I was at home in our shitty bungalow, watching her waste away."

I stare at the table and blink my cloudy eyes. Mom waited until she could no longer work to tell me about her pancreatic cancer. I came home right away and only had a few days left with her before she was moved to Hospice. And then she was gone.

"She told me she'd wanted me to focus on hockey." My voice is thick with emotion. I try, not for the first time, to understand where my mom was coming from. She must have been so scared and just wanted to protect us. She was always trying to do her best by us, right up to the end.

"She said the same thing to me. It just made me more angry with you. I understand now that it wasn't your fault, but at the time, I couldn't see beyond my own pain. I needed an outlet for that anger and you were the only one left. I'm sorry."

I nod, swallowing hard. I remember that loneliness well, but I had hockey to keep me going. Cody had nothing.

"I'd thought that last time I came to visit you was rock bottom, but things only got worse. I went on week-long binges where I didn't leave the house, just drank myself into oblivion. I'd manage to sober myself up long enough to find a job, just to wind up losing it a month later and start the entire process over again. I met Jenna around that time and actually managed to stay on the wagon for half a year. Things were good and I wanted to reach out to you, but I couldn't work up the nerve. And then she got pregnant with Amelia."

I'm leaning forward now, hanging on my brother's every word.

"I wish I could say that becoming a parent made sobriety easier, but I struggled. Suddenly, I was terrified of everything. What if something happened to Jenna and I became the world's most useless single father? What if something happened to Amelia? Or what if I fucked everything up and I lost them both? When I went back to school, it got worse. I started drinking again, occasionally. At first it was just to take the edge off before bed, but pretty soon I was sneaking whiskey into my morning coffee and staying buzzed all day. It got noticeable and Jenna begged me to get help. And for once, I listened. Started therapy just before Amelia's third birthday and joined AA at the same time. I haven't had a drink in more than six years."

"I'm really happy to hear it, Cody. I just wish you'd have reached out. I would have helped you any way I could have."

"I know you would have, little brother. But this was something I had to work through on my own. I already felt awful about how I shut you out."

I nod because his reasoning makes sense.

"Why didn't you get in touch after you got sober?"

He breathes a heavy sigh. "I wanted to. You'd just signed with the Otters and I didn't want you to think I had some kind of agenda. The more time that passed, the harder it got, and the less I knew what to say. But I gotta tell you; seeing you on the ice that day, I thought my heart was going to give out. I've been watching you on tv and seen pictures online, but it was different. You looked so grown up. And happy."

I think about how Beth looked as we were skating off the ice that day. Hair mussed, lips swollen from my kisses, and smiling. It's only been a day since I've seen her and I'm already aching to hold her.

Looking up, I catch my brother smirking at me and I feel the blood rush to my cheeks.

"So…you and Amelia's teacher, eh?"

"Shut up, Cody."

He laughs loudly. I attempt to glare at him, but I can't commit.

"My kid loves her. She's talked about nothing else since she started at the school."

"Yeah." I smile, because I can't think of Beth without becoming a sap. "She's pretty amazing. I was teaching her to skate for the school field trip."

"Aww. I can't believe they had to cancel it. Amelia's crushed. All the kids are."

"Yeah, Beth said the same thing." Even though it was completely out of her control, she said she felt like she was letting the kids down when I talked to her last night. I know there will be other skate days, but I also know that she was really looking forward to this one.

The alarm that I set on my phone starts to chime and I look at it to confirm the time. I feel like I just got here and wish I could stay longer.

"I've got to get going. We fly to Tampa in a few hours."

"Of course." He stands and starts to walk me back to the front door. "Thanks for coming over, Foster."

"Thanks for having me. I'm really glad you reached out."

"Maybe we could do this again sometime?" He looks at me hopefully.

"I'd really like that. I want to meet my niece properly. And Jenna."

"Do you–" He clears his throat looking suddenly nervous again. "I don't know if you have plans, but if not, we'd love to have you over for Christmas dinner. But I understand if it's too much, too soon."

I place my hand on his shoulder and say, "I'll be here."

My brother pats me on the back before stepping forward and throwing his arms around me. After nearly a decade, I'm hugging my brother. It's not the stiff, awkward kind you'd expect after so many years—this is the kind of hug that says everything words can't.

"I'm sorry I fucked up," he says, his voice breaking.

"Everyone fucks up," I answer, feeling him chuckle at our grandfather's words.

When the hug ends, we're both sniffing.

"Let me know what time to be here on Christmas," I say as I'm leaving. "And what I can bring."

"Just bring yourself."

I scoff, shaking my head. "I'm definitely bringing Amelia something. I've got nine years of presents to make up for and I want it to annoy you as much as possible. I'm thinking a drum set."

CHAPTER 38

BETH

"Thank you for making the time to meet with me. While there are several topics I want to cover, I promise not to take up too much of your time."

"Jesus, Beth," my sister Tara chides from the laptop in front of me. "You're acting like this is a job interview."

I feel like this is a job interview. To be honest, I put more preparation into this than I did when I was interviewing for positions I really wanted. The outline I made is next to me on the bed. Several prompts and talking points are highlighted in bright pink and yellow. I've mapped out all of the objections I'm expecting my family to raise and how I will respond to each one. They're there to remind me of the goals I'm trying to accomplish and help me stay on track.

But this is not an interview; it's a video call with my immediate family, minus Ally and Ben. Ally is on a night shift at the hospital. Ben's on his way to Florida with his team and while he offered to join the call for support, I told him I wanted to do this on my own.

No, I need to do this on my own. I may have only

requested the family meeting earlier today, but in a way I've been preparing for this for most of my life.

"First of all, I want to apologise for not telling you earlier that Foster and I were dating. I can understand if you felt hurt, but the relationship was new and we didn't–"

"I'm going to stop you right there, Sweetie." My dad holds his palm out to the screen, momentarily obscuring my mom's face. "You don't owe any of us an apology."

I blink in surprise. I mean, I don't really think I owe them an apology either, but I've found that people respond better to criticism when they feel mollified. "I don't?"

"Well, I, for one, would have appreciated finding out from you directly," my mother states in a tone that makes it clear she's still disappointed in me. "But I'm going to be the bigger person, as usual. So everything is fine. We're all very excited to see you on Friday. Foster is more than welcome to come, too. The more the merrier."

Slack-jawed, I glance down at my notes for direction, but this is not a scenario I prepared for. Four days ago they wanted me to end my relationship with Foster and move home. Now everything's peachy and they want me to bring him for the holidays?

None of this makes sense.

"Well, great. That's great." I should just accept this change of heart for what it is: a rare gift. But a nagging suspicion that they aren't telling me everything won't allow me to let this go so easily. "What changed?"

Six eyes stare back at me like they didn't understand the question.

"Tara?" I ask because, say what you will about my oldest sister, I can always count on her to tell it like it is.

"What do you think changed?" She scoffs. "They talked to Ben and he blessed the union."

And there we have it. This was not my parents coming to the conclusion that as long as I'm happy, they're happy. This was Ben giving the all-clear and them falling in line.

I'm not surprised. I'm not even disappointed. I'm just so tired of being treated like what I want doesn't matter.

"It wasn't like that." My dad looks sheepish. "I called your brother to talk about the recent line changes. He told me that he'd been wrong before and that he actually thought that you and Foster would be a good match. Then we talked some more about hockey and that was that."

"So, let me get this straight." I take a deep breath, trying to stay calm. "If Ben was still against Foster and I dating, you would be too? But since he's come on board, you no longer have a problem with us as a couple. Did I get that right?"

"I'm still pissed you didn't tell me," Tara smirks. "But I never had a problem with who your boyfriend was."

"I don't understand what the issue is," my mother titters as she waves a hand dismissively. "We're okay with you dating your brother's teammate."

"The first problem is that he's much more than Ben's teammate. The second is that you're okay with it for the wrong fucking reason."

My mother gasps audibly and my father's mouth hangs open. It's the first time I've ever used that kind of language in front of them, so I suppose it's understandable, but I'm not about to apologise.

"I'm tired of being treated like what I want doesn't

matter. It's always about what Ben wants or thinks. I used to resent him for the way our lives revolve around him, but you were the ones who made it that way. You missed most of my band concerts because Ben had a game. I had to have my tenth birthday party at a rink because Ben was in a tournament. Everything was always about him and even now that I'm an adult, nothing has changed. You care more about Ben's feelings than mine. You value his opinion more than mine. And I'm done pretending that I'm okay with that."

Tears blur my vision, but I don't fight them back. I'm done acting as though it doesn't hurt to have every decision I make questioned, every opinion dismissed with a patronising smile.

"I'm twenty-six years old and I've never done anything to make you question my character or judgement. I just want to feel like you'll support me regardless of my choices. Because being with Foster is one of those choices. He's kind, and supportive, and makes me feel like I can do anything I put my mind to. And even if Ben were to change his mind next week, I would still choose Foster because he is what and who I want."

The silence from my laptop speaks louder than words, but that's fine. I've said what I needed to say.

"I've got a lot to do before I turn in for the night, so I'm going to say goodnight. I'll see you in a few days. I love you all." I end the call and collapse in a sobbing mess on Tamara's couch. I'm not sure how long I cry for, but eventually the tears run dry and I'm spent. I feel better, I think. A bit lighter, like a knot that's always been inside me has finally started to loosen.

Just as I'm about to go wash my mascara-stained face,

my laptop chimes an incoming call. I'm startled to see that my parents are calling back.

I accept the call and my parents' faces come into focus. I see that I'm not the only one who's been crying.

"I had no idea you felt that way." Dad sounds more like a lost little boy than the man who raised me.

"Well, I do," I sniff, noticing that it's just the two of them. "Where's Tara?"

"You know how she gets when tears are involved," he chuckles. The second someone starts to cry, my sister can't get far away fast enough. "She told us you weren't wrong, then left."

"I'm sorry that I just dropped all of that on you," I hedge.

"No, Beth. We're the ones who are sorry." My mother's voice wobbles. "We were so focused on Ben's hockey career for so long, I don't think we could see how it was affecting you and your sisters."

"It was all-consuming for a while," Dad adds. "Once they told us he could make it to the NHL, we knew we'd have to make sacrifices. But we shouldn't have let it take over everyone's lives."

"And we never meant for you to feel like you don't matter. You matter so much, Sweetheart. I'm sorry if I'm a bit overbearing sometimes, but it's only because I worry, and I'm your mother and I want to protect you–never that I didn't trust you."

My mother just admitted to being overbearing. I can't believe I'm not recording this call.

"Really?" I ask, feeling the pressure behind my eyes build once more.

"Of course. Whatever decisions you make about your life, your father and I will support you."

"So you're okay with me dating Foster?"

"If he makes you happy, we're happy," Mom insists.

"And you don't mind that I live in Ottawa?"

"You can move anywhere you like and we'll come visit," Dad assures me.

"What if I decide to get bangs?"

My mother bites her lip. "I really don't think you have the bone structure to pull them off, but if you really want them I promise not to say anything."

I choke out something between laughter and crying. My parents aren't perfect, but I know that they love me and want me to be happy. I'll take it.

"Thank you," I say. "That means a lot. Because Foster makes me really happy and I love it here in Ottawa."

"We're so glad," Dad says thickly.

I add, "And I have no plans to get bangs."

"Oh, thank the good Lord," Mom breathes.

CHAPTER 39

FOSTER

"You have my permission to date my sister."

I take a break from gearing up to give a weary look at my current teammate and former best friend.

"I don't need your permission."

My response seems to catch him off guard. "Well, too bad. You have it."

I already knew from Beth that he apologised for his behaviour, but this is the first time he's talked to me since he left my place two days ago. I've been following his previous directive to stay away from him.

"Can I have permission to date your sister?" Austin asks from a few spots down. The bruise on his eye where Ben clocked him is still healing and is currently a deep purple. Even though he apologised for his behaviour at the bar, he doesn't seem to have learned his lesson.

"No," we say in unison.

"But you said you owe me." Austin points to the discoloured skin. Being able to torment Ben was clearly worth the punch to the face for him.

"I said I'd owe you a favour." Ben rolls his eyes.

"Exactly. And I want that favour to be permission to date Beth."

My glower must match Ben's because Will enters the fray.

"I swear to God, Crawford. If you keep running your mouth, I will not pull them off of you this time."

"Alright, alright," Austin shrugs before addressing the rest of the locker room. "Anyone else have a hot sister?"

We watch as our rookie gets pelted with several gloves, shinpads, and other various bits of equipment before finally sitting down and shutting up.

"I'm sorry for how I reacted when I found out." Ben's eyes are trained on the floor. I don't doubt the sincerity of his words.

"It's okay, man. We would have been open with you from the start, but you had a lot going on and we didn't want to pile on."

"Still. I never should have made it all about me. If I'd actually talked to either of you about it, I would have realised that you really care about one another. You and Beth have my full support from here on out. You're a good guy, Fozz. That's why you're my best friend."

I grin at him. "Thanks, man."

He opens his arms and I accept his hug as our teammates "awww" around us.

"Teammates by chance; friends by choice." Will holds up his hands to make a heart shape.

"That's deep, Will," Ben says, still hugging me. He lowers his voice, speaking directly into my ear. "Deep like the hole I'll bury you in if you hurt my baby sister."

"Understood." I nod at him as we pull apart and he grins, clapping his hands.

"Alright, boys! Let's go fuck shit up!"

❄

THE GAME WAS a massacre and we were the dominating force. There are times when a team gels so well that nothing can possibly stand in their way. Tonight was one of those times.

Watching our lines play together tonight was a thing of beauty. Each shift moved like a well-oiled machine, anticipating each other's moves with an almost telepathic connection. The forwards executed crisp, tape-to-tape passes, cycling the puck effortlessly in the offensive zone, while the defensemen pinched in at just the right moments to keep the pressure on. Breakouts were seamless, with players filling lanes and supporting each other perfectly. Every line change brought fresh energy, so we never lost momentum.

Not only that, it's obvious that everyone was having a blast.

When you play hockey at this level, the stakes are high. It's stressful and both physically and emotionally exhausting. But nights like these remind me how fucking lucky I am. I get to make a living playing the sport I love.

❄

THE FLIGHT HOME is a rowdy one. After tonight's win, we officially have the best record in the league this season and everyone's feeling festive.

No one even complains when Will starts a boisterous

rendition of Good Lord Stanley, changing all the lyrics to hockey references.

I spend the ride home from the airport staring out the window at the falling snow, thinking about how my life has changed the last few weeks.

I've got my brother back, something I gave up hope of happening a long time ago. Ben has not only come around about me and Beth, but he seems to be feeling more like himself again, the loveable goofball that wormed his way into my life all those years ago.

And I've got Beth. I wasn't bluffing when I said I didn't need his permission to date her. But knowing that us being together won't jeopardise her relationship with her family makes things a whole lot easier.

As the car pulls into my driveway, I'm thinking it's not possible for life to be sweeter right now.

That's when I see a familiar SUV parked in its usual spot.

In my haste to get inside I almost forget my bag. Throwing it over my shoulder, I jog to my house, careful not to slip on an icy patch.

Christmas music greets me as I push open the front door. Not the upbeat kind you dance to, the soft, hymn-like kind you might hear in a church. I put down my bag and kick off my shoes before entering the living room.

Beth is curled up, fast asleep on my couch. She looks like an angel in the glow of the Christmas tree lights and I stand there for a moment, just taking her in.

She looks so peaceful that I'm tempted to let her sleep, but I know she'll be more comfortable in my bed. Not to mention the fact that the couch isn't big enough for both of us and I need to hold her tonight.

I push a few stray locks of hair away from her face and she stirs. When her eyes flutter open, her sleepy smile threatens to make my heart give out.

"Welcome home," she whispers.

"Same to you." I kiss her, softly. My entire body relaxes at the reassuring pressure of her lips against mine. "Let's get you to bed."

I lift her up and she wraps her arm around my neck. As I walk us into my bedroom, I can't help but think how perfect she feels curled against me. It's as if she belongs there.

Because she does.

"My mom invited you for Christmas," she says sleepily as she nuzzles against my chest.

"Wow." I chuckle, completely taken aback. "That's quite the turn of events."

"I think I actually got through to them. Plus, you have Ben's stamp of approval which is essentially a Golden Ticket. But I told her you had plans with your family and she understood."

My heart squeezes and I hold her tighter. Part of me still can't believe that I'm having Christmas with my family. Cody had a sit down with Amelia and explained who I was and why I've been absent from her life up until now. Apparently she asked him three hundred questions before saying "Ok" and going off to play. I officially met her and her mom on Facetime yesterday evening. My niece did most of the talking during the forty-minute call. When it was time to say goodbye, she'd said "Goodnight, Uncle Foster" and my heart almost exploded in my chest. I hung up the phone and cried like a baby, then I called Beth and told her all about it.

"Please thank your mom for me." I kiss the top of her head. "And tell her I'd love to come next Christmas, if the offer still stands."

Beth's eyes shine up at me in the darkness. "I think it's safe to say that it will."

I feel her heart beating against me. My own heart thuds in my chest, beating only for her.

"I love you." The words slip past my lips as effortlessly as the air I'm breathing. "It's probably too soon to say that, right?"

"Yeah." She sighs contentedly against me. "I'm guessing it's also too soon to tell you I love you, too?"

"Most likely." Our mouths meet in the dark, ending the discussion. I listen to her breathe as she falls asleep, feeling happier than I ever have.

CHAPTER 40

BETH

The only way to describe the last twenty-four hours is chaos.

I arrived at school yesterday morning, bright-eyed and bushy-tailed thanks to the Foster James wake up method. Never have I ever had three orgasms before my morning coffee, but I am not complaining.

Bliss. That's what it's like being back home with Foster. Pure, undiluted bliss.

It's not my home for much longer, though.

A stone forms in my throat and sinks to my stomach knowing my time at Foster's place is limited.

But I'm not going to dwell on that right now. I'll move into my new place after Christmas and see Foster as much as I can. Things are good and they'll only get better.

I may be back on cloud nine, but this week my students were at an all-time low. Ever since they learned that Skate Day wasn't happening, they've been dragging themselves through the school days. You would think they'd cancelled Christmas itself.

Just before first recess yesterday, we received a high-priority email from the office. Apparently they were able to secure another rink for tomorrow at the last minute. Parents were being notified immediately, permission slips were being sent out, and transportation was being arranged.

But somehow, it all came together! Now as I'm walking the world's most excited fourth graders through the parking lot of the arena, skates in hand, I think I might be more giddy than they are. My first public skate. And on Otters home ice, no less.

"I can't believe they booked this place," Tamara says, glancing up at the tall building. "We normally go to a little community rink. This is insane."

"Christmas miracle," Jacob agrees. He looks like he might pass out from joy. "I've never been on the ice here before. Do you think they'll let us go into the dressing rooms?"

I raise an eyebrow at him and he reddens.

"You know," he clears his throat. "For the kids."

Right.

"What time is your flight?" Tamara asks as we approach the entrance.

"Seven-forty-five this evening." I can't wait to hug my sisters and see how strong Grandma's Egg Nog is this year. I wonder which ugly festive sweater my dad is going to wear on Christmas Eve. I'm even looking forward to my mother's passive aggressive comments about my physical appearance. That's how homesick I am.

But even though I've been counting the days until I see my family, leaving is bittersweet. I would have loved to have a bit of holiday time with Foster. I'm so happy he's having Christmas dinner with his brother, but I hate to think of him being all alone the rest of the break.

The students file through the zamboni entrance into the rink. I expect the noise from all the kids to be deafening, but instead an awed hush falls over them. Once everyone's inside, I follow after them and understand why.

The overhead lights aren't on in the arena, but the room is still bright enough that my eyes don't need to adjust. Hundreds of small snowflake lights circle the room slowly, dancing over every surface. I can't tell where the projector is, but they are everywhere.

Lined up along the zamboni path are several pop-up stands. I see balloon animals and cotton candy machines. There's a hot cocoa station and somewhere there must be Beavertails because I can smell their doughy, cinnamon goodness.

It's incredible. Like something out of a Hallmark movie.

I look at my students' faces to see their reaction to the splendour, but they aren't looking at the brightly coloured stalls. They're staring slack-jawed at the ice where several pro hockey players appear to be waiting for them.

Foster, Ben, and half a dozen other Otters stand smiling and waving to the kids from centre ice. While not in full gear, just jerseys, jeans, and helmets, they are still an impressive sight.

"Gooooood morning," an announcer's animated voice booms over the speakers. "The Ottawa Otters are proud to welcome Stittsville Public to the ice today as honorary Otters! Welcome to Skate Day!"

The players start to clap and cheer for the kids, most of whom are still speechless.

"Did you know about this?" Tamara asks. She's clearly as dumbfounded as the kids.

"I had no idea." How did Principal LeBlanc arrange this? There was no time to fundraise and there's no way we had money in the school budget for all of this.

Looking back at the ice, I see my brother lean in to say something to Foster before laughing and giving him a slap on the back. Foster's eyes meet mine and he gives me a tentative smile.

And that's when it hits me. The school didn't do this. Foster did.

I look around again at the brightly coloured stalls along the path. Hot cocoa, balloon animals, cotton candy. Not only did he save Skate Day for my students, he recreated the Winter Carnival I missed out on when I was a child.

Every impulse in my body tells me to run onto the ice and wrap myself around him, but given our audience, this is not the place and definitely not the time.

The next fifteen minutes is spent getting the kids ice ready. It's no small feat and I've never been so grateful for parent volunteers. But eventually their skates are all laced up and their helmets are secured tightly to their heads. I've been so focused on making sure my students are taken care of that I haven't had time to put my own gear on.

As the kids, parents, and my fellow teachers take the ice, I sit down to hastily put on my new skates. As I'm fumbling with the stiff new laces I sense someone approach.

“Need a hand with those?” Foster asks as he crouches down in front of me.

“That might be faster. Thank you.”

I grab my helmet from my bag. While I’m putting it on, I watch his hands as they lace up my skates. The look of quiet concentration on Foster’s face is so endearing. He looks so boyish right now that I fight a swoon. He finishes tying my second skate, gives my ankle a little pat, and looks up at me, smiling.

“You did all this for me,” I whisper. It’s not a question, it’s a statement.

“I did.” He must know I’m on the verge of tears because he gives my calf a squeeze. “Didn’t I tell you to get used to romantic gestures?”

“Yes, you did.” I grin. “How did you pull all of this off?”

He shrugs, a sheepish look crossing his face. "I called in a few favours and reached out to the owners. Ben got in touch with the guys on the team who hadn’t left for home yet and pestered them until they agreed to come. Cody handled everything with the school. Honestly, I didn’t do much."

“You did so much. Thank you.”

His cheeks flush as he helps me to my feet.

“I’ve never seen you in a regular helmet,” I laugh, giving it a little tap.

“I don’t like it,” he admits with a frown. “You can see too much of my face.”

“I like your face.”

“I’m glad.”

Foster leads me to the ice and I step onto the frozen surface with no hesitation and start to skate.

I've got this.

We skate around the perimeter taking in the scene. Will is leading a group of kids in a boisterous chorus of Rudolph The Red Nosed Reindeer while Austin leans against the boards, flirting with one of the mom volunteers.

Ben is surrounded by a group of boys and girls all vying for his attention. He's doubled over laughing at something one of the kids said. It's the happiest I've seen him in months and when he spots us skating by, his grin grows even bigger.

We approach Jacob, who stiffens when he sees us. I watch Foster give him a reassuring smile and nod as we pass.

"Hey, Jacob. Good to see you again, man."

Jacob's entire face lights up. "Ye-yeah. You too, Foster, man."

I have to bite back a laugh. Whatever crush he once had on me has been completely eclipsed by his man-crush on Foster.

"You're a pro," Foster tells me as we finish our first loop.

"I had a great teacher."

"Hi, Uncle Foster!" Amelia's squeal rises above all the other noise as she barrels towards us. Foster's lightning fast reflexes come in handy as he intercepts her before she collides with him. Completely undeterred, she jets off again. "Thanks, Uncle Foster!" she calls over her shoulder.

Foster shakes his head with a smile as his older brother follows hot on her trail. "You gotta teach her to stop, Cody."

He grins at him as he passes us. "She says she wants you to teach her."

I watch Foster swallow hard as his family skates away, and I squeeze his hand.

"This has been the best day ever," I tell him.

Those green eyes twinkle as he says, "It's not over yet."

A moment later the music cuts out on the loudspeaker with a record scratch. After a few seconds of quiet, it starts to blast the bass-heavy techno beats of 2 Unlimited. Right after the singer asks "Y'all ready for this?" Otto the Otter himself takes the ice in a Santa hat. The kids lose their minds, screaming as they skate towards him to join him in his dance routine.

I gape at Foster who grins back. "I told you I'd introduce you."

As we watch a seven-foot-tall otter do the floss, we're joined by Will, Austin, and Ben.

Austin is the only one who appears unimpressed. "Stupid Otto. He gets all the attention."

Will laughs as he drapes a huge arm over his shoulder. "Awww. Are you jealous of our mascot, Crawford? Did your mom not hold you enough when you were a baby or something?"

Austin scowls at him. "Probably not. But it's okay. Your mom's more than making up for it now."

Everyone laughs, Will loudest of all.

I turn to Foster. "Any more surprises I should know about?"

His expression becomes serious as he looks at the ice. Taking my hand, he skates backwards a few feet, pulling me with him out of earshot of the others. "No, but there is something I'd like to talk to you about. Later, at home."

Worry builds in my stomach at his words. Things have been good. Better than good. I'm not sure what could be causing him to look so uneasy.

Maybe he thinks we're moving too fast? No. He wouldn't tell me he loved me and spend his day off putting together this winter carnival for me just to turn around and ask to slow things down.

"Of course," I say with a lightness I don't feel. Forcing a smile, I add, "Race you to the hot chocolate?"

He grins down at me. "You're on."

❄

BY THE TIME I pull into Foster's driveway, I'm beyond exhausted. The field trip was an indisputable success. There were a few falls and a couple of squabbles, but no major injuries or incidents. Principal LeBlanc himself said it was the best Skate Day ever.

We got back to school shortly after one in the afternoon and spent the rest of the day watching *How The Grinch Stole Christmas*. Saying goodbye to the kids was hard and I wasn't lying when I told them how much I was looking forward to seeing them in the New Year.

I make my way to the house, juggling several gift bags filled with candles, chocolates, and gift cards from my students.

As I'm approaching the front door, it swings open to reveal Foster. His hair looks damp from a shower and he's dressed in what I swear are the only jeans he owns and an old sweatshirt.

In other words, he looks perfect.

He smirks when he sees all the gifts I'm carrying.

"My students spoiled me," I tell him as I enter the house.

He frowns. "That's my job."

Setting all the presents down, I wince as I slip my sore feet out of my boots. I look around for my slipper socks, but they aren't where I left them this morning.

Foster notices my confusion and says, "Be right back," before jogging off down the hall.

He returns a minute later as I'm hanging up my coat, and without saying a word, he drops down to one knee in front of me.

Oh God. I hope he's not going to propose.

Not today, anyway. I mean, we haven't been together that long and as much as I love him and want to be with him, I'm not ready to be a wife.

But he doesn't propose, thankfully. Instead, he holds out one of my slippers and, smiling, I place my hand on his shoulder for support as I slip my foot inside.

"Oh. My. God," I moan as the warm fabric envelops my aching foot.

Foster grins up at me. "I put them in the dryer for a few minutes. Figured your feet would be sore after all that skating."

I have no idea what I've done to deserve this man, but I'm keeping him.

After he slips the other one on, he stands and pulls me into his chest for a hug. "Better?"

"So much better."

We stay like this for a few minutes, just holding each other. His broad hands stroke my back and I'm lulled into an almost meditative state by his steady heartbeat. I could stay like this all evening.

"We need to leave for the airport soon," Foster says, interrupting my tranquil state. "Do you have much to do to get ready?"

Reluctantly, I let him go and take a step back. "No, I finished packing this morning."

"That's good." He clears his throat. "I'm going to miss you."

"I'm going to miss you, too," I tell him. Then, remembering what he said at the rink, I take a deep breath and ask, "What did you want to talk to me about?"

His mouth opens then closes again as he shoves his hands in his pockets and rocks back on his heels.

"You can say 'no,'" he prefaces, looking a bit pale. "I know that you're planning to move into the new spot next month, but," he swallows as he meets my gaze, "what if you stayed here? With me? I know we haven't been together long, but I've loved having you here and I don't want you to go."

I stop breathing. "Are you sure?" While I've been staying there for the past eight weeks, there's a huge difference between that and him asking me to move in and share his home.

Foster's eyes shine with sincerity as he reads my mind. "Beth, this wasn't a home until you got here and it won't be one if you leave."

Throwing my arms around him I bury my face in his neck, breathing him in, and whisper, "Yes." It's not just a word. It's everything I've been waiting to say. "Yes," I repeat, my voice firmer now. I pull back just enough to look into his eyes, my fingers tracing the line of his jaw. "There's nowhere else I want to be."

But as the words pass my lips, I'm reminded that there is somewhere else I need to be—the airport.

"I wish you could come with me," I groan into Foster's neck.

"I can, if you want me to."

I blink, my mind scrambling to catch up with what he just said. "Wait... what?" My voice comes out shaky, and I stare at him, half expecting him to laugh and tell me he's kidding. But he doesn't. Instead, he's watching me with the soft smile that always makes my heart flip.

"I'll come home with you, if that's what you want."

My mouth falls open as he gently sets me down. "You... you're serious?"

Foster brushes a strand of hair behind my ear. "Ben booked me a flight. It's his way of apologising for being an ass. I can fly to the Island with you now and come back first thing on Christmas morning. But I told him it was up to you. Do you wa–"

"Yes, please!"

He chuckles as his forehead comes to rest on mine. "Yes, ma'am."

I start to tear up again as I look up at the man I love. "I'm still not used to romantic gestures."

"Then I guess I'll have to keep coming up with them. How does that sound?"

Amazing. Wonderful. Perfect. Phenomenal. "Good."

"Good," he murmurs against my lips.

EPILOGUE

Ben

"What are we doing to celebrate our last night of freedom?"

Beth and Foster exchange a look as they walk hand in hand a few feet ahead of me. We just grabbed lunch at a new deli downtown and are making our way back to Foster's car. I adjust the brim of my ball cap to shield my eyes from the midday sun. Even though we're into September, it's thirty-five degrees today.

My sister glances back at me with a hesitant but kind smile. "I think we're overdue to have a quiet night in, if that's okay?"

It's not like I was suggesting we go clubbing. I don't do that anymore.

"Works for me. You guys want to watch a movie? I hear the new Secret Service one is good. You know, Bug; the one with your other boyfriend in it."

Beth rolls her eyes. "For the last time, Ben, I don't have a crush on Glen Powell."

"Sure you don't, Kiddo." She actually doesn't, but every time I insinuate she does, the veins in Foster's neck bulge like he's about to go from Bruce Banner to the Hulk. It's hilarious.

"Don't you have anything else to do tonight?" Foster frowns at me. His sunglasses hide his eyes, but I'm certain he's glaring at me behind them. "Laundry? Food prep? Making new friends?"

Beth elbows him in the ribs, but Foster merely throws an arm around her shoulders and pulls her closer.

"Mom did all my laundry yesterday."

"Of course she did," my sister snorts.

We got back to the city last night after a visit to Prince Edward Island. It was one of the best trips home that I can remember.

The weather was incredible. We rented a five-bedroom luxury cottage on the north shore of the Island while we were there, and for twenty-one days, it was nothing but beach, lobster boils, and family time. Having Foster there made it even better. It was nice to have someone to train with while home since Mom and Grandma seemed hell-bent on outdoing one another in the kitchen.

My best friend fits into my family like a missing puzzle piece. Dad loves having someone else to talk hockey with and Mom is thrilled to have someone new to mother. Even Tara, Destroyer of Worlds and Queen of Darkness, seems to like him.

Most importantly, he makes Beth incredibly happy. In the ten months since she moved here, I've seen her really come into her own. She's more confident, more sure of herself. When a permanent grade five teaching position opened up at Stittsville Elementary, she didn't hesitate to apply—and she got it. She loves it there, and I couldn't be more proud of her.

It's been an adjustment for me—not just sharing my best friend with my sister, but getting used to how much Fozzie smiles now that he's with Beth. It's like seeing Scrooge after his night with the haunted trio; you're happy for him, it just takes some getting used to.

Sometimes he's borderline cheerful. It's...unnerving.

"What Foster is trying to say is that we're just going to stay in and get ready for the busy week ahead of us," Beth explains as we come to a stop at an intersection and wait to cross.

In other words, I'm not invited.

"Of course, that makes sense," I say with a shrug. "I've got stuff to do, too."

I don't.

But Beth's not the only one making big changes. I've been working hard at following my baby sister's advice to stop thinking with my dick. It hasn't been easy. I've been letting that particular appendage call the shots for the last ten years.

Since Christmas, I've curtailed my night life, focusing on hockey, family, and friends–and it's been good. Weekly hangouts with Beth have helped us get to know one another better and now we're closer than ever. There have also been more poker nights with Foster, Will, and Austin. Foster's brother Cody joins when he can and has been a great addition to our motley crew.

My stats improved in the last few months of the season. We didn't make it to the finals, but we came close, ending up losing in the Eastern Conference Championship to the eventual cup winners. Still, by buckling down, I made my career my top priority. The late nights were taking a toll on my playing, but my summer training was intense and now my routine is tighter than ever. Training camp starts tomorrow and I've never felt so ready to get back on the ice.

Even with these positive changes, I still feel like something is missing in my life. While I've loved spending more time with Beth and Foster, it's hard not to feel like a third wheel, and I've been thinking of taking on a project to fill my spare time. Something that's just for me.

"I think I'd like to volunteer with Big Buddies this year." It's the first time I've voiced the idea out loud, but I've been considering it for months. Big Buddies is a local organisation that matches mentors with kids who need positive role models.

"Ben, that's a wonderful idea!' Beth beams at me. "I know students enrolled in the program and have only heard good things. Besides, you're so great with kids."

"Probably because he is one," Foster adds with a smirk.

"I liked you better when you were lonely, man. Dating my sister has given you too much personality."

"Deal with it," he chuckles happily. "Seriously though, I think you'd make a great mentor for someone. I definitely could have used someone like you in my life when I was growing up."

A lump forms in my throat at Foster's endorsement. He's not one to inflate my ego, so coming from him means a lot. "Yeah?"

"Absolutely," he says as we reach the car. "I think

you'll be a great role model for some kid and they'd be lucky to have you. In fact..." He pulls his car keys from the pocket of his jeans, "I'm going to let you drive us home." Foster tosses the keys at me and I catch them, stunned.

"Really? You're letting me drive Sexy Lexie?"

My friend frowns at me. "That's not her name."

"That's my name for her."

"You don't get to name my car."

"Too late, I already did."

" You're making me regret all the nice things I just said to you."

"No take backs," I laugh while jogging around to the driver's side and unlocking the door. Before I open it, my eye catches a glimpse of something across the street that stops me in my tracks.

Red hair. The colour of a sunset. The bright, intense kind that makes it look like the entire sky is ablaze; the kind of fiery hue that makes everything around it seem dimmer in comparison.

And I've only ever seen it on one person.

She can't really be here. I'm certain it's just my mind playing tricks on me like it's done every time I've seen a flash of red hair for the last decade. Conjuring up images out of pure longing that aren't really there. But the longer I look, the more sure I am that this time it's real. She's real.

Thankfully, there's no traffic, because if there were, I'd have walked right into it without even noticing. My feet move on autopilot, drawn into her orbit just like they were when I was sixteen.

Her head is down as she digs through an oversized

purse. Maybe for keys, or her wallet for the parking meter. I walk toward her slowly, like approaching a deer in the forest—any sudden movement, and she might bolt. I don't even blink out of fear she'll vanish.

"Ben?" I hear Beth calling from across the street. And so does Madelyn. I watch her entire body stiffen as she lifts her head and frantically scans the area. When her eyes land on me, she freezes.

All I can do is stare. Her blue eyes meet mine—those same eyes I've never been able to forget. So clear and honest, always seeing straight through me, even when I tried to hide. My gaze drifts over the freckles scattered across her nose and cheeks, down to her mouth—the lips I kissed more times than I can count. She wasn't my first kiss, but the moment my lips touched hers I knew I never wanted to kiss anyone else. Now, I can't help but wonder if they still taste like the strawberry lip balm she was always applying.

"Ben?" Her voice, barely audible, triggers a wave of memories I've spent a decade trying to forget. Memories of the happiest years of my life. When we were young, reckless, and stupidly in love. When I was hers and she was mine.

My Madelyn.

My eyes catch a flash of the large diamond ring on her left hand as it glints in the sunlight, and reality hits me like a freight train.

She hasn't been mine for a long time and it hurts more than I can describe. Because despite the years and distance, I'm still hopelessly in love with the woman standing in front of me.

"Hey, Madness."

Ben & Maddy's story will continue in

CHECK THE HALLS

coming October 2025

ACKNOWLEDGMENTS

Jon, thank you for not only supplying your usual tireless support, but for also being my technical expert on all things hockey. I love you like Foster loves pineapple coconut foaming hand soap.

Lucy, my all-time favourite ragamuffin. Being your mom is life's greatest adventure.

Carley, my editor and emotional support pillow. Thank you for your hard work and constant support. Your excitement for these characters made me more excited for what's to come!

Jeremy, I can't thank you enough for being my proofreader. Please stick around because I have no intention of learning how to use commas properly.

My critique partner, Trish, I'm so grateful for you! You not only help make my books better but you motivate me to keep writing and I'm so, so glad we found each other!

My cover designer, Fleurie. This is the fourth cover you've made me and it's my favourite! I'm so excited to continue working with you on this series.

I have incredibly supportive friends and family and I appreciate every last one of you. Yes, Peter—even you.

Everyone at Indigo Charlottetown, especially Callie & Deidre! Thank you for getting my books to new readers! I can't thank you enough for the support!

Finally, I want to thank my readers. Some of you have been with me since day one and some of you are just joining the party now. Regardless how you found me, I'm so glad you're here! Thank you not only for buying my books, but for reviewing them online and telling friends and family about them! I hope you stick around because I have a lot more to say.

xo K

ABOUT THE AUTHOR

K.M. Gillis drinks a lot of black coffee while creating her fictional characters and making them kiss. She loves cats and kills plants. She lives in Charlottetown, Prince Edward Island with her husband and daughter.

Also available by K.M. Gillis:

- The Love In 2C series
  - Running Into You
  - Raise The Bar
  - The Write Off

Printed in Dunstable, United Kingdom

73033555R00194